In for the Kill

In for the Kill

HAWKMAN SERIES #9

Betty Sullivan La Pierre

Visit www.booksurge.com to order additional copies.

In for the Kill

ACKNOWLEDGMENT

I want to thank Tom & Peggy Bratcher for their detailed information on the police procedures of Siskiyou County, California

I also want to thank Author, Sharon Booker for giving this book a wonderful title.

And

A great BIG thank you to Selma, Anne & Nancy.

I'd like to dedicate this book to my three sons,
Kevin, Stan & Tom
Who have always been there for me.

CHAPTER ONE

Jennifer sat at her computer, concentrating on the next book in her mystery series. When the phone rang, she let the answering machine pick up.

"This call is for Jim Anderson. If you're there, please answer."

She immediately jumped to her feet with a pounding heart. No one had used Hawkman's birth name since Dirk Henderson, the double agent who wanted to kill her husband several years ago. Trembling, she stared at the instrument's blinking red light. This could be another nemesis out to get him.

After a slight pause, the voice said, "I'll call back later."

The click of the hang-up left her reeling. She paced the floor and ran trembling fingers through her short, curly brown hair. This would definitely upset Hawkman. When he quit the Agency, he dreaded the day when someone from his past would find him. After Dirk had been caught and put into prison, he'd finally relaxed, figuring too much time had gone by now for him to be in danger.

Jennifer wrung her hands. *How'd this person find our number?* The telephone bill was in the name of Tom and Jennifer Casey. He obviously knew more about Hawkman than she cared to think about. The gnawing in her stomach told her she should call her husband right away. This man could be searching for him right now, and Hawkman needed to be on guard.

Jennifer picked up the phone and punched the number to his office.

"Tom Casey, Private Investigator."

"Hi, how's it going?"

"Just fine. Don't tell me you forgot to add something to this long grocery list?"

"No, but I just received a phone call for Jim Anderson."

A silence hung over the line for several moments.

"Who was it?"

"I don't know. I let it ring because I was busy and the machine took the message. He said he'd call back."

"This is very interesting. There's someone still out there looking for me. Maybe I'll recognize the voice."

"It's possible; the recording is fairly clear. No voice changer. Do you want to hear it now?"

"No, I'll wait until I get home."

"Do you think it could be just an old school buddy looking for you?"

"Hard to say. But I doubt it. Be sure to lock up and turn on the alarm after we've talked. I don't want to scare you, but no sense in taking any chances."

"Okay. Honey, watch your back. And remember I love you."

"I love you, too. I'll see you soon."

Hawkman hung up and tapped the receiver with his finger. It'd been a long time since the name Jim Anderson had entered his mind. A part of his yesteryears had come to haunt him again.

He opened the desk drawer and withdrew his shoulder holster. Lately, the habit of wearing it had not seemed so urgent, but the phone call from Jennifer had changed his perspective. As he buckled the gun around his chest, he could feel the old lessons taught at the Agency moving forward in his brain like a back-up computer disc. He forced it open and let the information flow into his mind, so he could recap all his training and be prepared.

It worried him this person had called the house and not his office. It meant he knew Jim Anderson had an alias. The message struck fear into Hawkman when he thought about

Jennifer being home alone. Shutting down the computer, he decided to leave. He wanted to hear the voice on the recording, and needed to discuss this situation with his wife.

He strolled over to the window, stood back, and surveyed the parking lot. All the vehicles looked empty, and no one appeared to be waiting to gun him down. But if this person had Agency experience, he could be parked down the street with a high-powered rifle and a pair of binoculars.

Hawkman took a deep breath, then exhaled loudly. Life had been mighty quiet and peaceful. He should have known it couldn't last forever. After unplugging the coffee pot, he stopped in his tracks when a knock sounded. He pulled his gun from the holster, moved to the side of the jamb, and flung open the door.

Hearing giggles, he glanced out in time to see two little girls running down the stairs, and turn the corner. He holstered his weapon, stepped forward and almost kicked over a covered basket sitting on the top step, but grabbed the handle before it tumbled down the stairs. A small beige and white head with sharp blue eyes peeked out from under the checkered cloth.

"What the heck!" Hawkman said, carrying the container to his desk.

When he pulled the cloth back, a well-fed kitten rolled onto its back and playfully swatted at the corner of the towel. Hawkman noticed a card attached to the side with a blue ribbon. He laughed when the cat batted at his fingers as he pulled the bow loose and opened the envelope.

"Hey, hold on a minute, you little critter. Let's see what you're all about."

Dear Jennifer,

In appreciation for all you've done for

my family. She will give you hours of pleasure.

God Bless, Marie and Girls

Hawkman put the note away, pushed back his hat, and eyed the young animal. "I must say, you're one cutie. But I don't know any Marie or the story behind you. I'm sure your new mistress will know what this is all about. At least, you'll give her something to think on besides a sniper."

He picked up the basket and headed down the stairs to his vehicle parked in the alley. After sliding it onto the passenger seat, and closing the door, he lifted the hood to assure himself no one had tampered with the engine. Confident everything appeared okay, he climbed into the driver's side and drove to the pet shop.

When he placed the container on the counter and the little kitten poked out her head from under the cloth, the cashier called the other employees. "Come look at this darling Ragdoll."

Everyone gathered around touching, and handling the cat.

Hawkman stepped back and rubbed his mustache. "Huh, I just need some food and a couple of toys. I have no idea what she eats."

One of the girls glanced up at him. "Where did you get this precious thing?"

"A gift from Marie."

She rolled her eyes. "Oh, you're so lucky. Her cats are the best in the world."

Hawkman looked puzzled. "Does she raise them?"

The young lady stepped back in awe. "Yes, didn't you know? She's the greatest Ragdoll breeder around; known all over the country."

He shrugged. "I'm not into felines, this is my wife's deal. The animal is for her."

"Oh, she's just going to love it."

He soon edged his way out the door trying to hold the cat in the basket with a bag of food and toys under his arm. "I think you've excited my pet."

They all laughed and gave him a wave as he struggled toward the SUV.

He sat the cat on the passenger seat, then took the newly bought food and two bowls from the sack. Setting the containers on the inside floorboard, he poured a little water from his own bottle into one, then sprinkled some food into the other.

Gently lifting the cat out of the basket, he placed her next to them. While she lapped up the liquid and ate a hefty amount of the dry crunchies, Hawkman scrutinized the area. He found nothing to cause suspicion, so climbed into the driver's side and waited for the cat to finish. When she started to preen herself, he picked up the animal and gently placed her into the basket.

"Okay, girl, we haven't got all day. We're heading to Copco Lake and you can take care of your personal hygiene when we arrive home."

On their way, Hawkman had a time keeping the little tiger from climbing out onto the seat, and ended up steering most of the way with one hand while rubbing her back with the other.

He breathed a sigh of relief when he drove into the garage. "Okay, wiggle worm, you ready to meet your new mistress?" He gently lifted the receptacle and carried it to the entry. He found the door locked and the alarm system set. So, he placed the basket between his feet, punched in the code and stepped into the house, then tried to grab the animal as she leaped from her confines.

Jennifer turned the corner just as a streak flashed across the living room floor.

"Oh, my gosh, what was that?"

"A bag full of energy for you, from Marie."

She clamped both hands over her mouth as she stared at two big blue eyes looking out from behind the chair. "She's beautiful!"

He frowned. "You act like you were expecting this little bundle of dynamite."

Reaching down and picking up the ball of fur, she nodded. "Yes, but I didn't know when. And I didn't think it'd be you who'd have the honor of bringing her home. I wanted it to be a surprise."

He plopped the basket on the counter. "Don't be disappointed. It took me totally off guard, and this little beast definitely kept my mind off snipers or someone stalking me."

A guilty smile twitched the corners of her mouth. "Good timing."

"The employees at the pet shop went bonkers over the sight of this creature."

"I can imagine. Marie's Ragdoll cats have the reputation of being the most beautiful in the area."

"I want to hear the whole story. But first, I'll bring in the food and stuff I bought for the new member of our family."

Once Hawkman deposited the items on the counter, Jennifer fussed over where she should put the litter box and then produced a good sized wicker pet bed she'd somehow stored away without his ever seeing it. She placed it in the corner near the fireplace.

The little cat had not let Jennifer out of her sight since she'd arrived and acted like she understood her instructions. Hawkman shook his head and meandered over to the phone. Staring at the flashing red button, he finally punched it and listened to the message.

Jennifer glanced at him when it finished. "Do you recognize the voice?"

"No."

"I pray it's not Dirk."

"We don't have to worry about him. He's in prison for the rest of his life, unless someone killed him. I'll ask Bill when I call."

"You're going to call Bill Broadwell, your old boss?"

"Yes."

"You believe it's someone from your Agency years?"

"I'm highly suspicious, because of his using the name, Jim Anderson. We'll see if he calls back. Screen the calls if I'm not here, and don't answer if you don't recognize the caller. I want you to keep the alarm on at all times and get your gun ready. We'll go out and do some practicing within the next day or two."

Jennifer stared at him with fear in her eyes. "You're serious aren't you?"

"Yes."

CHAPTER TWO

Since Jennifer had spent most of the evening chasing down the playful kitten, Hawkman decided he better help her get dinner on the table or it'd be midnight before they ate. "What are you going to do with her during the night?" he asked.

She wiped a hand across her brow. "I'm not sure. She's so nosey, and I don't want her to get into anything where she could get hurt or eat something that might make her sick."

"Why don't you put her gear and the litter box into the main bathroom so you can close the door. Put down the stool lid and she should be completely safe. Then in the morning, when you're ready, let her out to take over the run of the house."

Jennifer chuckled. "I understand cats take the mastering of a household very seriously."

"Why do those words not surprise me?"

"I think I'll put her in there right now, so I can eat in peace."

Jennifer quickly hauled the cat and all her possessions into the bathroom, then closed the door. "Whew, now maybe I can relax for a few minutes," she said, flopping down on the dining room chair.

"By the way, have you thought of a name?"

"Not yet. I need to think about it. Have you noticed when you pick her up how she just flops over your arm?"

Hawkman raised a brow. "Yeah, like a piece of cloth."

"The name 'Ragdoll' comes from that trait. Very easy to cuddle."

"Right," he laughed. "But you have to catch her first."

"She'll settle down eventually; she's just excited about exploring her new home."

"I have a feeling she's going to run you ragged for awhile."

"I'll call Marie and find out a little more about this breed's disposition, also, what I need to do as far as shots and getting her spayed."

"Speaking of Marie, would you mind filling me in on why she gave you this animal?"

"Last year when I took the chemotherapy treatments, I met her in the infusion room. She had the chair next to mine, and she looked so frightened. We talked for a long time until I sensed her relaxing. When I asked about her cancer, it turned out she had the same as mine. Based on my research, I informed her about the chances of survival and how lymphoma could be knocked into remission. The woman's whole demeanor changed and tears flowed down her cheeks in relief. She'd lost her husband in a construction accident a couple of years before, has three little girls, and thought her life had come to an end."

Hawkman reached over and patted her hand. "Sounds like you gave her courage."

"Whenever we met during treatment, we talked and laughed constantly. The last time I saw her, she asked if I liked cats and explained how she raised the Ragdoll breed. She told me I'd handed her a new lease on life and wanted to give me something personal. Marie promised when her best cat gave birth, I'd get one of the litter."

"I like the story. And the feisty little lion has now stolen my heart."

Jennifer grinned. "I understand they make wonderful pets."

"We'll soon know," he said, picking up their empty plates and heading for the kitchen.

Later they retired to the living room. Jennifer retrieved the kitten and played with her while Hawkman tried to watch the news.

"Are you calling Bill tomorrow?"

"I think so."

"What are you going to ask him?"

About that time, the phone rang. Hawkman raised his hand. "Let the answering machine pick up."

"I know you're there. Your lights are on in the house. I saw you eating dinner. What a great target." Then the line went dead.

Hawkman jumped out of his chair, and closed the drapes.

Clutching the cat to her chest, Jennifer stared at him in horror. "The voice sounded the same."

"Hit the floor," he said, flipping off the lamp next to his chair, leaving only the light from the flickering television to illuminate the room. His gun drawn and in a crouched position, he made his way to the kitchen window. Keeping to the side of the sashes, so his silhouette couldn't be seen, he peered out at the street. Seeing nothing, he hurried back to the bedroom, and grabbed his night binoculars off the dresser. He stepped out on the deck, and slipped his gun into the waistband of his jeans. Putting the glasses to his eyes, he surveyed the bridge and the land across the lake.

Jennifer followed. "Anything?"

"Nothing. No parked or moving vehicle anywhere."

"He must have driven by while we were having dinner, then called from down the road."

Hawkman moved back into the house, closed the sliding glass door, and pulled the drapes shut. He replaced the gun into the shoulder holster, then put an arm around her shoulders. "Again, I want to remind you to keep the house locked and the alarm on at all times. Don't answer the phone or the door unless you know who it is." He grimaced. "In fact, I'd like you out of here for a few days."

She tilted her head and looked at him sideways. "You know better than to even think along those lines."

He gave her a squeeze. "I knew you'd say that. But this guy sounds awfully close."

Jennifer pulled away, placed the cat on the floor and went to the bedroom. Even though her eyes had adjusted to the darkness, she had to rummage through the dresser drawers until she found the small holster fanny pack and buckled it around her waist. Hawkman came in, then followed her to his office. She took the flashlight he always kept on the top of the gun vault, worked the combination and opened the safe. She found her Beretta and a box of shells, then placed them on the desk before closing the heavy door. "I know how to shoot. I'll carry my weapon until we get this resolved."

She loaded the gun, put on the safety and slid it into the pack. "There, I'm ready for anything."

Hawkman stood beside her, clenched fists resting on his hips, his expression sober. "I don't like the idea of you being home alone."

Her eyes lit up and she grinned as she swooped up the kitten. "I won't be."

Frowning, he headed for the kitchen. "You think the little beast can save you?"

She shrugged. "Maybe I can teach her to be a watch-cat."

He chuckled as he surveyed the outside before closing the window blinds, then flipped on the light. "You're making something small out of this, but it could be very serious."

"I don't doubt the gravity of this situation. In fact, it scares me to death," she said, trailing behind him. "But we can't let it ruin our lives."

Hoping to change the subject, he turned and flipped a curl on her forehead. "I really like the way your hair is growing in. It's so curly, and with the blond highlights it gives you the appearance of a pixie."

"Thanks. I'm enjoying its easy care. But I understand it will go back to the original texture in a couple of years."

"Good. Two years is long enough for you to be an elf."

The ringing phone made them both start and stare at the machine.

"No need for you to turn off all your lights. I'm long gone, but I'll return. So watch your back, *Hawk Man*."

Jennifer cringed. "I don't like his threats. And this time, he called you Hawkman."

"It appears he's done his research." He picked up the phone and punched in a number.

She moved to his side. "Who are you calling?"

"The office. I want to see if he's left any messages there. If he has, he knows I'm now Tom Casey."

She stepped back and watched his jaw tighten as he gripped the receiver. When he hung up, the cat wiggled to get free of Jennifer's tight hold. She put her on the floor, then touched Hawkman's arm as he glared at the machine. "Obviously, he left a message. What did he say?"

"I can't escape. He knows all about us: where we live, your name is Jennifer, and I have an office over a doughnut shop." He glanced down at the kitten rubbing against his leg. "And you've received a kitten as a gift from Marie."

Jennifer's looked at him wide eyed. "Oh my, God!"

CHAPTER THREE

Jennifer tucked the kitten into the wicker bed, and she seemed content with the bathroom surroundings. Until this little girl could be trusted with the run of the house, it appeared a good remedy. Jennifer flipped on the night light, put down the toilet bowl lid and closed the door.

Hawkman had already slipped into bed, but left on the lamp. His eye-patch and gun lay on the end table next to his head. Even though his eyes were closed, she knew he hadn't fallen asleep. The covers came only to his waist and she could see the tense muscles of his chest and the shiny line of the scar running down his left arm. She remembered the agony he'd gone through while attending therapy classes, but he'd succeeded in getting back full control of the muscles. So well, no one would ever guess how badly he'd been cut by the horrible murderess, Tulip Withers. Jennifer donned her gown and crawled in beside him.

Leaning on her elbow, she put a hand on his arm. "Honey, how would he have known I received a kitten for a gift?"

He opened his eyes. "I'm not sure. It baffles me. I might need to question Marie."

She gasped. "Surely you don't think she has anything to do with this person?"

"It could be very innocent. Someone asking questions or looking over the litter, pretending he wanted to buy one. She could have told him she'd saved this particular feline for you. I wish I'd paid more attention in the pet shop. I blurted out to the workers I knew nothing about cats, and this one had been given to my wife as a gift from Marie. They created such a commotion over the little creature, it never entered my mind someone nearby might have been eavesdropping on the conversation."

"Do you want me to give her a call?"

"No. I need a little more time before I approach her."

Jennifer rolled over on her back and pulled up the cover. "Let's try to get some sleep; maybe we'll think more clearly in the morning."

She awoke early to an empty bed, and assumed her husband hadn't slept well. Letting out a sigh, she pushed her feet into her slippers and shrugged on the robe she'd tossed over the chair last night. She quickly ran a brush through her curly locks, then hurried to the other bathroom and opened the door. The kitten, playing with the small stuffed rabbit Hawkman had bought, batted it with her paw, then raised up and bounced on it with all four feet. Jennifer giggled as she picked up the feline and toy, then carried them down the hallway.

Hawkman had opened the drape covering the sliding glass door just enough so he could look out. He stood staring at the lake with a cup of coffee in his hand.

"Good morning. How long have you been up?"

"A long time."

"I figured you wouldn't get much rest." She knelt and put the cat on the floor. "By the way, she loves the toy you bought."

Hawkman glanced her way. "Oh, yeah, which one?"

"The stuffed bunny. Watch her go after it."

She flipped the rabbit a few feet away and the cat lunged, bounced on it, then rolled over with the ear in its mouth.

Hawkman chuckled. "Glad the little varmint likes to play. I have to say her antics are comical. Have you thought of a name yet?"

Jennifer went into the kitchen where she poured herself a mug of the hot brew. "No. It's got to be something catchy. It will come in time." She slid onto one of the kitchen bar stools. "What are your plans for today?"

"I've already called Bill."

She glanced at him in surprise. "Boy, I must've been sleeping like a log. I never heard you talking. So what'd he say?"

"He'll get back to me. Right now he has no idea who this guy could be. Said he'd do some research and give me a call in a day or two."

"Are you going into the office?"

"Yes. I have some work to do on a couple of cases." He raised a brow. "What are your plans?"

"I've got to check with Marie and find out if the kitten is old enough to get neutered. I want to get her spayed as soon as possible."

"Good idea. Lock yourself in and keep the alarm on. You can probably open the drapes during the day, but the minute the sun goes down, close them."

She nodded, took a sip of coffee, then narrowed her eyes. "Hawkman, I'm not going to barricade myself in this house for days on end. I'll take precautions and be alert, but if I want to go to the dock or town, I'm going. I certainly don't see you staying locked inside, even though you're obviously the target."

He sighed. "I figured you'd say that."

She shrugged. "Well, isn't it reasonable I go by the same rules?"

"Since you put it in such a manner, I guess so."

After her husband left the house, Jennifer couldn't find the kitten. Calling, she went through all the rooms, looked under the beds, in the corners, inside closets, behind books, then she panicked at the thought the cat might have dashed outside when Hawkman opened the front door. She hurried over to the dining room window near her computer area, pushed back the drape and scanned the side yard. Out of the corner of her eye, she spotted the little bundle of fur draped across the seat of her desk chair, sound asleep.

Hawkman chewed on a toothpick as he drove toward Medford. He'd racked his brain for an answer to who could be causing the torment. Should he consider the threats seriously, or could this just be a crackpot getting his kicks? Regardless, he felt like he should investigate the situation to make sure. He didn't like the idea the guy knew his original name and had mentioned the cat as a gift. These two items bothered him considerably. He hoped to hear from Bill Broadwell soon. Maybe he'd be able to give him a hint. Hawkman felt in his gut this person existed in his past life at the Agency. He had enemies, but who held such a vendetta that he'd come searching after all these years? The question baffled him.

When he reached the office, he popped into the bakery to buy a couple of pastries since he'd skipped breakfast.

Clyde, the baker, met him at the counter with a broad grin and a pan full of goodies. "You're in early today. These delicacies are right out of the oven. Take your choice."

Hawkman sniffed the air. "It always smells delicious in here. When I'm upstairs and you have those ovens pumped up, the aroma comes floating into my windows and through every crack in the walls. Makes my stomach grumble. You know I'm hooked."

The baker laughed. "Ah, yes. I'm glad you enjoy our goods. By the way, how is Ms. Jennifer?"

"She's doing great and still in remission."

"The last time she came by, she had on a turban. Has her hair grown back?

"Yes. It's curly and she looks like a mischievous little pixie. It's very becoming."

After Hawkman chose a couple of the sweet treats, Clyde put the rest into the display counter. "I'd heard hair can come back quite differently after chemotherapy."

"Yep, she thought it would never grow." He folded the sack top, started toward the door, then stopped and moved back to the counter. "Say, while I'm here, I need to ask you a question. Have you had any new customers lately, or noticed any strangers lingering around in the past couple of weeks?"

Clyde rubbed a flour covered hand down his apron and put the empty pan on a ledge behind him. "Let me think." He drummed his fingers on the counter for a moment, then raised his index finger. "I remember a man and woman came in the end of last week. I'd never seen them before."

Hawkman's interest piqued. "Did they come in together?"

"I'm not sure. I was tending to one of the ovens in the back." He pointed above the door. "That bell rings and alerts me of a customer, so I didn't actually see them walk inside. By the time I got out here, they were standing in front of the case chatting about the baked goods. But I don't think they knew each other."

"Why's that?"

Clyde chuckled. "A tall red headed woman, dressed to the hilt, who carried herself like royalty, just didn't fit with the guy in jeans, tee shirt and needing a shave. And they both bought their own doughnuts."

"What'd the guy look like?"

"Not quite as tall as you, with a fairly buff build. He had dark brown hair, with a tinge of gray at the temples, and green eyes. The right corner of his mouth had a twitch when he spoke." Clyde touched the middle of his nose. "Oh, and right here, he had a funny bump like it'd been broken. Also, he asked about your business hours. Said you weren't in your office and he didn't see a sign. I told him you usually made appointments with clients. The woman didn't say much of anything."

"Did you by any chance see either of them get into their cars?"

He shook his head. "No. Then he snapped his fingers. "I do remember when they left the shop, the guy stopped the woman a few feet outside the door and pointed to your shingle. She nodded and said something, then they parted, going in different directions. Later, my assistant, Gary, told me the woman performed weddings." He waved a hand in the air. "You know like a reverend. But he'd never seen the man before."

"Weddings?"

Clyde nodded. "Yeah. I thought it odd too."

"Did he mention her name?"

"No, but I'll ask him later today."

"I'd appreciate it, Clyde. Thanks."

Hawkman trooped up the stairs to his office wondering what the two had talked about outside the bakery. He hoped

Gary might be able to supply a name for the lady. He put on the coffee pot and while waiting for it to brew, punched up the messages on the answering machine. He recorded the threatening one he'd already heard when he activated it from the house. Maybe Bill would want to run these through the voice recognition system. Once he listened to the rest, he poured himself a mug of java and munched on the eclair as he opened the telephone book to the yellow pages. He flipped through until he reached 'Weddings'. After scanning the ads, he jotted down a couple of names and numbers of women who advertised themselves as ministers who performed such ceremonies. He doubted she had anything to do with the man or the threats, but might have noticed what type of vehicle he drove.

CHAPTER FOUR

Hawkman tried to concentrate on his other cases, but thoughts of threatening phone calls kept entering his mind. He picked up the receiver and punched the number for Jennifer's cell phone. When she didn't answer, he immediately dialed the landline and waited for the answering machine. "Jennifer, this is Hawkman, pick up."

"Hello," she said, sounding out of breath.

"You okay?"

"Yes, but this kitten is about to do me in. I hope she settles down soon or I'm not going to be able to keep her."

"What happened?"

"I found her nosing around in your closet. We're going to have to keep the doors closed since we've got mouse poison in there."

"Did she eat any?"

"No, I believe I caught her in time. She seems to be acting fine. I'll keep an eye on her."

"Maybe we won't need to put it out anymore with a cat in the house."

"That's a thought."

"Anything unusual going on?"

"Not that I've noticed. I haven't done much observing of the outside, been too busy with the cat. The house is locked up, the alarm system is on and I don't plan on going out today. Any news on your end?"

"Clyde, the baker, had a couple of new visitors at his shop last week. The man asked some questions about me. The woman is someone who performs weddings."

"What'd she look like?"

"Tall, redheaded, regal looking woman is how Clyde described her."

"Oh, that's Rita Rawlings."

Hawkman practically came out of his chair. "You know her?"

"I met her at a wedding. She even marries people in jail."

"Really? That's odd."

"Bet she had an event in your area and dropped by the bakery for a quick picker-upper."

"Sounds reasonable."

"Why are you interested?"

"She happened to be in the shop the same time this man came in. They exchanged a few words outside and he pointed at my sign, but Clyde didn't hear their conversation. I'd like to know what this guy said."

"Give her a call."

"I will, since I have her name now. Thanks."

"Glad to be of help. I better run and find the little pest. No telling what she's up to now."

Hawkman laughed. "Okay, hon, talk to you later."

He hung up and fished out the notepad from underneath a stack of papers where he'd written the two phone numbers earlier. After punching in the digits, he received a message instructing him to leave his name and number. She'd get back to him as soon as possible. He grimaced, but left the information and hung up. "Nothing's easy," he mumbled, tapping his pencil on the desk.

He thought about Clyde's description of the man and couldn't place a green-eyed, dark-haired guy in his past. Didn't mean an adversary didn't exist. Someone could hold a grudge due to an ugly incident without ever meeting face to face. Maybe Bill would come up with something. He hoped to hear from him in the next day or two.

Hawkman scratched his chin. Of course, this fellow at the donut shop might just have wanted my services, and had nothing to do with the threatening calls. Time will tell.

He felt stymied at the moment, with no clues on the caller. The phone I.D. was blocked, and the calls weren't long enough to set up a trace. He exhaled loudly, opened a folder and tried to focus on one of his current cases, only to have his concentration interrupted by a knock on the door. Reaching up to his holster, he flipped the cover. "Come in," he called.

A lovely, redheaded woman stepped into the room. She appeared quite a bit older than he, but the expertly applied make-up, twinkling green eyes, pale emerald colored silk blouse, skirt and beige cape, camouflaged her age. "Mr. Casey?"

"Yes." Hawkman straightened his jacket and immediately stood, as something about her stance made him feel obligated.

She strolled toward him and extended her hand. "I'm Rita Rawlings. I received your call. Since I was in the area, decided to stop by and see if you were in your office."

He shook her hand, then pulled a chair over to the front of his desk and motioned for her to take a seat. "I'm glad you did. I'd much rather talk face to face than over the phone."

Rita sat down and placed her purse on the floor. "I've heard a lot about you and your practice, but never had the pleasure of meeting you in person. However, I have met a Jennifer Casey, the mystery writer from this area. Is she by chance your wife?"

"Yes."

"She attended a wedding I conducted several months ago. Since then, I've read every one of her books. Tell her she's definitely made a new fan."

"Thank you. She'll be thrilled."

"Now what is it you wanted to know? You mentioned something about a man at the bakery in your message."

"First, would you like a cup of coffee?"

"Love one."

"Sugar or cream?"

"Black is fine, thank you."

Hawkman handed her a steaming Styrofoam cup and sat back down behind his desk. "I'm working on a case right now and the owner of the bakery downstairs told me you'd visited his shop last week. My interest is with the man who happened to be in the store at the same time. Do you remember him?"

She wrinkled her forehead. "Yes."

"Do you know his name?"

"No, I'd never seen him before, but thought it odd he asked so many questions about you and your services. Is he giving you static?"

"You remind me of my wife and her intuition. Do all women have this trait?"

She chuckled and took a sip of the hot brew. " A lot do."

"The answer to your question is, I'm not sure. I've received some threatening phone calls and am trying to track the culprit. This man may be innocent, but I thought I'd check out any reasonable leads."

She entwined her fingers on the desktop. "You're wise."

"What exactly did this person say to you inside and outside of the shop?"

"I don't know if I can tell you verbatim, but he asked the baker about your hours, which I thought innocent enough, until we got outside. Then he grabbed my arm, pointed to your sign and asked me what I knew about you. Needless to say, it made me a bit uncomfortable. Especially when he wanted to know if you'd ever been in the Agency." She threw up her hands and shrugged. "I told him I had no idea what sort of past you had, as I'd never met you. I'd only heard by word of mouth, Tom Casey ran the best private investigator service around."

"Thank you. Could you describe him?"

Hawkman took notes, even though she pretty much verified Clyde's description. "Did you by any chance notice his vehicle?"

"Yes, for my own personal reasons. As I said, he made me very nervous." She reached for her purse and dug into the contents. "In fact, I took down his license plate number."

Hawkman smiled. "Fantastic."

She finally located a small notebook, flipped it open, and tore out a page. "He was driving a bronze colored late model

Buick. Then she recited the number. It could have been a rental; you can't tell anymore."

He jotted down the information, then glanced up. "In my business, I have ways of finding out."

She grinned. "I bet you do." Tucking the paper and pad back into her purse, she stood. "Well, Mr. Casey, I've told you everything I know about this person. Wish I could have supplied you with a name. If he's the one causing you problems, I hope you catch him and bring him to justice."

"Thank you, Ms. Rawlings. I appreciate your coming by."

"It's easier than trying to set up an appointment, as my schedule can be hectic."

"I can imagine. My wife is the one who clarified who you were. She remembered you from the wedding."

"I'm flattered. Tell her to keep writing."

"I sure will." Hawkman walked her to the door and held it open as she descended the stairs. After she turned the corner, he immediately went to the computer and logged into a paid site where he typed in the license plate number she'd given.

CHAPTER FIVE

It took a few moments for the computer to search out the license plate number of the Buick. While staring at the monitor, Hawkman took a big mouthful of cold coffee and wrinkled his nose as he sat down the cup. Soon, the answer popped up: a rental company owned the car. He wrote down the information, then slouched back in his chair. It really didn't surprise him, but he'd hoped for a bit more information. How to find who leased the car could present a challenge. At least he had more data to go on, thanks to Ms. Rawlings' alertness.

He studied the description again, but still couldn't place the man in his past. Clyde and Rita had mentioned green eyes. They must've been an outstanding feature. His own were the same color, but they sure didn't arouse people's attention. He chuckled to himself. Of course, the first thing anyone noticed about him was the patch. A little hard to forget. Once he greeted folks, they never forgot who they'd met.

He leaned forward and shuffled the loose papers into a stack, then decided to take a couple of case files home. The thought of Jennifer being alone bothered him and he could work just as easily at his office there. He crammed everything into a briefcase and headed out the door.

When he reached the foot of the stairs, the baker's assistant hurried out the door, wiping his hands on his apron. "Mr. Casey, Clyde said you wanted to know the name of the lady who came into the shop last week. Her name is Reverend Rita Rawlings."

Hawkman didn't have the heart to tell the young man he already knew. "Thanks Gary. Helps a lot."

"She's a nice lady and did a great job in the wedding when she married my cousin."

Hawkman waved as he headed for his vehicle. "Appreciate your help."

When he arrived home, it relieved him to see the alarm set and the door locked. He deactivated the system and went inside. Jennifer sat at her computer and grinned, put a finger to her lips, then pointed toward the big window that overlooked the lake. The cat sat still as a statue on the wide ledge; only her tail twitched as she gazed out at the aviary where Hawkman's pet falcon, Pretty Girl, lived. He tiptoed toward the kitten, bent over and whispered harshly into the feline's ear. "Don't even think about it."

She leaped from the ledge, scampered across the carpet and hid behind the chair.

The air rang with Jennifer's peals of laughter. "Oh, she's so funny."

"How long has she been in the trance?"

"When she spotted Pretty Girl fluffing her wings, she snuck upon the window ledge and has been staring at the falcon for at least an hour. It's like she went into another world. I've actually been able to sit down and write for awhile."

"She'd better not get any ideas about catching that hawk. The bird would tear her apart with its claws and beak."

"Don't worry. There's no way I'd let her near the cage. But it's pretty harmless for her to daydream. After all, she's a cat." Jennifer crossed the room and put her arm around his waist. "You're home early. Everything okay?"

"I didn't get shot at, and no one followed me. No suspicious looking cars in the area. So far, so good. I did have a nice chat with Ms. Rita Rawlings."

She stepped back. "Really. Tell me about it."

He put his briefcase on the coffee table, and tossed his hat on the couch, then ran a hand over his mussed hair. "A very nice lady." He told Jennifer about her visit.

"You mean she actually thought fast enough to get the license plate number from his car?"

"Yep. Unfortunately, my computer search revealed it was a rental. Finding out who leased it will be a harder job. Those places aren't going to give me any information without a court order."

"Did the description of the man ring any bells?"

"No. I've racked my brain and can't remember anyone with dark hair and green eyes. I think his orbs must be pretty outstanding, as both Clyde and Ms. Rawlings mentioned them. I think if I had a name or some event to shake my memory a bit, I'd be able to place him. But right now, my mind's a blank."

"Have you heard from Bill?"

Hawkman shook his head. "No, not yet. If I don't hear from him tomorrow, I'll call again." He strolled over to the sliding glass door. "I better check on Pretty Girl and make sure the cat didn't give her a fright."

Jennifer laughed. "Right."

The falcon seemed in no distress while Hawkman filled her water and food dishes. She flapped her wings and scolded him. "I know, I know, you want to go hunting. I promise this weekend I'll take you out if all goes well. Just don't let the little lioness looking out the window scare you. She's harmless." The hawk tilted her head as if to say, are you kidding. That little twerp would hardly be a mouthful.

Hawkman snickered as he made his way back into the house. "I don't think Pretty Girl is very disturbed about the little tiger." He closed the drapes on both the windows, then headed back to his office. "I'm going to do a little work before dinner."

Jennifer watched as he ambled down the hallway. She knew in her heart, he feared for their safety, otherwise, he wouldn't have come home so early. The kitten strolled over and gave a pleading look. She picked her up, and placed the animal in her lap. The cat began batting at Jennifer's hands as she typed on the keyboard.

"Now, look, you little mess, you're causing me to make mistakes. I certainly can't concentrate with you fiddling around." She held up the ball of fur, and looked into her face. "You're so curious and have such pretty blue eyes. I've got to think of a name for you soon." She placed the kitten on the extra chair she always kept by the computer. "Why don't you take a nap and be a good kitty while I do a little work."

The cat soon jumped to the floor and tread regally toward her master's office. Jennifer grinned to herself, knowing the feline would eventually wind Hawkman around her little paw. He'd proved to be a real softy when it came to animals, regardless of how gruff he sounded on the outside.

She could hardly stand the suspense of what might happen, so she quietly rose and tiptoed down the hallway. The door stood partially open and Jennifer heard Hawkman talking.

"Now you little scalawag, what the heck do you want? You're about the nosiest little critter I've ever seen. What are you after anyway? If you're not careful, you're going to get stuck."

Jennifer assumed he'd risen when she heard the squeak from the chair he'd never got around to oiling.

"Oh my, wait until we show your mistress what you discovered." He opened the door and almost jumped out of his skin. "Good grief, woman, you do know how to startle a man."

"When the kitten headed for your room, I just had to spy and see what she'd do."

"She's turning out to be quite a little detective." He held up the gold bracelet Jennifer had lost a couple of weeks ago.

Her eyes lit up as she took it from his hand. "Where'd she find it?"

"She obviously spotted the shiny object in the crack between the gun vault and the printer cabinet. She kept reaching back there and finally brought it forward."

Jennifer clasped the jewelry around her wrist, reached down and gave the kitten a pat. "Thank you, my little investigator, I thought I'd lost it forever."

The cat looked up and gave a soft mew, contentment written all over her face.

At that moment, the whole house shook from a loud bang and the sound of broken glass echoed through the air. When the lights flickered and went out, Hawkman grabbed Jennifer's shoulders, then pushed her deeper into the room. "Stay in here."

CHAPTER SIX

Hawkman quickly drew his gun from the shoulder holster. Using the furniture as cover, he crept toward the living room. Jennifer unzipped her fanny pack, gripped her Beretta, and crouched behind the large oak desk.

He could see the drapes blowing in the breeze from the broken window, but saw no one inside. Leaning against the wall, his weapon poised, he continued around the corner and edged toward the front entry. The power failure had disabled the alarm system, so he opened the door and slipped outside.

Hunkering close to the house, he made his way around to the side where he spotted the silhouette of a person climbing the steps, going up to the deck near the dining room window. He pointed his pistol and called, "Who goes there?"

The figure turned and raised his hands. "Hawkman, it's me, George, from next door. Wife and I heard a loud bang and all the lights went out. Looks like the transformer in front of your house has exploded. I knocked on the front door, but got no response, so decided to come around back to see if I could get your attention."

Hawkman glanced at the pole and could see the smoke curling out of the big box. His gaze traveled down the road and he caught sight of a strange car parked off to the side near the bridge. Suddenly, the headlights came on, and the vehicle took off across the river. It looked like a Buick. He holstered his gun and moved toward his neighbor. "You see anyone fooling around the area?"

George shrugged. "No. We've been watching television most of the evening. You think someone shot out the transformer?"

"Very possible."

"I'll give Pacific Power a call and see when we can get a repair crew out here," George said, walking toward his home.

"Thanks."

After his neighbor left, Hawkman went back inside the house. "Jennifer, you okay?"

"Yes." She came from his office carrying a couple of flashlights and handed him the extra. "I heard you talking to George."

"Yeah, looks like the transformer out front blew and knocked out power all the way down the street. We're probably going to need candles or a lantern for several hours."

She flipped on her light and ran the beam across the dining room carpet. "The transformer didn't throw this," she said, pointing at a large shiny rock resting in the middle of a pile of broken glass. "Looks like it came from the edge of the lake as it's still glistening with water."

"Don't touch it. If we're lucky there might be some prints. He quickly picked up the straying kitten and handed her to Jennifer. "You better take care of this little one so she doesn't get her paws cut on any sharp slivers."

"I wondered where this little stinker went," she said, cuddling the cat close to her chest. Then she glanced at Hawkman with a solemn expression. "Who would throw a rock through our window?"

He frowned and tapped the flashlight against his thigh. "I don't know. But I spotted a car taking off across the bridge and it looked like a Buick."

When the phone rang. Hawkman stared at it as the machine answered.

"Hiding in the dark? This time I only sent a boulder through the window. Hope it didn't shred your cat."

After a siege of wicked laughter, the party hung up.

Hawkman's jaw tightened. "The man's sick. I think we're dealing with a psycho, which makes him even more dangerous.

He's calling us from a cell phone and they're hard to track, unless I can get the FBI in on this. But they probably wouldn't touch it until the man commits murder."

The clear sky and full moon gave a glow to the room, so they were able to move around without much difficulty. Jennifer opened the drapes in the living room, flipped off the flashlight, then made her way to the couch. She cuddled the cat in her arms and sighed. "What are we going to do?"

He stood in front of her with his fists on his hips. "I'd like you to get out of here. Why don't you take the furry critter, and the two of you go down to visit Sam in Sunnyvale."

She shook her head. "You know better than to suggest my leaving. I couldn't stand it. And anyway, his apartment isn't big enough for me to go stay for any length of time. He only has one bedroom and would insist I use it. It wouldn't be fair to force him out of his own bed while he's working. He needs his rest. And there's no way anyone could sleep on his horrible couch. No, I'm not going anywhere, so get that notion out of your head."

Hawkman turned away and slapped his hands against his sides. "I wish you weren't so stubborn. This man's a nut case. And he knows where we live. He could approach you during the day when I'm not here, and do you harm."

"I guarantee I'll leave my mark on him before he has a chance to do anything to me.

Hawkman glanced toward the kitchen window. "Sounds like the Pacific Power truck's here. I think they've set a record." He went to the front door and peered out. "I'm going to talk to them."

"Okay." Jennifer took the cat into the bathroom and placed her in the straw bed, then tossed the stuffed bunny in beside her. The kitten immediately bounced on it. "Sorry girl, I can't let you out to run around until I get the glass cleaned up. Don't want you to hurt yourself." She closed the door and went into the kitchen where she could watch the crew from the window. Their powerful floodlights lit up the area like day time. Hawkman stood talking to one of the men and pointed to the transformer as they lowered it to the ground. Once they released it from the cable, he and the worker examined the outer shell.

After a few minutes Hawkman came inside. "Should have power within the hour."

"Good. Then I'll be able to pick up the mess. I've gathered up some of the bigger pieces, but it's going to be a bear getting the slivers out of the carpet. We'll have to wear shoes around this area until I'm sure it's clear." She frowned. "I don't know what I'll do about the kitten."

"I'll help you clean it up. I think the drapes stopped most of the glass from flying all over the place."

"Why were you examining the busted transformer?"

"I wanted to see if it had a bullet hole."

"Did it?"

"Yes."

Her shoulders drooped. "Well, there's not much Pacific Power can do, if they don't have an inkling who did the shooting."

"Nope, but if they ever find out, it would be a hefty fine and possible jail time. Unfortunately, we couldn't hear any gun discharge due to the explosion, so I couldn't be sure why the transformer went until I examined the shielding."

"So you think this man planned all these distractions, right down to the stupid phone call?"

"Sure looks like it."

"He's definitely got a warped mind."

Once the power came on, Hawkman helped Jennifer clean up the glass. Then he nailed a piece of plywood across the window until they could get it replaced.

The next morning, Jennifer typed on her computer, while the kitten sat on the desk, her tail twitching as if waiting for the right moment to pounce.

Hawkman grinned as he watched. "How can you get anything done with the little imp at your elbow, just waiting to attack your fingers?"

"I'm getting used to her antics. She's even given me some ideas for my books."

He chuckled. "I can imagine. What are you going to name her?"

She glanced at him with a mischievous twinkle in her eye. "I haven't decided yet, but have a few ideas. I might have her named by the time you get home this evening. You are going to the office today, aren't you?"

"Not sure. I hate to leave you alone with that maniac on the loose."

She stood with her hands on her hips. "I'm not going anywhere today. My deadlines are approaching and I've got to get this book finished. I'll lock up the house, turn on the alarm system and stay glued to this computer for the next eight hours. So, please, go."

"Promise you'll call if anything suspicious happens."

"Don't worry. I will."

Before leaving the lake, Hawkman circled the area to make sure the Buick wasn't nearby. Driving up Quail Lane, he came to an immediate halt in front of Ken and Peggy Bronson's house. "Why didn't I think of them earlier," he said aloud. He glanced around and noticed neither of their Sheriff's vehicles were on the property. "They must be on duty," he mumbled. "I'll talk to them this evening." He hit the accelerator, made a U-turn, and headed toward the bridge.

When he reached his office, he noticed the blinking red light on his answering machine and punched the play button before sitting down.

"Mr. Casey, this is Rita Rawlings. I need to talk to you. I might have some information of interest."

Hawkman jotted down the number on a paper pad, then put on the coffee pot. After settling in his chair, he picked up the receiver and tapped in the digits.

CHAPTER SEVEN

Hawkman's gut told him this woman had something important to tell him and he needed to reach her as soon as possible. When her answering machine responded, he left a message, banged the receiver back on the cradle, then crumpled the top sheet on his memo pad and threw it into the waste basket.

He poured himself a cup of coffee, then strolled to the window while sipping the hot brew. Glancing out over the parking lot, his shoulders stiffened when he spotted a bronze colored Buick at the far end. He placed the cup on the filing cabinet, grabbed his binoculars and focused on the person in the driver's seat. Immediately, he realized the man also had a pair of glasses trained on him, and actually waved before driving off.

"Who are you?" Hawkman mumbled, as he stepped back and returned the binoculars to their resting place.

He sat down at his desk, and called Jennifer. "I want you to be extremely watchful in about an hour. The idiot knows I'm in my office and may come out there to terrorize you."

"I have my gun. Everything's locked up and the alarm set. I'll keep a watchful eye."

"Look for the bronze colored Buick I told you about. I doubt he'd have time to change cars before getting there."

"Okay, I'll give you a call if I spot him."

Hawkman hung up and punched in Bill Broadwell's number. When he reached his office, he gave a special code, which routed the call through a different channel. A man's voice soon answered.

"Bill, Tom Casey. Have you had a chance to look through the files on the situation I told you about?"

"Yeah, I was going to call you today. This is a strange circumstance to arise after all these years. But I've come up with three possible names. These guys are no longer with the Agency. They've either retired,quit or we've lost track of them. They may even be dead."

"Give me the names and a little history. I'll check them out."

"Bob Hudson got passed over for promotion several times and the honor usually went to you. He left the group shortly after you disappeared."

"I remember him," Hawkman said. "A real whiner, but good at what he did."

"Then there was Jack Hargrove. Carried a chip on his shoulder and spoke out more than once to his colleagues on how he hated Jim Anderson. No one really knew why, because at the time he came into the Agency here, you were already gone and presumed dead. But he did make a threat once, that one of these days he'd find you. He didn't think you were really deceased."

"That's odd."

"And another strange thing is he didn't even work around your department, he was in a completely different field, so his threats are a mystery."

"Then the last name I have is Hal Brokers. He had a mean streak and at one time or the other mentioned your name when he and colleagues spoke about people they'd like to see dead. He had it in for anyone who pushed ahead of him on the totem pole and you were one of them."

"I vaguely remember him. Tall blond guy, right?"

"Yeah, he never smiled. Always had a frown on his face."

"What does Jack Hargrove look like?"

"Hold on a minute, let me grab his file. I don't ever remember meeting him myself."

Hawkman could hear the rustle of paper and Bill grumbling.

"That's strange. There's no description or picture in his file. Looks like someone has removed it. This isn't good. Let me get back to you."

"Okay, but before you go. Dirk Henderson is still incarcerated isn't he?"

"Oh, yeah. He'll never get out from behind bars. In fact, that's the first thing I checked when I got your call."

"Thanks, Bill, appreciate your help."

Hawkman studied the three names. He could pretty well mark off Bob Hudson. Not the type of man to hold a vendetta, even though he did a lot of complaining. Jack Hargrove he couldn't place. He didn't recall ever hearing the name. Hal Brokers was a mean devil, but he couldn't see him going after an associate. He was the kind of guy who would always defend anyone in the Agency, regardless of how much he hated the person. He had lots of honor. And neither of these two men had green eyes. Of course, with colored contact lens now, one couldn't even go by eye color anymore.

He circled the name Jack Hargrove and put a question mark beside it. This one bothered him. And for Bill to find the file incomplete made him suspect Hargrove either removed the identification or had someone do it. Something about the name kept jogging the recesses of his mind, but wouldn't come forward. He wondered what the guy had to hide. He'd be anxious to hear from Bill when he found out. Leaning back in the chair, he tapped the piece of paper with his pencil eraser. His thoughts were interrupted by a knock at the door. He reached inside his jacket and lifted the flap on his holster. "Come in."

Rita Rawlings poked her head around the door jamb. "I'm glad you're here."

Standing, Hawkman motioned toward the chair. "I've been waiting for your call, but much happier to see you in person."

"It's very hard to catch me at home. I'm all over the place and I also play bridge several afternoons during the week. But I do check my answering machine throughout the day, and caught your return call."

"Cup of coffee?"

"Yes, please," she said, taking the seat. "Oh, while you're up, you might check out the window and see if the brown colored Buick is parked out front."

Hawkman glanced outside while carrying the two cups of coffee. "Yes, it's there." He frowned, as he turned toward her. "What's going on? He just left here a little while ago. Don't tell me he's following you?"

"I've caught him a couple of times in my rearview mirror."

Hawkman placed the steaming brew in front of her. "You take it black, right?"

"Yes, thank you."

"This is very curious. Why would he tail you?"

"It all started last week, after we had our meeting. Of course, I didn't pay any attention whether he was around when I left your office. But that evening I stopped for a beer at Lonnie's off Main Street."

Hawkman nodded. "Yes, I know the place."

"The bartender and I go way back. We were chatting when our friend in the Buick came in the door. I asked Bud if he knew him. He told me he was a newcomer and had visited his place several times in the past couple of weeks. When I asked his name, he said he really didn't know, but he'd heard a couple of customers call him J.J. and one had called him Judd."

He chuckled. "Say, can I hire you as my assistant?"

Rita grinned. "I don't think I have the time. But it sounds exciting."

"And sometimes dangerous. This man could be threatening. I've come to the conclusion, he's not stable."

She reached into her purse and placed an item on his desk. "Well, he better not get too close. I'll take care of him rather rapidly."

Hawkman reared back his head and guffawed. "I can't believe a lovely woman like you carries a stun gun."

A sly smile formed at the corner of her lips. "Fortunately, I've never had to use it, and I'm not even sure I'm legal. I've had it for years, but I've carried it in my hand numerous times and make sure it's fully charged. My job takes me into dangerous areas and I need some sort of protection."

He shook his head. "You are something else. My wife tells me you even marry people in jail."

"Oh, yes. I don't carry the gun in there. I'd never get by the metal detector and I'm sure the guards could protect me. Strange as it may sound, most of my marriage services are performed in the prison."

"That's amazing. Why would anyone want to marry someone who's behind bars?"

She rolled her eyes and threw up her hands. "Because they're 'in love'. Many times I've tried to talk these young women out of it, but it's like talking to a stone wall. They tell me they're going to change him. Shows how naive women can be. Men are similar, but not nearly as bad."

"You've obviously been doing this for several years; you don't need me to warn you to be careful."

"I'm very business like, especially when in the jail environment."

"Getting back to our friend in the Buick. I want to thank you for giving me his name."

"I wish I could figure out why he's following me, unless my dear bartender friend told him I'd been asking questions. He might have thought I had a personal interest."

"That's possible. You're a lovely woman, and he might be impressed with your attention. However, his knowing you're in here now could be risky. As he's really out to get me. I want you to be extremely careful. We sure don't want him to construe your visit here to the point he thinks you've become his enemy. So if he ever confronts you, you tell him you've hired me to find a long lost cousin or whatever story you want to concoct, and I'll go along with it."

"Good idea." She stood and checked her watch. "I've got to be going. Glad I caught you in and hope the information helps."

"Yes, I appreciate it. Promise me you'll keep in touch, especially if our mutual friend approaches you in any way."

"I'll certainly keep you informed."

"By the way, do you have a cell phone?"

"Yes."

He wrote his number down on the back of one of his business cards and gave it to her. "Keep this handy. I can always be reached through my cell."

After Rita left, Hawkman went to the window and observed the Buick following her out of the lot. He didn't like it one bit.

CHAPTER EIGHT

Hawkman couldn't do much about the guy stalking Ms. Rawlings, but figured she could probably handle herself. He stared into space in deep thought for several minutes, then shook himself free of the abstraction, picked up the phone, and contacted the glass shop. He gave the measurements of the broken window and asked how soon they could do the work. They assured him they'd get out to Copco Lake first thing in the morning.

Next, he called the pet shop, asked about Marie, the cat breeder, and how he could get in touch with her. They gave her name as Marie Paulson, but only provided a phone number and explained he'd have to set up an appointment. When he dialed the number and the answering machine came on, he groaned. This didn't appear to be his day for getting in touch with real people on the first try. He left a message and asked his call be returned as soon as possible.

Checking his watch, he assumed school had let out and Ms. Paulson was probably carting her daughters to some sort of lessons. But to his surprise, she rang back within fifteen minutes.

"Mr. Casey, is everything all right with the kitten?"

"Oh, yes. She's just fine."

"Thank goodness. It scared me when I got your call."

"Jennifer has her hands full, but she's having fun."

Marie laughed. "Ragdolls make lovely pets, tell her she'll settle down real soon. You want another?"

"Oh, no! One is all we can manage."

"So what is it you needed to talk to me about?"

He cleared his throat, feeling a bit uncomfortable. "I wondered if I could drop by your place in a few minutes. I'd like to talk to you about an important matter."

"Sure," she said, a question in her voice. "I'll be here the rest of the afternoon."

Hawkman took down her address. "I'll be there inside the hour." Before leaving the office, he glanced out the window to see if the Buick happened to be parked in the lot. Not seeing any sign of the vehicle, he locked up the office and left.

Driving toward the Paulson residence, he kept an eye on the rearview and side mirrors to make sure no one tailed him. He felt responsible for Rita's dilemma and didn't want to involve Marie in a similar situation. She had children and he didn't want to put any of them at risk.

He drove through a tract neighborhood with nice lawns and trimmed bushes. When he came to the address, he parked at the curb in front of a white house with pale brown trim. Two little girls, turning cartwheels on the lawn, ran giggling to the side yard as he approached the front entry.

A woman in her early forties, wearing jeans, tennis shoes, and a long-tailed denim shirt with rolled up sleeves, answered the door. Raking loose strands of her short brown hair behind her ears with her fingers, she smiled. "Hello, Mr. Casey. I'm Marie. Please come in." She led him into a small living room, cleverly furnished so it appeared much bigger. A large Ragdoll cat scurried from under the couch and headed down the hallway.

"I'm sure you're wondering what I want to talk to you about, " Hawkman said, as he sat on the edge of an overstuffed chair.

She chuckled. "Yes, I must say, you've certainly aroused my curiosity. Can I get you something to drink?"

"No, I'm fine, thank you."

Marie made herself comfortable on the couch, where another cat sauntered in, hopped upon the cushion, and snuggled against her side. "I'm very pleased Jennifer likes her new pet. Has she named the kitten yet?"

"No, but she's thinking about it."

"I should have known," she said, smiling. "So like a mystery writer to concentrate on picking out the right name."

Hawkman shifted in his seat. "I don't want to take up your time, so I'll get right to my question. This may sound frightening, but I don't mean to scare you. It's hard to describe the information I need without causing you a bit of apprehension."

Marie knitted her brow. "Please go on."

"Jennifer and I are being harassed, and I'm in the process of trying to find the man who's doing it."

"I don't know how I can help, but I'll try."

"This person knew you were giving Jennifer the kitten."

Her mouth dropped open. "How?"

He shrugged. "I'm hoping you can tell me. Before you gave her the cat, did you have other customers looking at the litter, and by any chance tell them you were saving a certain one for my wife?"

Marie looked thoughtful for a moment. "I took Misty, the mother of Jennifer's feline," she pointed at the cat beside her, "to a show at the hotel downtown. I'd kept her litter about a month after they were weaned because of the upcoming event. I normally sell them shortly after they're off the mother's milk. That's why Jennifer's kitten is close to six months old." She threw up her hands. "Sorry, I got off on a tangent. But do tell Jennifer the cat has already been spayed and her shots are up to date. Anyway, the place was packed and several people were interested in the Ragdolls."

"Do you recall a man with brown hair, gray at the temples, a nose that appeared to have been broken at one time, and intense green eyes, asking questions?"

She snapped her fingers, causing the cat beside her to stand up for a moment, then she settled back down against Marie's thigh. "Yes, I do remember a man of that description. He had a strange twitch to his mouth when he spoke. And yes, he had very intense green eyes. Sort of spooked me. He asked about the kitten I gave to Jennifer. I told him she was saved for someone very special. And he asked me who in the world could be so lucky. I remember just laughing, and said a mystery writer married to a private investigator. I wouldn't have told him her name. But I didn't dream such a little bit of information could cause any harm."

Hawkman raised a hand. "Don't worry, Marie, you did what any normal person would do. But you have verified information very important in this case." He rose from the chair. "And I want to add, Jennifer is going to be thrilled when I tell her I met the beautiful mother of her little panther."

She laughed as she stroked the cat's back. "Yes, she's the prettiest one I have. And has an excellent disposition. I think you'll both be happy with her offspring."

"Thank you for seeing me. And if you should ever spot this man again, please give me a call." He handed her his card.

"I certainly will."

"I'll tell Jennifer the information on the cat, as she's mentioned several times she needed to get in touch with you."

Hawkman left the residence, and as he drove out of the area, checked all the side streets to make sure the Buick hadn't followed. Then he headed home. When he walked in the door after deactivating the alarm, he stepped into the living room and found Jennifer on her knees, raking a long wooden yard stick back and forth under the couch. "What the heck are you doing?"

"Oh, Miss Marple batted one of her toys under here and she can't reach it. I'm trying to get it out."

He scratched his sideburn. "Pardon me. Who's Miss Marple?"

She got up from the floor with a small furry ball in her hand and tossed it toward the corner. "There you go." Then she faced Hawkman with a grin. "I've named the kitten, Miss Marple."

"I see. Could you let me in on how you came up with such a handle. It's quite a mouthful."

She waltzed into the kitchen. "Remember Agatha Christie's books? She created a character named Miss Marple. When her stories became movies, an excellent actress who played the role was Joan Hickson. She appeared quiet, nosey, seemed innocuous, but solved many crimes." Jennifer pointed a finger at him. "And she had intense blue eyes. I thought the description fit our new little pet to a tee."

Hawkman rubbed a hand across his mouth to suppress a smile. "Sounds like you've hit the nail on the head. Miss Marple it is."

Jennifer glanced up at the clock and frowned. "Why are you home so early? Has something happened?"

"There's been an incident that's left me concerned." He told her about Rita Rawlings coming to see him. "I don't like this guy following her. It could be dangerous. He's a loony and might think she knows something."

"Well, if he ever approaches her, he'll go down, since she carries a stun gun."

He wrinkled his forehead. "How'd you know that?"

She grinned. "We had a wonderful conversation after the wedding."

"I obviously didn't attend, as I remember nothing about it. When did this event occur?"

"Several months ago. You were out of town. You didn't know the young couple anyway. They were Sam's friends from high school."

"Ms. Rawlings told me about her weapon at my office. Oh, by the way, I did meet Miss Marple's mother today."

Jennifer snickered. "Sounds like we're trying to outdo each other." She pulled a pitcher out of the refrigerator. "Want a glass of ice tea?"

"I'd rather have a beer."

She set the big container on the cabinet, then stopped with her arm extended inside the cooler, and glanced at him with a questioning look. "Did you say you'd met Miss Marple's mother?"

He nodded. "You want to hand me a beer or are you just going to stand there cooling the kitchen."

She quickly grabbed a bottle and shut the door. "So you went to see Marie?"

"Yes, a very nice lady. And she said to tell you your cat, uh, Miss Marple, is six months old, has already been spayed and her shots are up to date."

"Oh, good. Of course, I'd have called her before I made the appointment with the veterinarian. At least I won't have to go through that mess." She poured herself a glass of tea, then led him into the living room. "Now, tell me about the rest of your conversation."

They sat in their matching chairs and Hawkman told her of his visit with the cat lady.

Jennifer gnawed her lip in silence, then leaned forward. "I don't like the way things are going. Are you positive you weren't followed?"

"Pretty sure. I kept a good lookout, and scouted the area when I left."

"If this guy really wants to get you, all he has to do is kidnap one of Marie's little girls."

"He doesn't have to follow me to find out her name. All he'd have to do is call the hotel and ask about the cat breeders who attended the show."

She sighed. "You're right."

I'm going to run over to Ken and Peggy's tonight to inform them of this situation. Maybe they can keep an eye out for Jack and his Buick. Especially when I'm not here."

"I hate to have the Deputy Sheriffs watch over me when I can look out for myself."

"You're not a law officer, and I can't be in two places at once. Besides, they're local and this is their territory."

Jennifer looked concerned. "This whole situation is getting scary. It's not just you and me anymore. Now Rita, Marie and the local law enforcement are involved."

CHAPTER NINE

Hawkman stared at his wife. "You really know how to blow my evening. I thought about the danger of drawing Rita and Marie into this mess, but I had to speak to them."

"Of course you did. They held valuable information you needed. I guess what worries me the most is, they're both single. Rita doesn't bother me as much, because she's survived many years without a man around. But I'm afraid Marie might be vulnerable, since she's only been widowed for a couple of years. And she's got those three little girls."

"I gave her my phone number so she could let me know if she sees him around the area. I'm sure Marie understood my underlying meaning and will keep her daughters under close supervision."

Jennifer leaned over and patted his knee. "I'm sure she will. I think I'm super sensitive to little girls getting kidnapped after the Tiffany Ryan ordeal."

"I can definitely relate." Hawkman rested his elbows on his knee and rolled the beer bottle between his palms. Miss Marple leaped from the side of the chair where she'd been eyeing his movements and almost batted the bottle from his hands. He laughed, grabbing the beer before it went sloshing across the floor. "Why you little rascal, I'd almost forgotten you were here. I'm going to have to keep a closer eye on you." He picked up the animal and put her in his lap. "You are a cutie." He rubbed her tummy as he continued his conversation. "I've been thinking about one of the names Bill gave me."

"Which one?"

"Jack Hargrove. The 'J' fits in with what Ms. Rawlings heard at the bar. Someone called him J.J. and then she heard the name Judd also. So his middle name could also start with a J." He shook his head. "Wish I could remember this guy, but the name doesn't raise any memories."

"It would have been nice if Bill could have faxed you a photo."

"Oddly enough, he found the ID picture missing. He's going to get back to me once he finds out who's been tampering with the file. And he wasn't familiar with the man either, so he's going to see what he can uncover."

"You know, there's a chance this fellow you're dealing with isn't even associated with the Agency. Maybe he's a complete stranger."

"It's possible, but how would he know my real name?"

She slapped her thighs. "Maybe someone from way back, possibly in your college days. Did Rita or Clyde give you an inkling of how old the guy might be?"

"No, but I gather with the dark hair, graying temples, and buff build, he's close to my age."

Jennifer grinned. "Well, I don't know about the buff build."

He held up the kitten and looked into her face. "Miss Marple, don't you think she's mighty ornery to her sweet husband?"

Jennifer rolled her eyes. "I guess you think you've got a comrade just because she can't tell you what she thinks."

"Not sure she's my buddy yet. Have to wait and see how she and Pretty Girl get along."

Jennifer kicked off her shoes, and pulled her legs beneath her. "Back to this mystery man. I hope Bill calls you soon. This whole situation is making me very jittery."

Hawkman put the cat on the floor, rolled a ball across the carpet, and watched her bound after it. "That reminds me, the window people will be here in the morning to replace the glass."

"Good, that plywood makes the room dark."

When the phone rang, they glanced toward the kitchen bar as the machine picked up. "This is the Medford Hospital, we need to reach Mr. Tom Casey."

Hawkman vaulted from the chair, leaped across the cat and grabbed the receiver. "Yes, this is Tom Casey."

"We've just admitted Rita Rawlings to the hospital and she's asking for you."

"I'll be there within the hour."

He hung up and turned to Jennifer. "Put the cat to bed and grab a jacket, we're going to Medford."

She quickly slipped on her shoes and jumped up. "What's happened?"

"Rita Rawlings has just been admitted to the hospital and is asking for me."

As they exited onto Interstate 5 from Hornbrook, Jennifer put on some lipstick and fluffed her short hair with her fingers. "Did they give any indication why Rita was brought in?"

"No. I didn't want to take the time to find out. I figure since she'd asked for me, it has something to do with the mystery man."

"I don't understand why he'd go after her."

"Me neither, unless he's figured out that she's passed on some information and he wants to shut her up."

"Does he think he can remain anonymous with all the phone calls, then throwing a rock through our window?"

"As I said, he's sick and his thinking is warped."

She stared out the passenger window into the darkness. "I certainly hope Rita's okay."

"We'll soon know."

Jennifer changed the subject. They talked about the cat and miscellaneous topics until they approached the hospital. Hawkman pulled into a slot near the emergency entrance, and they climbed out of the SUV. A flash of lightening crossed the sky, followed by a rumble of thunder. A few sprinkles hit Jennifer in the face as she hurried toward the cover of the entry.

"Oh my, I didn't know we were getting rain tonight." She

pulled her jacket tightly around her chest. "And it's turned downright cold."

"I heard the forecast on the radio, but didn't pay much attention since I didn't expect to be out in it."

They entered the building and made their way to the check-in desk. "I'm Tom Casey, here to see Rita Rawlings."

"Oh, yes, Mr. Casey. We've been expecting you. Please follow me."

They journeyed down the long hallway with Jennifer bringing up the rear. They soon came to a room for patients waiting to be transferred elsewhere. The attendant turned to Hawkman. "She's in here. Detective Williams is with her now."

"What happened?"

"Her car went over an embankment."

"Is she hurt bad?"

"Nothing life threatening, but she's banged up a little. We'll keep her overnight for observation."

The woman left, and Hawkman opened the door a crack and peeked inside. The detective in a chair next to the bed, glanced up and gave a wave.

"Hawkman, come in."

When they stepped into the room, Jennifer immediately scooted toward Rita's side. "Are you okay?"

"I think so, just bruised a bit," she said, removing an ice-pack from her mouth. "My head slammed into the steering wheel when I hit the tree."

"Oh, you poor dear," Jennifer said, brushing some hair strands from Rita's face. "Looks like you got a fat lip, but I don't see any other cuts."

Williams stood and turned to Hawkman. "Ms. Rawlings tells me she was forced off the road by a man you know about. She said you could fill me in on the details. So what's going on?"

Hawkman told him about the incidents leading up to Rita's involvement. "Believe me, I never thought it would turn out like this. She has nothing to do with this problem, and it baffles me why he's after her."

"I think I can answer your concerns," Rita said.

Hawkman stepped to her side. "I'm listening."

"Remember when I told you about my being in the bar having a beer last week and asking the bartender if he knew the guy?"

"Yes."

"I went by there tonight after I finished a wedding and Bud informed me J.J. had the hots for me. I asked how in the world the man ever came to the conclusion I'd be interested. He said he'd told him I'd asked his name." She raised a fist. "I thought I'd kill Bud on the spot. And to make matters worse, I didn't realize J.J. was in the bar. I left in a huff. On my way home, I noticed this car following me, and the person kept blinking the bright lights. I kept moving, and before I knew it, the vehicle pulled alongside me. The driver motioned for me to pull over. I shook my head and kept driving. The next thing I knew he bumped into me and I went flying off the side of the road."

"Did you recognize the car?"

"Yes, the bronze colored Buick."

CHAPTER TEN

A nurse entered the room. "We're going to move Ms. Rawlings now. If everyone will go to the waiting area down the hall, I'll let you know when we have her settled. It'll probably be close to thirty minutes."

"What's the room number?" Jennifer asked.

"Two twenty-three."

"Thank you."

Hawkman and Jennifer decided to head down to the cafeteria to see if they could find something to eat. Williams joined them.

"What do you think of Ms. Rawlings' story?" the detective asked.

Hawkman shook his head. "Hard to say. She could be right. But just because she wouldn't pull over, isn't a good reason to run her off the road. The behavior of this man has been erratic and unstable. I'm not sure what to make of it."

"Do you have any information about him?"

"None. I don't even know what he looks like, other than the description given to me by Rawlings and Clyde. She did give me a clue about his name. Everything has happened so fast, I haven't had a chance to get the information I need." He snapped his fingers. "Remind me to give you the rock that sailed through our window. I have it in my vehicle. Maybe your guys could check it for fingerprints."

"It's almost impossible to pull them off a rough surface."

"This one is fairly smooth."

Williams nodded. "We can sure give it a try. Ms. Rawlings said you had the license plate number of the Buick."

"Yes, it's at my office. The car is registered with a rental agency. There's no way they'll give me any information without the proper authority, but you could find out. You've got a hit and run on your hands now." Hawkman frowned. "By the way, who reported the accident?"

Williams raised a brow. "An anonymous male caller."

"That's interesting."

"It would sure save me some time, if I had the license plate number. I could send it out over the dispatch immediately. I'll keep your pretty wife company if you want to go get it."

"I'll go right now." He stood and took the last bite of his sandwich. "While I'm gone, Jennifer can tell you about Miss Marple."

Williams knitted his brows and stared at her. "Who?"

Hawkman hurried down the hospital steps and headed toward his 4X4. The rain had subsided and he could see the stars through the breaks in the clouds. "Crazy weather," he mumbled as he scooted into the driver's seat.

Pulling out of the parking lot, he glanced into his rearview mirror and stiffened at the sight. A bronze colored Buick followed right on his tail. It pursued him through town, then suddenly turned off onto a side street. He breathed a sigh of relief. Surely there's more than one such colored Buick in the area. But he still kept vigilant, in case the car showed up somewhere along the way before he reached his office.

He entered the parking lot, and discovered he had the area to himself, so stopped in the center under one of the lights. He surveyed the area, nothing seemed amiss, but uneasiness crept through him. Pulling his gun from the shoulder holster, he climbed out of the SUV, and locked it up. His gaze took in every shadow around the building. Not seeing anything out of the ordinary, he took the stairs two at a time to the office entry. Standing to one side, he pushed open the heavy steel door, reached around the jamb and flipped on the light. Everything seemed in order. Holstering his gun, he secured himself inside before going to his desk where he'd left the piece of paper with the license plate number. He scribbled a quick copy for the detective, and stuffed it into his pocket. Before leaving, he went to the window and checked outside. The lights sent an eerie glow across the blacktop, but all appeared clear. Hawkman headed down the stairs.

Jennifer and the detective finished their snack, cleaned off the table and strolled down the hallway. She checked her watch.

"Hawkman should be back by now. I'm going to call and find out what's keeping him." After several seconds, she scowled. "That's odd, he's not answering his cell."

"Maybe I should run over to his office."

"Let me call there too." The phone to her ear, she shook her head. "No answer."

Williams stopped and grimaced. "Doesn't sound like him. He'd have notified one of us if he'd been delayed. I think I'll drive over."

"Good idea. I'll go on up to Rita's room. Be sure and let me know if everything's okay."

They parted and Jennifer proceeded to the elevator as Williams went out the door.

The detective kept an eye out for Hawkman's SUV as he drove down the road. When he pulled into the complex, his gut tightened as he parked beside his friend's empty 4X4. He glanced up at the office windows and saw no sign of lights. Jumping out of his unmarked car, he pulled his gun and cautiously advanced toward the building.

About half way across the blacktop. he gasped, "Oh my God!" Ripping his cell phone out of his jacket pocket, he called 911, then rushed to the face down, limp body of Hawkman. He placed his fingers on his neck. Finding a pulse, he breathed a sigh of relief. Blood seeped from the wound on the back of Hawkman's head and trailed down the collar of his shirt. The red smeared cowboy hat lay upside down at the side of his body. Williams picked it up and examined the crown. It appeared someone had attacked from the rear, as a big gouge penetrated the leather.

Suddenly, Hawkman groaned and Williams placed a hand on his shoulder. "Take it easy big man. Help is coming."

When the ambulance tore into the lot and screeched to a stop, Williams waved them over. "He's got a bad head injury."

The paramedics had Hawkman strapped onto a gurney, rolled into the vehicle and took off with siren blaring in a matter of minutes. Meanwhile, the detective called his officers to meet him at the scene. When they arrived, he gave instructions for a thorough search of the area and gave one of the men Hawkman's hat to tag for evidence. "I'll check back later. Call me if you find anything significant."

Williams returned to his car and took off for the hospital. He immediately went to Ms. Rawlings room and poked his head inside. "Uh, Jennifer, could I talk to you a moment?"

She scurried into the hallway, her expression full of concern. "What's happened?"

"Hawkman's been attacked. I don't know how bad he's hurt. The ambulance has brought him here. I'll meet you in the emergency area after I talk to Ms. Rawlings."

Before he finished his sentence, Jennifer dashed for the elevator. When she spotted it would be awhile before it stopped on the second floor, she rushed to the stairwell and ran down the steps.

Meanwhile, the detective moved into the room. "Ms. Rawlings, I need to ask you some more questions."

Rita pushed herself up with her elbow. "I don't like the look on your face."

"Mr. Casey went to get the license plate number of the Buick and someone assaulted him outside his office."

She put a hand over her mouth and dropped back onto the pillow. "Oh, no! How bad is he hurt?"

"He's conscious and aware. When I find out anything, I'll let you know."

"Do you think the man who ran me off the road is responsible?"

"I'm not sure, but I want you to give me another detailed description, and a recount of anything else that might help in identifying him."

After giving a clear report of her assailant, she told the detective about the donut shop and bar incident, then she pointed to the cabinet at her side. "If you'll hand me my purse out of the third drawer, I'll see if I still have the slip of paper with the license plate number."

He shoved the pad and pencil into his pocket, and knelt beside the bed. "That would really help," he said, retrieving the handbag.

She fumbled through the many pockets and finally came up with a crumpled piece of paper. "Ah, here it is."

The detective quickly jotted down the information, then handed it back to her. "Keep this, in case you need it again."

Smoothing out the page, she tucked it inside her checkbook. "Next time I'll know exactly where I put it." She set the bag beside her. "You better get down to the emergency room and find out about Mr. Casey. Ask Jennifer if she'd please let me know his condition."

"I'll have her come up as soon as she can. You take care and stay alert." He patted the metal foot of her bed and headed out the door.

CHAPTER ELEVEN

Detective Williams joined Jennifer in the emergency waiting room. "Heard anything?"

"He's conscious and wanting to get out of here. But the doctor insisted on doing a CT scan on his head, but he doesn't think there's any brain damage. He felt whatever hit him was deflected and Hawkman didn't get the full impact. However, he did need a few stitches."

"His hat might have saved him, it took a beating. It had a big gouge in the back. I found it at the scene and turned it over to my officers. Maybe we can find out the type of weapon used."

Jennifer grew silent for a moment, gnawing on her lower lip.

The detective studied her expression. "Okay, what's going on in your mind? You're as bad as your husband. I can hear the wheels grinding."

She grinned. "That's a nice compliment. If you really want to know my thoughts, I'm not only concerned about Rita, but also Marie Paulson."

He frowned. "Hawkman mentioned a Marie, but didn't elaborate. What does she have to do with this guy?"

Jennifer explained about the kitten and how Marie might be the next victim. "She's recently widowed and has three little girls. I haven't had a chance to talk to her, but Hawkman assured me he'd made her aware of the danger."

Williams scratched his head. "How many others are involved in this mess?"

"I don't think there's anyone else. But it might be wise if you stationed a guard outside Rita's room for the night."

He glanced toward the ceiling. "Yeah, that's a good idea. It certainly can't hurt and this is about the only thing brewing tonight." He stood. "I think I'll take off and get some business done. If Hawkman has a turn for the worse, just give me a call on the cell. I'll assign an officer to stay here, then I'm going to find out who owns the rental car place. I think it's time to start getting some answers."

She nodded. "You know my husband; he won't be staying here for the night if he has anything to do with it. And will more than likely be contacting you first thing in the morning."

"I'll be expecting his call." Williams waved and walked out the door.

❧

The detective pulled up the collar of his coat as he stepped from underneath the awning of the hospital entry. Torrents of rain overwhelmed the gutters and drains making large puddles in the parking lot. He splashed through a couple, and felt the water soaking through his shoes and socks. Shivering from the plunge in temperature, he jumped into his car and turned on the heater. Rubbing and blowing on his hands to warm up, he finally backed out of the space. A small tree limb, propelled by the high wind, bounced across his windshield as he bumped out of the exit. "What a night," he mumbled, turning onto the asphalt.

He called the station and made arrangements for one of the officers to stand guard outside Ms. Rawlings' room for the night. Driving slowly down the street of the car rental agency, he didn't expect to find anyone there at this hour, but remembered people turned cars in late at night. Since this guy sideswiped a vehicle, there'd be dents and he probably wouldn't want to face the owner. So maybe he parked it in the lot after hours.

The detective stopped in front of the building, and left the motor running. He squinted through the rain splattered windshield, and could make out a driveway alongside the building. He turned in, but came to a sudden stop when he spotted a body lying in the middle of the wet pavement. Leaping from the car, he dashed to the person's side and immediately tapped in 911 on his cell. He felt for a pulse just as the man groaned and tried to move. "Stay still, fellow."

The man's eyelids flickered open and he stared at Williams. "Who are you?" he whispered.

"I'm Detective Williams and help is on the way."

"You gotta catch that guy; he brought in a damaged car," he said, pointing toward a bronze Buick. "He slugged me when I told him he couldn't leave until he talked to the boss."

"What's your name?" Williams asked.

"Fred Baxter. I'm the night watchman for several of these buildings and had just started my walk through of this place when this guy drove in. I immediately saw the damage to the side of the car and told him I'd better call Mr. Fielding."

The emergency vehicle swerved in and the paramedics jumped out. "Hey, detective, you're keeping us busy tonight," one of the men said, pushing the gurney toward the victim.

Williams stepped aside so they could examine Fred. The rain had stopped for the moment, but thunder could be heard in the distance.

"What's his condition?" the detective asked.

"His vitals are fine. We'll take him in and have him checked by the doctor."

"Let me ask Mr. Baxter a couple more questions before you roll out of here." Williams stepped up to the rear of the vehicle. "You want me to call anyone?"

"Naw, I have my cell phone. I'll call my wife. It won't scare her if she hears my voice."

"Do you have a phone number for Mr. Fielding?"

"Yeah, I know it by heart." He rattled it off and Williams wrote it down.

"I'll want to ask you more questions. Where can I reach you?"

Fred gave another number. "That's my cell and I always have it with me."

"Thanks." Williams moved back and gestured for the paramedics to close the door. "Okay, boys, take him away."

After the ambulance left, the detective retrieved his flashlight out of the car, then strolled over to the Buick and examined the marks on the side of the vehicle. It definitely had hit something, and the color left on the metal appeared close to the same shade as Ms. Rawlings car. He took out his cell phone and punched in the digits of the manager.

"Mr. Fielding, this is Detective Williams of the Medford Police. I'm at your place of business and discovered your night watchman has been attacked. The ambulance has taken him to the hospital, but I think he'll be fine. He talked to me about a man who'd returned a damaged vehicle. When he told him he needed to contact you, the assailant slugged him. I'd like for you to come down here and give me the information on who rented this Buick. I'll be waiting."

Williams climbed back into his car, turned on the engine and flipped the heater to medium. He'd stood outside, enduring the cold temperature with his damp clothes clinging to his body until he felt chilled to the bone. The warm air felt good and he hoped it would partially dry his shoes and socks. His feet felt like two big cubes of ice.

Fifteen minutes passed before a late model, white Cadillac sedan pulled into the driveway and parked beside him. A short, obese man struggled out of the driver's seat and hobbled over to his car.

"Detective Williams?"

"Yes."

"Let's go inside the building so I can get the paperwork." He turned and pointed a stubby finger at the Buick. "Is that the one we're talking about?"

Williams climbed out and followed him. "Yes."

Mr. Fielding unlocked the back door, reached in and flipped on an outside light which illuminated the area. He quickly strolled around the Buick, surveying it with a sharp eye, grumbling as he examined the bent metal. "It's heavily damaged. I'll need to contact the man and my insurance agent."

The rain started to come down heavier, and they hurried inside the rental office. The manager slipped on a pair of reading glasses. "Would you be so kind as to show me your credentials?"

"Sure." The detective flipped open his badge and the man studied it for a few seconds, then went straight to the corner filing cabinet behind the counter. He sorted through some folders, and eventually retrieved one. "Here it is." Removing a couple of pieces of paper, he placed them on the surface. "This is the information we took from his driver's license."

Williams glanced at the sheets. "Do you have a scanner?"

"Yes."

"Could you make me a copy, please? Did you rent the car to this man?"

Fielding shook his head as he placed them on the copier. "No, I just overlook the business. I'm seldom here." Glancing at part of the invoice, he pointed at a line. "Charles rented it, and he's on vacation right now. He'll be back in about three days."

Williams studied the report once Fielding handed it over. Fortunately, the driver's license picture had come out bright and clear.

CHAPTER TWELVE

Detective Williams studied the address on the license. "I see Mr. Hargrove is from out of state. Did he mention why he was in Oregon?"

"I couldn't say; you'd have to ask Charles."

He waved a hand. "That's right. You weren't here."

"If you'll wait a minute, I'll see if I can get hold of Mr. Hargrove at the motel where he's staying."

"Good idea."

Fielding opened the phone book to the yellow pages, held the receiver between his fat chin and shoulder, then punched in numbers as his finger tapped across the page. "Please ring Mr. J. Hargrove's room." His eyebrows rose. "I see. Did he leave a forwarding address?"

He hung up and glanced at Williams. "He checked out about two hours ago, and didn't leave any information on how he could be reached."

Williams turned toward the door. "Thank you for your time, Mr. Fielding. If I find this man, I'll let you know. I have a feeling he's left you with a big bill. But I'm going to ask you not to have the car repaired until I have my lab crew go over it."

"I understand. I won't send the automobile into the shop until I get your okay." A slight grin curled the corners of his mouth as he held up one of the sheets. "I do have Mr. Hargrove's credit card number, so he might get a little surprise on his statement."

The detective stepped into the peppering rain, stashed the report under his jacket, and dashed to his car. Once inside the vehicle, he twisted the key in the ignition, then checked the name of the motel and drove into the street. He entered the driveway of the establishment, and parked under the large fancy overhang. When he approached the plush front desk, he flashed his badge and asked to see the manager.

Williams spoke with him for several minutes, but received no more information. Back in the car, he wondered if Hargrove had left the area. Since he'd be on foot, he'd more than likely take a taxi to his destination. The detective called one of his officers and instructed him to check the taxicab businesses and the bus station while he inquired at the airport.

After several hours of studying each airline's passenger list, and finding nothing suspicious, he made copies of the pictured license and distributed them to the attendants in case Hargrove tried to board on a 'standby' status. He talked with his officers after he'd finished and they'd also come up empty handed. It appeared the man had disappeared into thin air. "Where the hell has he gone?" he mumbled, getting into his vehicle.

He'd done all he could today, and the hour approached midnight. Rubbing the back of his neck, his thoughts went to Hawkman. More than likely Jennifer had him home and tucked into bed by now. Williams chuckled to himself, as he pictured his friend's resistance.

✒

At the hospital, Hawkman slowly walked into the waiting room. Jennifer jumped up and went to his side. "Have they dismissed you?"

The doctor, who'd followed him out, interrupted. "He doesn't have a concussion, only a bad lump on the head and a few stitches. But I want him home in bed as soon as you can get him there. A couple days' rest and he should be good as new." He handed Jennifer a prescription. "This is for pain pills, if he needs them."

Jennifer tucked it into her purse. "Thank you." She hung onto Hawkman's arm as they moved into the hallway. "Why don't you wait here while I run up and tell Rita goodbye."

"I'm fine. I'll go with you."

"Are you sure? You're staggering."

He put a hand to his forehead. "Okay, I think you're right," and he flopped into a chair against the wall.

"Don't move. I'll be right back."

Jennifer hurried up to the second floor and started to enter Rita's room, but found herself stopped by the strong arm of the officer guarding the door.

"Just a moment, I need to see some identification. And may I ask why you're here?"

"I'm a friend," she said, showing her driver's license.

He poked his head into the room. "You know a Jennifer Casey?"

"Yes, yes. Let her in, please," Rita called out.

Jennifer moved briskly to her bedside. "I can only stay a minute. Hawkman's waiting for me downstairs."

She looked puzzled. "You keep calling your husband 'Hawkman'."

"It's a nickname and I'll explain it to you at another time; right now I have to hurry. Just wanted you to know he's okay and I'm taking him home. Call me tomorrow when you get out of here." She headed for the door, then turned. "By the way, who's picking you up?"

"One of my bridge buddies. Glad your hubby's okay. I'll talk to you tomorrow."

Jennifer dashed out the door and down the steps. She didn't know what her better half might do if she didn't get back to him. When she arrived by his side, she found him bent over, holding his head in his hands.

"Man, I've got a terrific headache. And they've shaved off a big swatch of my hair. Where's my hat?"

"Do you want me to get the pain pills?"

"No."

"Williams has your hat at the police station. I think it's ruined, so you'll have to shape another one. Do you feel like walking to the car or do you want me to bring it around?"

He stood up and swayed a little. "I think I can make it okay."

When they got outside, it was pouring rain.

"You wait here so you don't get wet," Jennifer said. "I'll get the car."

Hawkman leaned against the side of the building without an argument and she ran into the cloud burst. She soon had the SUV at the door and he climbed inside. He pushed against the seat and lowered the back rest. Before Jennifer drove out of the parking lot, he'd closed his eyes, breathing in a soft rhythm. She smiled to herself.

The storm eased as she approached Copco Lake and had diminished to a sprinkle by the time she pulled into their driveway. She jumped out, ran to the entry, deactivated the alarm and opened the front door. When she reached the passenger side of the vehicle, Hawkman had awakened and glanced around.

"We home already? Boy, you must have broken the sound barrier."

"No, dear, I drove the speed limit. Let's get you into bed; then I'll move the 4X4 into the garage."

She got him tucked in, put the car away, then went to the bathroom to let Miss Marple out for a run. When Jennifer opened the door, she burst into laughter. "Oh, no, you've been one busy little cat."

"What'd she do?" Hawkman called from the bedroom.

"Hope you don't mind a big roll of toilet paper. She's unrolled the whole thing and it's draped all over the tub, the toilet and the sink. Our little kitten has had a heyday."

"She's probably mad at you for leaving her so long."

"I wouldn't doubt it."

Miss Marple launched out of the room like a rocket, passed Jennifer, and headed straight to where Hawkman lay on the bed. After leaping up on the end of the mattress, she sat down on her haunches and stared at him.

Jennifer rolled up the paper the best she could, giggling as she worked. Then she crept into the room and watched the feline from a distance. Miss Marple inched herself closer to Hawkman's leg and snuggled as close as possible without disturbing him. It fascinated Jennifer how the animal had taken to her husband.

When the phone jangled, Jennifer hurried into the kitchen. Her full attention focused on the answering machine.

"Guess I didn't hit you hard enough. I saw them take you to the hospital and your pretty wife brought you home. The police think I've disappeared. But have no fear, I'm still around. So watch your back, *Hawk Man*. I'm not through with you."

Jennifer hit her fist on the counter. "Who are you and why are you doing this?" she asked aloud. She left the phone and booted up her computer. Her nerves felt raw and stretched like tight rubber bands. It would take awhile to unwind, and that message didn't help.

CHAPTER THIRTEEN

The next morning, Hawkman awoke to see two big blue eyes peering at him. "What the heck are you doing in my bed?" he quizzed the cat.

Jennifer rolled over and took Miss Marple into her arms. "I didn't have the heart to make her go to her room. She's so worried about you."

He sat up and groaned. "Did she tell you this?"

"Not in so many words, but her actions speak tons."

"You know, you're spoiling her. Now, she'll never be happy sleeping anywhere but right here."

"How are you feeling?"

"Much better. I have a very sore scalp."

"The doctor said not to get your stitches wet. So I'll help you wash around them."

His eyes lit up. "You gonna take a shower with me?"

"I don't think I could reach your head," she quipped.

"Darn. You're such a party pooper."

He climbed out of bed and looked over the lake from the sliding glass door. "Looks like a much nicer day than yesterday. At least the sun is shining."

"April is unpredictable. It could cloud up and snow tonight."

"You're right. I remember a couple of years ago when it snowed in May." He turned and stretched his arms. "Man, I'm sore all over."

"You took a bad blow and probably fell hard."

"I better give Williams a call."

"Before you do, you might want to listen to the message we received last night."

He jerked around and stared at her. "Why didn't you wake me? I didn't even hear the phone ring."

"There wasn't anything you could do about it."

Hawkman padded into the kitchen in his bare feet and underwear; went straight to the phone and punched the play button. After he heard the man's voice, he mumbled. "Who is this guy?" Scowling, he punched in the detective's number, then put it on speaker.

"Williams, Hawkman."

"How are you feeling?"

"Sore and have a headache. We received another threatening phone call from our mystery man."

"Interesting, I found out his name."

Hawkman's attention piqued. "What is it?"

"J. Hargrove. The car rental had the information, along with the motel where he'd been staying. When I talked with the management at the inn, they informed me he'd checked out. So I hurried to the airport. Another futile trip, along with checking the bus depot and taxi drivers. It's like he disappeared into thin air. I also checked the other car rentals in the area. Nothing."

"He's obviously still around; listen to this." He hit the play button.

"When did that come in?" Williams asked.

"Late last night, after we got home from the hospital."

"It appears our guy wants to play games."

"He can't get far without wheels. Have you checked the used car lots?"

"In the process right now. Leaving a picture at each one. I'll let you know if anything turns up. Also, Ms. Rawlings filed a hit and run report this morning after they dismissed her from the hospital, so we've got our eyes peeled."

"You've got a picture?"

"Yeah, off the license. Want me to fax it to you?"

"Please."

After Hawkman hung up, he prepared to receive the fax and within minutes it came through. He lifted the paper from the tray, studied the photo, and shook his head. "I've never seen this guy."

Jennifer looked over his shoulder. "Isn't that one of the names Bill gave you?"

"Yes, but I've never met this man. I'd remember those eyes, if nothing else."

"If he worked for the Agency, how come you don't recognize him?"

"It's a big place."

Hawkman heard a noise and glanced toward the kitchen window. "Looks like the guys are here to install the glass in the broken window. Get the bell while I run in and throw on some clothes."

Jennifer tightened the belt around her robe and ran her fingers through her hair. She deactivated the alarm and opened the door. Her knees felt weak when she looked at one of the men. "Are you guys here to replace the broken window?"

"Yes, ma'am."

"Just a moment, please. I'll get Mr. Casey." She closed the door, threw the dead bolt and dashed to the bedroom. "One of those men looks like the guy in the picture."

"Are they from the glass place?"

"That's what they said. I told them to wait outside and I'd get you."

He snatched his gun from the holster and slid it into the waistband of his jeans, covering it with his tee shirt. "I'll go take a look."

Jennifer trailed him to the kitchen. He moved to the window, and glanced out. "The logo on the truck matches the company I called."

"The shorter man is the one who looks like the photo," Jennifer said, pointing.

The two men had meandered out to the center of the driveway and Hawkman took a moment to study them.

"His body build doesn't match Clyde and Ms. Rawlings' description of Hargrove. That guy's not as tall. And the pot belly hanging over his belt, doesn't match what I'd call buff." Hawkman removed his gun and handed it to Jennifer. "I don't think I'll need this. Would you put it back?"

"Sure." Jennifer retreated to the bedroom to get dressed. She slipped the gun into Hawkman's shoulder holster and put her hands on her hips as she observed Miss Marple curled up on his pillow. "You little squirt. I think you're more fond of the mister of this household." She ran her hand down the silky fur. "Hey, I'm the one who feeds and plays with you."

The cat gently batted Jennifer's hand, then turned and rubbed her head along Hawkman's pillow.

"Come on, time to get off the bed." Jennifer picked up the kitten, placing her on the floor while she smoothed out the covers and tucked in the spread.

She showered, dressed, and came into the room where the men were installing the new pane. Hawkman had brewed some coffee and sat at the kitchen bar reading the paper while sipping the hot liquid.

"Looks like they're almost done," she said, pouring herself a cup.

"Doesn't take long once they've removed all the old glass. I'd given them the measurements, so they had the piece cut. Just a matter of setting it into place."

The men soon finished the job and Hawkman handed them a check. "Thanks, fellows, nice work."

Hawkman turned to Jennifer after they left. "I talked with them awhile, and both have been with the company for over five years. So, he definitely wasn't Hargrove."

"Thank goodness. My heart almost stopped when I saw him. He really resembled the picture."

"Yeah, but his eyes weren't green, they were more hazel and not near as piercing as Hargrove's."

When the phone rang, he stood back and listened to the beginning of the message.

"This is Detective Williams. If you're there, give me a buzz."

Hawkman punched on the speaker phone. "Yeah, I'm here."

"I had the feeling you might be monitoring your calls, so thought I'd better identify myself."

"Glad you did. What's up?"

"Got the lab results on your hat. The techs found some rust embedded in the leather and came to the conclusion you were hit with a metal pipe of sorts. They figured a tire iron from the looks of the crease it left in the leather. "

Hawkman reached up and touched the bandage on his head. "Good Lord, no wonder I have such a horrible headache. Did they find the weapon?"

"No, sorry. Not a sign of it on the property, or in the garbage bin."

"Should have the rental place guy check the inside of the car."

"My lab men are going over there today. They'll search it from stem to stern. Do you want your hat back?"

"Is it wrecked?"

"I doubt you'll wear it again. Got a big hole in the back. It's sitting here on my desk; be glad to save it for you."

"Might as well keep it for evidence. I've got plenty. Just breaking them in is the hard part."

"Didn't come up with anything on the used car lots either. No one recognized the guy."

Hawkman scratched his chin as Jennifer looked on. "The man will need some sort of transportation. Have you had any reports of stolen vehicles?"

"I'm checking it out."

"We're not dealing with someone who has scruples. At this point, he's apt to steal a vehicle from a little old lady at the grocery store."

"I believe it. I'll get back to you if anything worthwhile shows up."

CHAPTER FOURTEEN

Hawkman scooted off the kitchen bar stool and crossed over to his favorite resting place in the living room. "What do we have here," he chuckled, as he reached down and picked up Miss Marple off the cushion. "I thought you were Jennifer's pet." He gently placed the cat in his wife's identical chair.

She immediately jumped to the floor and stood at his feet, staring up with pleading blue eyes.

"Honey, you need to give this cat more attention. She's begging."

Jennifer glanced up from her computer and smiled. "She's definitely taken an interest in you. Wonder if somehow she knows you're hurt."

"I think animals sense something different. Whether she knows what, is hard to say. But she didn't move from my side all night. I didn't dare shift positions in case I'd roll over and hurt her."

Resting her chin on the palm of her hand, Jennifer's expression turned to concern. "I'm surprised you weren't hurt worse after hearing Williams talk about the weapon being a pipe of sorts. That sends shivers down my spine."

Hawkman shrugged. "Guess it pays to wear a good hat."

"It's obviously ready for the trash can. You're going to have to shape another."

He nodded. "I'll do that later. What really bothers me is they've found no sign of Hargrove." He threw up his hands. "It's like he's 'evaporated'. But we know he hasn't."

"Maybe he changed his appearance and flew out of here. If he spent some time in the Agency, he's probably got several identities."

"True. But we received the call after we arrived home from the hospital, so he's still around. And it wouldn't surprise me if he stole a vehicle off of someone's driveway."

"It could take a week for a report to come in."

He raised his brows. "Why?"

"Spring break. Kids are out of school, and people take off. If they had an extra car in their garage, or out in front of their house, they won't know it's gone until they return."

He started to hit his forehead with the palm of his hand, but gave it a second thought. "You're right. I'd completely forgotten. Without Sam here, I lose track of the vacations." He grimaced. "Sure could put a delay in knowing what kind of vehicle to look for."

Jennifer arose from her computer, strolled into the living room and sat down in her chair. "Unless someone spots him."

"I doubt he'll hang around Medford. He knows he's a wanted man."

"Any idea of where he might go?"

He shook his head and immediately put his fingers on his temples. "Still smarts to move."

"You should be in bed."

"Oh, sure. You've got a lot of nerve to talk. Remember when I tried to get you to go lie down during your chemo treatments?"

She laughed. "Yes. But it still doesn't keep me from trying to entice you to rest."

"The only way I'll go, is if you go with me."

"Right. A row in bed is the last thing you need."

His eyes twinkled. "Try me."

"Hawkman, you're awful."

About that time, the cat leaped upon his lap with the stuffed bunny in her mouth.

"How does she manage to sneak around without us even seeing her?"

"She's a little pussy foot sleuth."

He took the toy and ran it down the arm of the chair. Miss Marple stood up on his thigh and batted it with her front paws, then immediately fell into the crack between his legs. He laughed and tossed the bunny to the floor. She jumped down and leaped on the soft toy. Shoving it around for several minutes, she ended up pushing it behind the couch leg. She played peek-a-boo with the toy until she finally tired, and flopped down beside the sofa.

Hawkman chuckled. "We just enjoyed a show far better than what's on television."

"She's a case, isn't she?"

"So you think you'll keep her?"

Jennifer swung her head around and glared at him. "Of course. Whatever gave you the idea I didn't want the kitten?"

"I figured maybe you'd give her to me, since she likes me better."

She grabbed one of the pillows off the couch. "If you weren't hurt, I'd throw this at you. I'd say you're one spoiled husband."

He hooked a thumb toward his chest. "Who, me? By the way, when are we going to eat?"

Jennifer sighed and rolled her eyes. "See. You're rotten."

After they ate, Hawkman retired back to his chair. "Man, I hate feeling like this."

She glanced up from loading the dishwasher. "Are you hurting?"

"Have a dull headache, and my body's sore."

"Just rest awhile, you'll feel better soon. If you're bored, why don't you shape one of your hats? You have a closet full of new ones. You need something on your head, especially since you've got a cute bald spot." She turned her back to him so he couldn't see her grin.

"You had to bring up my bare scalp. I'd just about forgotten it was there."

She put a hand over her mouth. "Sorry."

"But you're right," he said, hoisting himself up and strolling into the bedroom.

Jennifer could hear him rummaging through boxes. Miss Marple sat on the floor with both ears pointed toward the hallway. Jennifer wondered how the animal knew this wasn't a good time to bother her master.

Soon, Hawkman returned to the living room with the Stetson El Patron in his hand. "I think it's time I broke in this baby."

She smiled. "I wondered when you'd get around to it."

He slipped the hat onto his head, then quickly removed it. "Ouch! Don't think I'll be able to wear it for another day or so."

After he sat down in the chair, she walked behind him. "Let me take a look at the wound."

"You can't see anything, there's a bandage covering the stitches."

"I can see through it."

"Sure you can," he scoffed.

She pulled the tape up on one side and Hawkman winced. "Be still. Hmm."

"What does that mean?"

Patting him on the shoulder, she stuck the adhesive back in the same spot and moved away. "Nothing. I'm teasing. It appears to be healing just fine. It's still a bit swollen and bruised."

"I could've told you that."

Jennifer headed for her computer. "I've got some work to do."

Hawkman placed the hat on the coffee table, then snapped his fingers. "I should call Ken and Peggy. I want to inform them of the situation." He glanced at Jennifer. "How about, if they're available, having them over for cocktails tomorrow evening?"

"I'd love it. They're a fun couple to be around."

He punched in the Bronsons' number. "Hey, Ken, how's it going?" Hawkman laughed. "No sleep for the wicked, huh? Well, it doesn't surprise me since you two are the only Deputy Sheriffs for miles around. If you and Peggy are free tomorrow night, why don't you drop by for cocktails? Also, got a little business I need to discuss." He listened for a few seconds, then gave Jennifer the 'okay' sign. "Great. See you then."

After hanging up, he picked up his binoculars. "Think I'll go out on the deck."

Miss Marple followed him to the sliding glass door.

Jennifer hopped up and caught her before she could get outside. "Nope. You're an indoor cat," she said. "I don't want you to get fleas, and besides, we haven't completed all your shots."

Hawkman checked Pretty Girl's food and water, gave her some encouraging words, then paced back and forth in thought. Soon, he ventured down to the gangplank leading to the dock, then looked through the glasses and inspected the area. The lake looked peaceful, but the slight nip in the wind would definitely make it uncomfortable to try and fish off the dock. He strolled back to the deck and sat down on the chair beside the small butcher block. Laying down the binoculars, he happened to notice the cover on the outside electrical outlet stood open. He reached over and snapped it shut.

He settled back and wondered how someone could have snuck up behind him as he came down his office stairs. There were no cars around and nothing looked disturbed at his place nor at the bakery. The perpetrator had obviously hidden behind the stairwell for the right moment. He had a feeling Hargrove planned on doing more damage than just knocking him out. But why?

He felt for a toothpick in his pocket, then remembered he had on a tee shirt. Standing, he picked up the binoculars and went into the house. Going to the kitchen cabinet, he grabbed several of the small sticks from the box, put one in his mouth, carried the rest to the small table next to the picture window and placed them on a napkin. He flopped down in the chair, but immediately put his fingers to his temples and groaned.

Jennifer looked up with raised brows. "You sat down too fast."

"Man, did I. Felt like the top of my head exploded."

"Honey, you're so restless. Go ahead and watch some television; it won't bother me."

Jennifer focused on her writing as Hawkman turned on the news. When she heard a faint snoring, she saw his head droop to one side. Then she noticed Miss Marple sitting in the middle of the carpet, staring toward their bedroom. Her ears were perked and her tail twitched. Strange, why is she staring in that direction? Suddenly, Jennifer felt a cold draft hit her legs. Her hand went to her fanny pack and wrapped around the pistol. Standing, she brought the Beretta to firing position and moved slowly down the hallway.

CHAPTER FIFTEEN

Jennifer hesitated a moment. The cool air rushed in from either the master bedroom or Hawkman's office. Those two rooms had sliding glass entries you could come in from the outside, and as far as she remembered, both were closed. The inside office door was shut; the bedroom was open. She sidled against the left wall and listened for any sound. Hearing nothing, she took a deep breath, stepped into the open with her gun aimed straight ahead. The vertical drapes bellowed in the wind. Her gaze darted around the walls. She took a deep breath, dropped to her knees, quickly scanned under the bed, then checked the closets and bathroom more closely. Once assured no one had hidden inside, she hastened across to the opened glass slider, closed and locked it.

Miss Marple had followed at her heels and jumped upon the bed. Jennifer flashed a glance at the cat, who seemed relaxed as she sprawled on the spread. About that time, Hawkman walked in and stared at the gun in her hand.

"What's going on?"

"I'm not sure. Did you forget to lock the slider?"

He scowled, and glared at the window. "No. Why?"

When she told him what had happened, he immediately took the Glock 30 pistol from the bedside table. "Stay inside," he said, as he slipped out onto the deck.

She sat down on the bed, the Beretta in one hand and rubbed Miss Marple's back with her other. "You're a good little watchdog, kitty."

Soon Hawkman came into sight. He stood outside the glass for a moment and examined the door. "Someone's jimmied this lock."

"Did you see anyone suspicious?"

"No. Not even a car." He stepped back into the house, went straight to his closet and removed two poles. One, a small metal rod, which he slipped into the hole at the top of the sliding door frame, leaving a hanging string attached at the end for easy removal. Then he took the old broom handle which he'd cut sometime ago to fit into the rail behind the gliding part of the window and dropped it into the space. "Those should prevent anyone from opening it again. Even if they try, it will definitely make a noise."

"Why would someone break open the door and not come in?"

He stared into her eyes. "Don't you get the picture? We're being harassed."

Jennifer flipped the safety on her gun, returned it to her fanny pack, stood and hugged herself. "I don't understand the reasoning behind any of this. And in broad daylight too."

Hawkman placed a hand on her shoulder. "I don't either, but I'm going to get to the bottom of it soon."

She wound an arm around his waist as they walked into the living room. "How's your head?"

"Much better, until this happened."

"It's going to be a little hard not being able to open a window for fresh air."

"This isn't going to last long, I guarantee you. But I think we'd better keep the alarm activated even when we're here, just to warn us if someone's messing with the doors or windows."

Jennifer's arms stiffened as she curled her fingers into fists. "I feel like I'm living in a prison."

"Think on the positive side. It's still not warm enough for you to fish on the dock."

"You're missing the point. If I have the desire, I want the freedom to go."

"Bear with me. It won't be long." He opened the coat closet door and threw the switch to activate the alarm throughout the house. "Just remember it's on."

She grimaced and moved into the kitchen. "How about a big Dagwood sandwich tonight?"

His eyes lit up. "Sounds good."

The next morning, Hawkman arose feeling more like himself. The stitches on his scalp itched and he hoped in another day or two the doctor would remove them. He flipped off the alarm, then picked up the new Stetson hat from the end table and cautiously placed it on his head. Shrugging his shoulders, he smiled to himself as he tugged at the brim until it fit low on his forehead. He strolled out the back door, and examined the area near their bedroom, looking for any telltale signs he might have missed yesterday. After examining the lock again on the slider, he knew whoever opened it had used a pick. This guy was no amateur. It nagged at his mind why this person had chosen him to make life miserable. He hoped his old Agency boss, Bill, would have some answers. If he didn't hear from him soon, he'd call again.

Hawkman checked Pretty Girl and considered taking her hunting. He'd neglected his pet falcon long enough. It would keep him busy and out of Jennifer's hair for at least a couple of hours. He meandered toward the front yard, pulling a weed here or there. When he reached the front fence, he leaned his forearms on the top rung and studied the landscape beyond the fire house.

"Hey, heard you got into a little fray in town."

Hawkman turned his head toward the voice and recognized his neighbor from down the road. "Bob, how's it going? Haven't seen you in awhile. Appears you and the wife do a lot of traveling around the country." Then he pointed toward the mutts scampering across the grass. "Looks like you've got the dog patrol this morning."

"Yeah, these rascals get fidgety." He rested against the end post. "And I'm getting tired of driving all over the place. I'm hoping to keep the little woman home for awhile so I can get my energy back." He laughed. "So what's the scoop?"

Hawkman gave him a quick description of how he'd acquired the head injury. "Have no idea who did it. Not sure if I interrupted a robbery or what. But I sure took a wallop."

"The police don't have any suspects?"

"Nope."

"Well, you take care of yourself. I better get these monsters home."

"Oh, Bob, have there been any house break-ins on your end? "

His neighbor looked at him with concern. "No. Why?"

"We suspect someone tried to get into our house. Just wondered if you've noticed any strangers lingering about or different vehicles?"

"That's a bit scary to hear. Usually the residents don't have those types of problems. It's the ones who only come a few months out of the year and their houses are left vacant the rest of the time. But even then you seldom hear about such incidents." Bob rubbed his chin while staring at the ground. "You know, I did spot an old red Willys jeep cruising about yesterday. Never seen it before, but the kids go crazy over those types and it might just be a new toy for someone."

"True. Could you tell if the driver was a young person?"

He shook his head. "No. Could have been though; he had on a baseball cap, pulled down low over his eyes."

"Thanks, Bob. If you see the jeep again, will you give me a jingle?"

"Sure." He gave a wave and whistled for his dogs, then headed down the road toward his place.

Hawkman stood at the fence for several more minutes, thinking about the red vehicle. It could very well have been Hargrove. He walked back toward the garage, stopped at the sprinkler controls and twisted them on. After adjusting a couple of the sprayer heads, he went into the house.

Jennifer sat on the couch, her coffee cup on the table as she tossed the stuffed bunny to Miss Marple. When he walked in, the cat stopped her play immediately, headed straight for his feet and rubbed against the leather of his cowboy boots.

"The little twerp," Jennifer laughed. "I do think she likes you better than me."

He raised his brows and grinned. "Told ya."

She went into the kitchen with her empty mug. "I saw you talking to Bob. Has he noticed anything unusual?"

"Have you taken lessons from Richard on how to lip read?"

She chuckled. "No, but I know my husband. Any conversation will have some pointed questions."

"You're right, I did ask him if he's seen any strange vehicles in the area."

Filling her mug, she carried it to the kitchen bar and sat down on one of the stools. "Well, what'd he say?"

"A red Willys jeep."

Jennifer eyed him over her cup as she blew on the hot brew. "Bet it's Jack Hargrove."

Hawkman frowned. "What makes you think so?"

"Because, I have a feeling he's going to hide out in the hills. And he needs a four-wheel drive."

He stared at her in silence.

CHAPTER SIXTEEN

"Why are you looking at me like that?" Jennifer asked.

Hawkman rubbed his mustache. "Sometimes you scare me."

She smiled. "How?"

"You come up with these uncanny scenarios and they make sense. Do you realize how many times you've helped me solve a case?"

"I just blurted out the first thought that popped into my head. Do you really think he might do such a thing?"

"Yes. The police are on his tail. He either wants to kill me or make me suffer. Since he hasn't accomplished either, he's got to hide until he achieves his goal." Hawkman crossed the room, opened the dining room drapes and pointed. "He wants to be close enough to hassle us, and there's no better place to hang out than up in those hills. I think you might have well hit on his plan."

"So what are you going to do about it?"

"I'm going to track him."

She wrinkled her forehead and stood. "Honey, you can't until you've recovered completely."

"It'll be a couple of days before I do anything, and I want to talk to the Bronsons."

She refilled her mug and sat back down. "Well, that's a relief."

"Tomorrow I'll try to contact Bill Blackwell at the Agency and see if he has any more information, I've got to figure out what beef Hargrove has with me. Also, maybe Detective Williams will have some information. If a Willys jeep has been stolen, then we can pretty well bet Hargrove's behind it." He reached up toward his head. "And I've got to get these stitches out. The itching is driving me crazy."

"Let me take a look."

He removed his hat and bent his head forward. "I took off the bandage so it could get some air."

"The cut looks real clean and smooth. Hair is already growing back. You seem to heal fast. Today's Wednesday, so I'd bet by Friday the doctor would remove them."

"Could you make an appointment for me? I doubt they'd take a walk-in. Doctors are so busy these days, they don't have fifteen minutes to spare."

"Sure."

"I think I'll take Pretty Girl out for a hunt today. I've neglected her badly."

"That's a good idea."

❧

Jennifer gazed out the window as Hawkman prepared to take the falcon from the aviary. The bird appeared to sense the hunt. She flapped her wings and made a loud pitched noise as she climbed onto the long leather glove protecting Hawkman's arm.

He carried her to the old pickup parked in the side yard where he'd installed a permanent perch inside the cab. Jennifer watched until the truck disappeared up the road toward Topsy Grade. Before he left, he'd thrown on the alarm, and checked to make sure all the doors and windows were locked. His last words were 'stay inside'. She could keep the drapes open during the daylight hours, but still felt like a prisoner inside her own home. It must be a psychological thing she thought, as she headed for her computer. There are many days I don't leave this house while I'm writing. She let out a sigh. But let someone tell me I can't leave, and I rebel.

In her heart, she knew Hawkman had more than one objective in mind when he left. She figured he planned on scouting the area while Pretty Girl hunted.

Jennifer started to sit down at her computer, but put a hand to her mouth and tittered. "Miss Marple, you're in my seat. Since your master isn't here, you decided to pay attention to me." She lifted the ball of fur and looked into her eyes. "You know, you're pretty fickle, but you're still a doll."

Placing the cat on the floor, she turned on the computer. While it booted up, Miss Marple jumped upon the chair next to Jennifer, then hopped upon the table and settled across some of the notepads.

Jennifer studied her for a few seconds. "My gosh, I think you've grown three or four inches in just a few days." She ran a hand down the cat's furry back. "Okay, if you promise to be still, I'll let you stay there."

It didn't take long before Jennifer's fingers flying across the keyboard caught Miss Marple's eye. She literally pounced on her hand, causing a row of unreadable print across the page. Jennifer burst into laughter. "Oh, you little rascal. I'll never get anything written." She transferred the playful feline to the floor, moved the chair out of range, fetched the stuffed bunny, along with several other toys, and took a few minutes to play with the kitten. Once she had her distracted, Jennifer returned to her work. She found it hard not to peek around the computer to watch the cat's antics as she pounced on the toys. This animal had definitely proved herself to be a delight.

Jennifer ran into a block on her story and stared out over the lake, trying to think where she wanted to go with the plot. She straightened in her seat as she spotted a red jeep coming down the road on the other side of the lake. Hastening to the window, she watched it lumber pass the bridge and head toward Topsy Grade. It definitely looked like an old model. She knew she'd never seen it before.

Hawkman stopped at the Miller Ranch, but found no one home. They must have all been out in the fields or at work in town. He'd kept his eyes peeled at every turnoff and open space in hopes of spotting the red jeep, but so far had seen nothing resembling such a vehicle. Driving on up the grade, he headed for Richard's place, knowing Pretty Girl liked to hunt from the knoll behind their house. Surrounded by trees, the area thrived with ground squirrels and other varmints. Uncle Joe, who worked in town, told him he had permission to come anytime. Richard no longer lived at home, as he had a job in another state and only came back on holidays.

Hawkman chewed on a toothpick and shook his head. "Pretty Girl, these boys grow up fast."

The bird let out a squawk as if she understood. Hawkman bounced across the rough road leading up to the small hill. The falcon ruffled her wings, moving her head up and down, as if she recognized the landscape.

They were soon situated at the top, and Hawkman turned the Peregrine loose. She took off and disappeared into a cluster of oaks. He pulled off the glove, and reached under the seat for his binoculars. Setting the glasses to his face, he scanned the surrounding area as far as he could see in all directions. The countryside seemed mighty quiet. Not even a dust cloud appeared in the sky. Soon the falcon returned and soared above his head playing in the wind current. He observed the beautiful bird for several minutes before he pulled on the long leather glove and whistled. She took several sharp turns then came down and landed softly onto his arm.

"You were a little messy with your dinner," Hawkman said, as he took a soft cloth from under the driver's seat, and wiped blood specks from her chest feathers. After tethering her to the perch, he turned the key in the ignition.

When they returned home, the sun sat low in the sky and the breeze had a cool nip. He put the bird into the aviary, gave her fresh water and filled her food tray, even though he knew she wouldn't need any nourishment tonight. Cold air whipped around the corner of the house, so he drew the tarp down over the cage. He glanced at the big window overlooking the lake and chuckled. Miss Marple sat on the inside ledge, watching his every move.

He had to go around to the front door to deactivate the alarm, and as he headed down the steps, he noticed the cover on the electric socket stood open again. Reaching over and flipping it shut, he frowned. Jennifer knows better than to leave it open, he thought as he headed around the house.

When he stepped inside, she glanced up from preparing some hors d' oeuvres for their expected company. "I can see Pretty Girl looks mighty content, and noticed you flipped the tarp down. It must be getting cold outside as I definitely felt the draft across my feet when you opened the door."

"Yep, it's pretty nippy tonight; feels like an Alaskan front moving in." He pointed toward the deck. "Before I forget, I wanted to ask why you aren't closing the cover on the electric outlet."

She looked puzzled as she carried a platter to the living room and placed it on the coffee table. "I haven't touched it in ages."

"That's odd. I've closed it twice in the past week."

"Maybe some curious raccoon has been investigating."

He scratched his sideburn. "I doubt the animal could open it. The spring's pretty tight. But it's possible. Their nimble little paws can do lots of mischief. However, they might get quite a shock if they poke a finger into the socket."

"I saw something interesting today."

"Oh yeah, what?"

"A red jeep."

His curiosity piqued, he followed her to the computer center. She shut down the machine and reached over to move the chair she'd scooted aside.

"Why's that clear over here?"

"Miss Marple decided to use it to get up on my desk. The little stinker is fascinated with my fingers on the keyboard. She wouldn't leave me alone, so I removed her ladder."

"I see. Okay, back to the jeep. When did you see it?"

"Shortly after you left."

"Where did it go?"

"Up the same road you did. I thought maybe you'd spot it."

"No, I didn't. And I kept an eye out for anything red. I stopped by the ranch, but didn't find anyone home."

"They're all working at other jobs just to make ends meet. It's really rough on people right now. They can't make a living off the land anymore."

"Yeah, it's sad."

The jangle of the phone caused them both to glance toward the machine. Hawkman strolled toward the kitchen bar.

"Hello, Jim. I'm still around. You haven't seen the last of me yet. Tell your pretty little wife she better not drive on the road for awhile. It could be dangerous for her health."

Hawkman slammed a fist on the counter. "Damn him! Why threaten you. If he's after me, come for me, not my wife."

Jennifer edged close to him and put an arm around his waist. "Honey, he's just hassling you. He probably wouldn't do a thing to me."

"He's a fool. Look what he did to Rita. We can't for one minute believe he wouldn't hurt you if he had the chance."

CHAPTER SEVENTEEN

Hawkman cleared off the end of the kitchen bar and arranged it so he could mix drinks for his guest. Placing several glasses and an ice bucket on the cloth, he noticed Jennifer's eyes sparkling with anticipation.

"You really like Peggy, don't you?"

"Yes. I'm glad they're our friends. She's not only charming, but you'd never know by looking at her five foot, three petite build, that she totes a gun and serves as a law officer for Siskiyou County. And when I think of all the things she's done, like learning how to fly a plane and becoming an accomplished horse rider, I'm amazed how she's packed all those things into her life."

"Yeah, she and Ken are a good pair. Remember when I asked him one time who he called if he needed a back-up? He told me, 'Peggy'."

Jennifer laughed. "Shows they trust each other."

Soon a knock sounded on the door and Hawkman greeted the Bronsons. He gave Peggy a hug and shook Ken's hand. "Good to see you two. It's been awhile since we've gotten together."

Ken took off his cowboy hat and placed it on a bar stool. "What a day! Traveled from one end of the county to the other." He took a handful of almonds, then flopped his lanky six foot frame down on the leather easy chair. "Oh, man, does it feel good to sit in something besides a patrol car."

After Hawkman fixed cocktails, he joined the group in the living room. He noticed Miss Marple went right to Ken, then to Peggy, giving each a loving rub. After showing her approval, she flopped down on the rug in front of the hearth as if she were a guest.

"Oh, my gosh, " Peggy exclaimed. "When did you get that adorable cat?"

"Meet Miss Marple," Jennifer said, waving a hand at the kitten. She gave them a quick rundown of the story about how she'd acquired the pet.

"Now, she's a pretty little thing," Ken said. "And did you say, she's a Ragdoll breed? Never heard of it."

"Yes," Jennifer said, as she picked up the feline and handed her to Ken. She will just lay over your arm like a rag."

"Well, I'll be damned," Ken said. "Peggy, look at this," as he lifted his arm with the cat's body dangling over each side. "She's just like a limp noodle."

Peggy laughed. "Ken, put her down. You're going to scare the poor little thing."

He gently placed the animal on the floor and immediately, Miss Marple wound herself around his boots, purring."

"She definitely likes you," Jennifer said, smiling.

"You want to take her home?" Hawkman asked. "She really knows how to shred toilet paper."

Ken guffawed. "I'm not so sure how she'd like our big black lab, Du."

"That little cat could make up to anything," Hawkman said, as he pointed toward the window where their dog had her nose pressed against the outside glass.

"That lab is such a lover, she'd probably protect Miss Marple with her life. However, I'm not giving my cat away," Jennifer said, with a toss of her head. "So don't get any ideas, Ken Bronson."

"Wait a minute. He just asked me if I wanted her."

"She's not his to give away."

Ken shrugged and glanced at Hawkman with a mischievous grin. "Okay, guess I'll leave her here. You heard the boss."

Hawkman chuckled. "Can't say I didn't try." After several more minutes of small talk, Hawkman brought up the dilemma he faced. Then walked over to the phone and punched on the latest recording.

Both officers scooted forward on their seats, as they listened.

Peggy turned toward Jennifer. "You should not be left alone. This man could be dangerous, especially after hearing his threatening message and what you've told us about Rita. Has he bothered Marie?"

"Not that we know of," Jennifer said. "I'm sure she would've called, and so far she hasn't."

"If you see me in the Sheriff's vehicle out front, think nothing of it. I'll stay close by and patrol the area. If I get a Code 3, emergency call, and have to leave, I'll let you know. Otherwise, I'm on Code 5 which means 'stake out'."

"I hate for you to have to do this," Jennifer moaned.

"That's what your tax dollars pay for; we're here to protect you. It's our job."

Ken glanced at Hawkman. "The same goes for you. Since this man comes from the Agency, he knows the tricks of the trade. You need your back covered. I'll check with Detective Williams and see if Medford's issued a warrant yet. If Ms. Rawlings has already posted a hit and run, that's enough. If a red jeep has been stolen, there's a good chance every officer is on the lookout in Oregon and California. I'll check with headquarters tonight and see if anything's come in. If he's the one who conked you on the head, I don't want you looking for this crazy man by yourself. It's too risky."

Hawkman saluted. "Yes, Sir!"

"Don't give me any of that 'yes, sir' business, just heed my word." Ken pointed at him. "The next time you start searching the country side, I want to be with you."

"Thanks. Sounds like a good deal. And if I expect my wife to pay attention. Guess I better do the same or she'll have me strung up."

Jennifer nodded. "You got that right."

After the Bronsons left, Hawkman plopped down on his chair. "I feel better now with them aware of the situation. We'll have extra protection this way."

The next morning, Hawkman prepared to leave for the doctor's appointment Jennifer had set up to get his stitches removed. Getting those blasted sutures out would make his head feel a lot better. His scalp itched like crazy, but he didn't dare scratch.

Before leaving, he took a tour around the outside of the house and checked all the windows, noticing the outlet cover hadn't been bothered for a couple of days. Things appeared normal. Satisfied, he went back inside. When he stepped into the kitchen, the phone rang. He immediately moved closer just as Jennifer walked from the back of the house with Miss Marple close at her heels. She stopped at the edge of the counter, her expression somber.

"Hello, Tom, Bill Broadwell. Give me a call."

"He immediately punched the speaker phone. "Hello, Bill, Hawkman here."

"I can't get used to calling you Tom Casey, and now you want me to call you Hawkman."

"Whatever's easiest. I'll answer to anything."

"Fair enough. I think we might have some of this mystery about Jack Hargrove partially solved."

"I'm listening."

"Do you remember a Raymond Skokie?"

"I'll never forget him. We were on an assignment together and he stepped on a land mine. It almost blew off his leg."

"He's Jack Hargrove's stepson."

Hawkman flopped down on the bar stool. "You jest?"

"No. Turns out Jack married Ray's mother, who was a widow at the time, and Ray was just a little guy, three or four years old. They weren't able to have children, so Jack raised the boy as his own. He had high dreams of his stepson becoming a super spy. After the accident, all those dreams blew up in his face as Ray was never allowed in the field again. Two years ago, Jack's wife passed away of cancer, and he retired. I spoke with Raymond, who still works here. He said his dad hasn't been the same since his accident. And the death of his mom seemed to have pushed him over the edge."

"How in the world does he connect me to Ray's calamity? We were out in the field heading toward different sides of a building when it occurred. I wasn't near the man."

"Ray doesn't blame you. But he said his dad felt like since you were the most seasoned agent, it should have been you going in the direction where the bomb had been placed."

"That's sick. How would I have known about a bomb? And I wouldn't have sent any man into an area if I thought he'd be in harm's way."

"Ray said he couldn't understand his dad's thinking. He worked for the Agency and knew how things ran. Ray said he'd asked his dad numerous times how he'd have managed the situation."

"How'd he respond?"

"He said Jack made comments about how he wasn't a haughty, bullheaded man like Jim Anderson. Ray even tried to explain how he liked you and asked to be on your team. But it didn't appear to make any difference. His dad still blamed you for crippling his son."

"This is not good news. I always liked Skokie. He was an excellent agent and I'm sure he's good at whatever he's doing now."

"Ray also told me his dad took the I.D. pictures out of the file, because he didn't want people remembering what he looked like."

"Did you tell Skokie what we suspected?"

"Only after he told me his dad had disappeared and he had no idea where he'd gone. He's quite concerned. I have a feeling Ray might contact you."

"It could help."

After hanging up, Hawkman rubbed his face and exhaled loudly. Jennifer gazed at him with concern.

"It appears Bill's news has upset you."

He nodded. "Immensely."

"You want to talk about it?"

"Yeah. Let me get a cup of coffee."

He sat back down and thumbed his fingers on the counter. "This is really bad. How the hell does one go after a sick man? And he's obviously deranged."

"Do you think if Ray came out here, he could talk some sense into his dad?"

"I don't know.," Hawkman said, shaking his head. "Skokie hasn't had any luck so far. I'm not sure it would do any good."

"It might be worth a try."

"Maybe. If he calls, I'll see what he thinks."

Hawkman left for the doctor's appointment and returned within a few hours. While driving over the lake bridge, he spotted Peggy's vehicle parked near the mailbox under a shade tree. He gave a wave as he turned the corner and drove into the driveway. After disarming the alarm, he stepped into the house, gave Jennifer a quick kiss on the cheek and grabbed a beer from the refrigerator. He moseyed onto the deck and stood looking out over the water. Jennifer picked up the cat and whispered. "Miss Marple, your master has a lot on his mind. I think it best we leave him alone for awhile."

Later that afternoon, Hawkman spoke with Detective Williams and no local car theft had been reported. But as Jennifer had said, people were gone during the Spring break and more than likely they wouldn't hear anything until the weekend.

He strolled back to his office. Miss Marple followed a few feet behind and stopped at the doorway. She sat on her haunches and watched as Hawkman rummaged through a cabinet hanging on the wall. He placed two small survivor kits on the desk.

He sat down, opened up the larger day hunter kit, measuring 6x4x2, which held everything he needed and could be carried on his belt. Taking out the tin inside, he popped it open, dumped out the smaller items and took inventory. He checked off the essential articles: Things needed to light and make a fire, a mini-match magnesium fire starter and steel striker. Water and food:

purification tablets, water bag, fishing tackle kit. Signaling: mirror. Navigation: compass. Knives and tools: folding wallet knife, cable saw and two X-Actop knife blades. Medical: small packet of antibiotic ointment, gauze pads, and two butterfly closures. Multipurpose: thread, magnetized sewing needles, magnifier, tweezers, pencil, waterproof paper, laminated instructions on water purification and fishing knots, safety pins and aluminum foil.

He left the room to find some replacements for a couple of bent pins, bandages and water. When he returned, he caught Miss Marple in his chair about ready to hop onto the desk. He swooped her up into the crook of his arm.

"Oh, no you don't, little lady. Those things are not toys and could be mighty dangerous to a kitten." He put her back on the floor and scolded. "There are some items in this house you're not to bother and this is one of them."

Miss Marple flopped on the floor, stretched out her back legs and gave him a big yawn.

Hawkman snickered. "I don't think you believe a word I've said."

Jennifer poked her head into the room. "Is Miss Marple giving you a hard time?"

"No, I'm giving it to her. She thinks her paws should be into everything. One nosey and curious animal."

"You want me to take her out of here?"

"She's fine. I need to teach her she can't stick her little sniffer into every opening. It might not be safe."

Jennifer put a hand on her hip. "And may I ask how you plan on accomplishing the impossible?"

He glanced up from his chore of placing the items back into the kit. "Not sure, but I'll think of something."

She moved to the desk and studied the articles scattered across the surface. "What are you doing?"

"Getting my survival kits ready for when I go trekking into the hills to find Hargrove. I might not even need them. But they're good to have, just in case."

"Oh," she said, putting a hand to her throat. "When do you plan going on this trek?"

"Tomorrow."

"I'm assuming you'll let Ken know."

"I'll give him a call. But if he can't make it, I'll go alone."

Jennifer glared at him. "I see. You sure pay attention to the authorities."

"I can't expect the man to drop everything and go romping into the hills on a possible false run."

"So, how long do you expect to be gone?"

"Not sure, that's why I want to carry these."

Jennifer knew better than to argue. She sighed and turned away. "I'll make you some sandwiches and put them in the refrigerator. And we have bottled water."

"Perfect." He closed the one similar to a fanny pack and set it aside, then opened the red medical kit.

Jennifer headed toward the kitchen.

This one had some duplications, but the lip balm, blister pads and moleskin could come in handy, along with tissues, Handiwipes, surgical gloves and a Mini Maglite. It appeared complete, so he zipped it closed and pushed the two to the corner of the desk. He leaned over toward the cat. "Okay, Miss nosey, you want to see what I have up here?"

She came to her feet and stretched, then meandered over so he could pick her up. He placed her in his lap. She put her front paws on the top of the desk, looked around, then jumped to the floor and stalked out of the room.

Hawkman guffawed. "Not near as interesting as you thought." He came out of the office laughing as he closed the door behind him.

Jennifer glanced up as she squatted in front of one of the kitchen cabinets. "What's so funny?"

"Miss Marple."

"She can definitely make a person smile with her antics."

He glanced at the counter and picked up some envelopes. "When did you get the mail?"

"A few minutes ago. Don't tell me I'm not allowed to walk to the mailbox?"

"You should be okay in broad daylight with Peggy patrolling the area, but don't count on it. Just make sure you have your gun and take notice of your surroundings."

"Don't worry, you've instilled those instructions into my brain. There wasn't a soul around, not even Peggy."

"It might be best you go right at noon, when everyone is heading for the box to pick up their mail. There's safety in numbers."

"You're probably right. Tomorrow I'll make it a point to go when the neighbors are there."

The jangle of the phone interrupted their conversation. They each looked at one another, then shot a glance toward the instrument.

"I'm ready to unplug that blasted thing," Jennifer mumbled.

"I'd like to speak with Jim, uh, excuse me, Tom Casey. This is Ray Skokie. Would you please call me..."

Before he could give the number, Hawkman picked up the receiver. "Hello, Ray, this is Tom Casey."

CHAPTER EIGHTEEN

Hawkman replaced the phone and glanced at Jennifer leaning against the counter.

"I couldn't make heads or tails out of the conversation, you didn't say much," she said.

"Ray wants to come out here next week and help me search for his dad."

"You think that's a good idea?"

"He's very crippled and if we go into the hills. I'm afraid he'll slow me down considerably."

"Maybe he's more agile than you think. After all these years, he might have adjusted to his handicap."

Hawkman rubbed a hand along the back of his neck and grimaced. "I doubt it; the man's leg was badly maimed. I'm not sure if he has an artificial one or they just repaired the limb. But regardless, it's rough terrain and I doubt he could manipulate it very well."

"You're not really sure Jack Hargrove is in the hills, are you?"

"No, I'm not. But lots of evidence points to it. And I have a feeling he's not far away. Since you saw that jeep going toward Topsy Grade and I never saw a sign of it when I came down the road. My guess is he's making his camp close."

She tapped the counter top with her fingernails. "I have a feeling you're right. He wants to be near enough to give us a hard time without having to travel a long distance."

"Plus, if he stole the Willys jeep, he'll keep it hidden and only use it in case he needs a getaway vehicle. Taking into account Rita's and Clyde's description, the man's obviously in good shape. After all, he was with the Agency, and worked in the field, so he'll know how to survive. I figure he'll be on foot most of the time."

Jennifer folded her arms across her waist. "So what's your plan? I hope you're including Ken."

Hawkman shrugged. "I want to find Jack before Skokie gets here."

"How long do you think it'll take? Are you going to be so far away you can't return home in the evening?"

"I don't know, but I won't stop searching, so I might be gone overnight."

"What will you do if you find his hiding place?"

"Nothing. I'll leave, then take Skokie there when he arrives and let him try to talk some sense into his dad. But if Jack discovers me sneaking around and tries anything foolish, I'll have to take him down. I don't want to kill the man, but I might not have a choice."

Jennifer silently crossed the kitchen, bent down in front of the cabinet and removed a couple of items. "I have two flip top cans of pork and beans. Would you like me to pack those?"

"Yes, thanks. I won't need a lot of food, but I'll exert plenty of energy hiking around, and it'll be nice having something to munch."

❧

The next morning, Hawkman went into Medford and stopped by the police station. He poked his head around the door jamb of Detective Williams' office. "Didn't know if I'd find you in, but took a chance."

"Same old stuff. My autograph is really in demand lately. I'm beginning to feel like a movie star."

Hawkman snickered. "I don't think it's quite the same."

"Boy, you sure know how to break a guy's bubble. I was beginning to like the job again." He tossed his pen on the desk and leaned back. "Now that you've ruined my day, what can I do for you?"

"Wondered if you'd had any stolen vehicle reports?"

"Let me make a quick call." He moved forward, picked up the phone and punched in an extension. "Maggie, Detective Williams. Anything new on stolen vehicles?" He glanced up and whispered. "She's checking."

Hawkman nodded.

"Yeah, thanks. Make a copy and send it over." He hung up. "You might find this one of interest. By the way, Ken Bronson called this morning and told me you had a talk with him and Peggy. He also wanted to know about Hargrove."

"I like the feeling of having more eyes on the house. I don't like Jennifer there alone."

In a few minutes, a skinny middle-aged woman walked into the office. "Here you go, detective."

"Thanks, Maggie."

He looked it over, then handed the report to Hawkman, who read the description aloud. "A 1954 CJ3B red Willys jeep stolen from the driveway at..." He didn't have to read the rest as he figured the jeep had been spotted at Copco Lake. "I think this is the one Jennifer saw. I haven't spotted it yet, but the description fits. Can I take this printout?"

"Sure. The license plate number is listed, along with all the extras. You think our hit and run man has it?"

"Very probable. I think he's hiding in the hills. I'm going to see if I can find him."

"Let me know, and we'll contact the Bronsons to go capture our villain and recover the vehicle."

"Will do. Thanks, Williams."

Hawkman decided not to tell the detective about Jack's stepson just yet. He left the station, stopped by the grocery store, then headed home.

He parked in the garage, then stumbled inside with his arms laden with sacks. Jennifer quickly grabbed them and put the perishables away.

"So did Williams have anything to report?"

"Yeah, a stolen red jeep. I've got the picture here in my pocket. I want you to take a gander at it and tell me if it resembles the one you saw," he said, handing her the paper.

She examined the copy. "Yes. It looks just like it. So when do you plan on taking off for the hills?"

"As soon as I can get ready."

He went to the bedroom, changed into hiking boots, and a long sleeved shirt. After fastening his shoulder holster back around his chest, he took a small bedroll from his closet, tucked it inside the backpack along with the stun gun and a box of extra shells for his Beretta Cougar. He decided to wear a medium weight jacket as the nights turned cool. Picking up his sunglasses, he zipped them into the pocket.

He carried the backpack into the kitchen where Jennifer loaded it with sandwiches and water bottles. Miss Marple stood at his feet, but didn't attempt to rub against his boots. In fact, she sneezed and shook her head.

Jennifer laughed. "I don't think she likes your different footwear."

"Probably because of the wild scent. She's a house baby and doesn't recognize the smell."

"Maybe it will make her like me better."

He grinned as he closed and buckled the pack. "I want you to drive me up to fishing access three. I've got a hunch about where Jack might be hanging out."

"Really, where?"

"On the south side of the road, about a half mile into those hills. There's a deserted, run-down shack, and it's well hidden from the road. Sam and I found it on one of our hikes. If I remember right, there's also an old trail a jeep could probably maneuver. I know of two or three vacated places in the area, but I'm going to check out this one first."

She placed the walkie talkies on the counter. "I've loaded these with new batteries and would feel a lot more comfortable if you took one. I won't try to contact you, but you can call me if you get into any kind of trouble."

"Good idea, I'd forgotten about them." He placed one in a Velcro fastened pocket of the backpack. "Okay, I think I've got everything, so let's hit the road."

Jennifer dropped him off at the specified spot, made a U-turn and watched him climb up the steep bank. When he disappeared over the crest, she sighed and headed home. She spotted Peggy parked on the road near the house and pulled alongside .

"Where's Hawkman?" Peggy asked. "I saw the two of you leave together."

"I just dropped him off up in the hills. I wanted him to talk with Ken first, but he seemed set on doing this alone. He doesn't want to confront Hargrove, he just wants to find him before Jack's son gets here. Hawkman hopes to take him to his dad and maybe a son to father talk will bring Jack to his senses."

Peggy studied Jennifer, her smoky blue eyes questioning the story. "You say Hargrove's son is coming?"

"Yes."

"That's odd."

"Why don't you come over to the house and I'll tell you about it over a cup of coffee."

"Good idea."

She followed Jennifer home and parked in the driveway.

"You sure look sharp in your uniform," Jennifer said, deactivating the alarm and opening the door.

"Thanks." She walked straight to the phone and called Dispatch. "I'm 10-6. Here's the phone number." After hanging up, she sat down at the kitchen bar. Okay, tell me about this son

Jennifer poured them a cup of coffee and sat opposite Peggy, then related the story about Ray Skokie.

"So, he's a stepson raised by Jack?"

"Yes."

Peggy scowled. "They must have been very close, yet something about the story doesn't fit."

Jennifer raised her brows. "What?"

"Not sure, can't put my finger on it. But I'll think about this turn of events and talk to Ken. I'll get his reaction and get back to you. By the way, has Hawkman got some way to contact you if he gets into trouble?"

"Yes, he's got a walkie talkie."

"Good, if you get any distress signals, contact me immediately." Peggy stood and headed for the door. "Lock up," she yelled over her shoulder.

Jennifer waved, shut the door, set the alarm, closed the drapes, then picked up Miss Marple and cuddled the cat in her lap. Blowing out a breath of air which rippled her bangs, she settled in for what she figured would be a forty-eight hour prison term.

CHAPTER NINETEEN

Hawkman continued to climb and felt the tension in his legs. The forest had thickened and the trees grown quite tall since he and Sam discovered this hideout several years ago during one of their hikes. If he found the old place still standing, at least he'd have an advantage of staying hidden.

He ducked behind a row of bushes and got his bearings. If his memory served him right, the shack stood huddled in a stand of trees several yards ahead.

Even though he saw no evidence of jeep tracks in the grass, he skirted close to the tree line, and stayed in the shadows as he surveyed the area. When he spotted a pile of fallen lumber among the big oaks, he hesitated, then moved closer, and cautiously ventured inside the grove. There he discovered the small building had rotted and toppled over. No way could it be used for any type of shelter. He sat down on a partially decaying stump, took out one of the water bottles, and calculated his next move.

He still had plenty of light, and decided to go east toward Topsy Grade. There were several buildings still standing near the ruins of the old hotel and hot springs. Hawkman figured Hargrove wouldn't want to be spotted, and some of the structures were too close to the road. But he remembered a few shacks deeper into the hills, used by workmen during the era when the recreation area thrived. Some of those might still be usable, and could be easily reached by the jeep. Also, there'd be plenty of places to hide the vehicle.

He soon topped a hill overlooking the back of the hotel. Plopping down on the ground at the base of a big oak, he studied the area with his binoculars, but could only see a short distance before the forest closed in. He scanned the adjacent grounds for any signs of activity. Not seeing any movement, he searched for other clues. Near the edge of the trees, he detected parallel lines of fresh crushed grass leading into a shadowed opening. They looked very much like fresh tire tracks. He decided to investigate.

Bears and mountain lions were often seen in this area, so he pushed the stun gun into his belt. He didn't know if it would stop the furry beast, but it'd be worth a try if one surprised him. He'd use his .45 only if he needed to protect his life.

It would be dark within the hour, and so as not to lose sight of the trail, he made his way down the hill and followed the tracks into the woods. The darkness, silence and coolness enveloped him the deeper he trod. Suddenly, in the stillness, he heard an engine turn over. He quickly jumped behind the thick brush and hunkered down. After several seconds, Hawkman could tell by the sound, the vehicle had started moving. He stole a peek, as the red Willys jeep bounced past him. Jack Hargrove sat in the driver's seat.

Hawkman waited until the vehicle moved out of sight, then jogged down the trail. He soon approached a small building with a chimney. The shack had probably housed a workman or two for the hotel. He examined the door and found it securely fastened with a new padlock. Walking around the outside, he noted the windows had long since lost their glass, and were covered with towel-like cloths. Poking at one, he realized they'd been tacked to the frame on the inside. He shoved his finger into the corner and pushed back the material enough to view the inside. The gloominess forced him to use his Maglite to see the interior. A cot sat on one end, topped with a sleeping bag and pillow. In the corner stood a covered potty bucket. A rickety table sat on the opposite side holding a box of crackers, bottle of water, bag of chips and a kerosene lantern. A three-legged milk stool served as a chair. He couldn't see directly under the window where he stood, but figured it didn't matter as the man had set up living quarters. And from the looks of things, he planned on staying awhile.

His ears perked at hearing a low rumble. Glancing in the direction of the noise, he could see the beam of headlights bouncing off the tree trunks as it made its way along the rough trail. Hawkman quickly darted into the trees and hid. The jeep stopped in front of the hut, and Jack climbed out with a paper bag. Hawkman wondered where he'd gone, as he certainly hadn't been away long enough to drive into town, and the store at Copco Lake was closed. Jack dumped small pieces of dried timber out of the sack into a small circle of rocks at the side of the building, and lit a small fire. After several trips inside the shanty, he brought out the three legged stool and prepared to roast several wieners over the flame.

Once his hot dogs were well done, Hargrove hurried into the little house, and returned with buns and mustard for his dinner. He snapped open a soda and crunched on chips. Smelling the food and watching the man eat made Hawkman's stomach growl. He quietly slipped a sandwich from his pack.

After eating, Jack collected the remnants, covered the fire with dirt, and disappeared into his makeshift dwelling, closing the door. Within a few minutes, a soft light glowed through the covered windows and stayed on for about half an hour.

Pitch blackness engulfed the area when Jack extinguished the light. Hawkman could have kicked himself for not finding a good place to bed down beforehand. The cloud covered sky kept the stars and moon from throwing forth any brightness. He hoped it wouldn't rain tonight. But just as the wish passed through his mind, he heard drops hitting the leaves and felt splatters on his face.

Only one thing to do. He eased toward the jeep and carefully opened the back door hoping it wouldn't squeal or creak. He quietly crawled inside, moved a stack of stuff to make an area clear enough so he'd have room to curl up and get a few winks. Tugging the night roll out of the pack, he lay down and covered up. Just as he settled, the rain came down in torrents.

A few drips came through the cloth top, and he had to move his head to avoid them. At least he didn't get completely soaked.

He'd dozed for a couple of hours when the rocking of the jeep jarred him completely awake. Hargrove had climbed into the vehicle and started it up. Hawkman crunched down and covered his head, in hopes Jack hadn't spotted anything different about the reshuffling of items. He had no idea of the time, but darkness still prevailed, but the rain had stopped. Hargrove backed up the jeep, then drove out the bumpy road to the blacktop. After approximately fifteen minutes, Hawkman thought he heard the rush of the river. When the jeep stopped, Jack jumped out without even glancing back. Hawkman quickly looked out the windshield and realized they were parked in the City's construction lot next to his own house. He hurriedly climbed out the back, tossed his pack and bed roll beside the parked road grader and followed Hargrove as he approached the deck of his house.

Hiding behind the woodpile, Hawkman drew his gun and watched Jack tiptoe up the back stairs. What the hell's he doing, he thought, preparing to move foreword as he watched the man reach down and pull something out of the wall. The moon peeped out from behind the clouds and Hawkman could see Hargrove winding a cord around his hand, then shove it into his pocket. As Jack hastened down the steps, Hawkman moved around the woodpile, never taking his eye off the sneak who now headed toward the jeep. When Hawkman saw him flip open a lighted object in his hand, he realized Hargrove had just used the electrical outlet to charge his cell phone.

"What a cheap SOB," he muttered under his breath.

Hawkman stayed hidden and watched until the jeep turned around, headed across the bridge, and turned east on Ager Beswick Road. He strolled over and picked up his backpack, and crossed toward the deck where he piled his gear. Checking the electrical outlet, he grumbled. The cover stood open. He flipped it shut, and went around to the front door, where he deactivated the alarm and let himself inside.

He turned on the kitchen light and immediately threw up his hands. Jennifer stood in front of him clutching her gun with the barrel pointed at his chest. "Don't shoot. It's me, your husband."

She dropped her arms to her side and let out a loud sigh. "What are you doing walking in at this hour?"

"Long story. You want to hear it now or later?"

Miss Marple had followed her out of the bedroom, and stood at the sliding glass door, meowing loudly. Jennifer placed her gun on the counter, walked over to the cat and picked her up. "What's with you, baby. You've acted strange for about an hour."

"What do you mean?" Hawkman asked.

"I had her in bed with me, suddenly, she raised up, climbed over me, then looked toward the outside. She did this a couple of times, and even nudged me with her head."

"You should have paid attention. She sensed someone out there."

She twisted around. "Are you serious?"

"Yes." He told her about how he ended up in the back of the stolen jeep and slipped out when Hargrove parked by the bridge. "I watched him come up to the deck and would have made a move if he'd tried to get into the house. But I could see he had something else in mind." He reached over and gave the cat a pat on the head. "Miss Marple may be more of a detective than you imagined."

CHAPTER TWENTY

Jennifer frowned. "I don't understand what Jack Hargrove was doing on our deck?"

"Are you ready for this one?" Hawkman asked, raising a brow. "Charging his cell phone."

"What!"

"Yep. So he can make those harassing calls."

She put her hands on her hips. "Of all the nerve."

Hawkman grinned. "I'd like to fix that plug so he can't get it open or at least give him a shock."

"Not sure it's a good idea either way. You might make him mad enough to throw another rock through the window."

"Good point."

"Oh, before I forget. Peggy caught me coming back from taking you to the hills. She's not happy about you going without Ken."

"I didn't need him. He'll understand."

"I guess it's a man thing." She shrugged. "I think I'm going to head back to bed and see if I can get some sleep." She glanced up at the wall clock. "Good grief, it's three in the morning." Carrying the cat, she put her in the bathroom. "You're going to have to sleep the rest of the night in here, little one. I need some shuteye."

The next morning, Hawkman opened the door and snickered. "Oh, boy, Miss Marple, you're in deep yogurt."

Tying the belt on her robe, Jennifer moved up behind him. "What's she done now?"

"You forgot to take the toilet paper away when you put her to bed, so we're going to have to suffer through a gigantic roll again."

"Oh, shoot, that little rascal. Well, I can't blame her, I should have removed the temptation. I think I'll just put it in a box, it's a heck of a job to roll it back on the spindle."

"Now you're thinking."

She tapped her finger on her chin. "Oh dear, when is Ray Skokie going to be arriving?"

"He'll probably call today and let me know. I figure he'll come tomorrow or the next day."

"I'll have to move her stuff into our bathroom. I didn't think about having a guest when I put her in here."

A mischievous grin played on his lips. "It means he gets a good roll of toilet paper and we have to use it out of a box."

Jennifer gave him a playful punch on the arm. "I don't think Mr. Skokie would appreciate your humor."

Hawkman reached down and picked up one the cat's toys from the floor. His eyes twinkled as he shook the cluster of small bells.

Jennifer glanced at him with a puzzled expression. "What've you got in mind?"

"Not sure, but this might come in mighty handy."

She pushed past him and gathered up the long streams of paper draped across the room. "What a mess," she mumbled.

Hawkman laughed. "Your fault."

"Don't remind me. One definitely won't gain weight taking care of a kitten." She carried the bundle into their bedroom and dumped it onto the foot of the bed. "Now to find a box, preferably one with a lid."

While Jennifer busied herself with restoring the bathroom to its original order, Hawkman strolled out on the deck. He bent down on his haunches and studied the flip cover of the electrical outlet. Even though the contraption had a place where he could insert a padlock, he'd rather set a trap for Mr. Hargrove and catch him in the act. He glanced at the stairs and smiled. Heading back inside, he went to the hall closet and pulled out his fishing tackle box. He set it on the kitchen counter and removed an almost invisible fishing line from the contents.

Jennifer studied him as she swished past with an armful of dirty towels. "Are you going fishing?"

"Nope. This is going to be much more fun."

She dropped the laundry on the washer and moved back to where he stood. Scratching her head, she watched him loop the line around the cat's bell toy. "What in the heck are you doing? I hope you're not going to give that to Miss Marple, it could be dangerous."

"Don't worry, I won't." He held up the string with the toy attached to the end and gave it a shake. It rang with a nice loud jingle. "Perfect."

She wrinkled her forehead. "I think you're losing it."

"I might be. I'll know if it will work tonight when I test it out."

"Okay, quit dodging the issue. What are you up to?"

"I'm going to set a trap for Mr. Jack Hargrove."

"I see. Would you explain a little more, please?"

Hawkman picked up the roll of fishing line, took the toy off the end and crossed to the dining room. "I'm going to run the string out the window, attach it to the railing and run it across the stair walkway. I'm hoping the line won't glisten in the dark. I'll tie the toy to the end inside the house and hope Mr. Hargrove walks into the taut line. The ringing of the bells will alert me when he's on the deck."

"You know he'll run the minute he feels it."

"True, but it will do my heart good to let him know I've caught on to his using my electricity to charge his cell phone."

Jennifer rolled her eyes. "Men! I'll never understand the way you think. I thought you wanted to catch him."

"Not just yet. I'll wait until Skokie gets here. I think he wants the opportunity to reason with his dad before Williams arrests him."

"From what Bill told you, it doesn't sound like Ray has had much luck so far."

"No, and it's probably going to be a wasted trip. But I think he'd like one more chance."

She grimaced. "It must be awful to have to cope with a father who's doing bad things."

Hawkman nodded as he threaded the string through the window. He poked a pencil into the middle of the container and handed Jennifer the roll. "Could you hold on to this while I go out on the deck and measure how much I'll need?"

"Sure."

He marched outside, took the line hanging from the window, and pulled it toward the end post. After wrapping several extra feet around the wood, he went back inside and cut the thread with his pocket knife. "Thanks, that should do it."

"I've got work to do before I can get to my writing." She headed toward the bedroom. "Good luck with your project."

Hawkman continued working on the trap. He kept going in and out the sliding glass door until Jennifer strolled into the living room.

"Have you seen Miss Marple?"

He looked at her in shock. "Dang, I haven't paid attention and left the slider open several times."

Jennifer dashed onto the deck . "I don't want her to get fleas. She'll carry them into the house and then we'll have an infestation of those horrible pests."

"Wait!" he yelled as Jennifer headed down the stairs, hit the fishing line with her legs and fortunately grabbed the wooden handrail before she fell the rest of the way down the steps.

Hawkman hurried to her side and helped her up. "You all right?"

She dusted off her hands, wiped them down her jeans and glared at him. "Yes. I might have a few splinters, but otherwise, I'm okay."

He took her by the shoulders, turned her toward the aviary and pointed. "Miss Marple is very interested in Pretty Girl. It doesn't look like she's moved from that spot for several minutes." He tucked his thumbs into his front jeans pockets. "It appears she's in a trance."

Jennifer stood back and watched the cat as she stared at the falcon. Miss Marple never moved so much as a hair on her head, but her tail twitched back and forth. "Now what do you suppose she's thinking?" she whispered.

"If her mind's on food, she might as well forget it. The falcon would make a meal out of her in a matter of minutes."

"I don't think we ever want to take them out together."

Hawkman turned back to his project. "Hope you didn't hurt yourself."

"No, the jeans saved me from getting cut, but I could have broken my neck."

He shook his head. "Naw, you're too agile. You caught yourself the minute you felt your body falling."

"What do you think will happen to Jack if he stumbles over it?"

He pointed toward the yard. "He'll be coming up the stairs, it's a bit different. He wouldn't get hurt, he'd just sprawl out on the deck with a big thud. And it wouldn't bother me a bit if he acquired a few bruises, especially after what he did to my head."

She walked over and picked up Miss Marple. "Do you think he'll attempt to come tonight?"

"Not sure. All depends on how well his cell phone holds a charge or how much he's talked on it today."

"What if this makes him really mad and he does something bad, like break another window, or hurt the falcon."

Hawkman jerked up his head. "He better not even think about injuring my bird."

CHAPTER TWENTY-ONE

Hawkman worked in silence as he looped the fishing line over the last post and threaded it into the window. He couldn't help but think about Jennifer's comment. Would Jack be mean enough to harm the falcon? If he just turned the bird loose, no harm. Pretty Girl would return. But if he hurt her, it would make Hawkman very upset.

He glanced at the aviary, wondering if he shouldn't move the bird to the truck for the next couple of nights. It couldn't hurt, and might save her life. He'd drive the pickup to the other side of the house near his bedroom; then he'd hear her squawk if anyone bothered her. There was a problem with the aviary: the back, nearest their bedroom, was solid and made of heavy wood. The front part was screen which faced the sliding glass door off the dining room. All sounds went in that direction. He or Jennifer had never heard her make any noises at night. But he knew she must have scolded raccoons when they ambled onto the deck.

Going inside, he picked up the cat's bell toy and tied it to the end of the fishing line and let it drop to the wall. Immediately, Miss Marple came bounding to the area when she heard the jingle. Hawkman placed the toy high enough so she couldn't reach it. He watched in amusement as she stood on her hind legs trying to get to the plaything. "I'm only going to borrow it for a few nights, little girl, then I'll let you have it back."

He swooshed her up into his arms. "To help get your mind off this toy, let's go find your stuffed bunny."

꒰ꜛ꒱

Jack Hargrove stood on the top of a shaded knoll not far from Copco Lake. He didn't move a muscle as he gazed through the binoculars perched on the top of his nose. His field of vision focused on the first house after crossing the bridge. Soon, he dropped the glasses to his chest and plopped down on a large boulder. He reached down into the knapsack he'd placed on the ground, pulled out a sandwich and twisted off the cap of a bottle of beer. As he munched on the snack, his eyes narrowed as he stared toward Hawkman's place. He'd noticed the Sheriff's car parked near their house and wondered if they were staking out the place in hopes of catching him. He'd keep a wary eye when he made his runs to charge his cell or other mischief he might have in mind.

"You son-of-a-bitch," he mumbled. "You're going to pay for what you did to my son. You ruined his life. Why should you live the life of luxury, while Ray stumbles around, hardly able to keep his footing? He has no one but himself because of his horrible limp. No woman gave him a second look after he got so crippled."

He squashed a beetle with the heel of his boot. "That's what I'm going to do to you, but first, a little torture."

Removing his cell phone from his pocket, he flipped open the lid and pushed the button. "Ah, you're still not answering your phone. I don't know what to call you, Jim, Tom or *Hawk Man*. Heard you go by all three names. By the way, I know you're home. I saw you fiddling around on your back deck. Still healing, huh? Had any bad headaches? That's just a sample of what I've got planned for you. Tell your pretty little wife to be careful."

He slammed the phone shut and the echo of his laughter rang through the forest. Wiping the tears from his eyes, he slung the backpack over his shoulder and left the rock. Jack hiked back to his makeshift home. When he reached the front entry, he checked his little hidden traps to make sure no one had entered his new abode while he'd taken care of business. Finding everything secure, he unlocked the padlock and opened the flimsy door. He dropped the bag on an old rug, then sat down on a new stool he'd found in the ditch. A broken mirror lay on the table. He picked it up and studied his reflection. "I look like a damn mountain man with fierce green eyes," he mumbled, patting his shaggy mustache and beard. Removing his hat, he ran his fingers through the tangled mess of uncombed hair, and winced in pain.

Hawkman and Jennifer hovered over the phone as the message came through.

"He obviously wasn't close enough to make out what I was doing on the deck. But he's out there." He grasped her arm. "I don't want you out of this house."

She pulled away and slapped the palm of her hands on the counter. "You keep saying that. Peggy's watching. She's not going to let him get close. And I can't stop living just because some idiot makes threatening remarks. He's only saying those things to ruffle your feathers."

"Well, he's doing a damn good job of it."

Jennifer sighed. "And you're letting him push your buttons."

"He wouldn't, if I didn't think him deranged enough to do something hideous."

She rubbed her arms. "What do you mean,'hideous'?"

Hawkman exhaled loudly. "He's a jerk. No conscience, no feelings. My imagination can conjure up all sorts of nasty things."

Jennifer hugged herself. "You're scaring me."

"I mean to do just that." He picked up a pencil and popped it in two pieces. "The man's a nut case. You don't know what he'll do. One can't be too careful."

He ambled across the room to the small table between the chairs and picked up his binoculars, then went outside on the deck. Studying the terrain in all directions, he wondered where Hargrove had set up his post. He removed the glasses from his face and stood staring into space. Not knowing what the man knew bothered him. How close did Hargrove dare to get and how much could he see? Hawkman went back inside and yanked a set of keys off the board above the calendar and headed toward the front door.

"Where are you going?" Jennifer asked.

"I'm moving the old truck to the other side of the house."

"Why?"

"You've made me nervous with your comment about Pretty Girl. I'm putting her in it for the night."

Her gaze followed him out the door.

Hawkman climbed into the pickup and drove it around near the master bedroom window. He contemplated parking the truck so the passenger door opened up toward the house, but figured it wouldn't matter. If Hargrove had intentions of hurting the falcon, he'd do it regardless of which way the truck faced. He decided when he put Pretty Girl inside, he wouldn't tether her to the perch. This way she might have a chance to escape or give Jack a hard time if he entered the cab. He rolled the windows down just enough so she couldn't wiggle out, but would have plenty of air. Throwing on the emergency brake, he left the vehicle and went back inside. Hanging up the keys, he turned to Jennifer. "I won't move Pretty Girl until almost dark. Then I'll put her back into the aviary at daybreak."

"What if Hargrove sees you? He's obviously spying on us."

"That's why I'll wait until later. He'll have trouble making out what I'm doing, unless he's using night binoculars. Pretty Girl usually squawks if a stranger comes around. This way I should be able to hear her."

Jennifer partially stood and glanced around the room. "Miss Marple, where are you?" When the cat didn't respond to her calling, she searched behind the chairs and under the computer desk. The cat seemed to have disappeared from this end of the house.

Hawkman headed toward the back, where he met Miss Marple coming out of the bathroom. "Just needed a little privacy, didn't you, girl."

He picked her up and brought her to Jennifer.

"Where was she?"

"In the bathroom."

Jennifer blushed. "Oh."

The afternoon soon turned to evening, and Hawkman closed the drapes. His stomach churned and a weird feeling kept circling inside his gut. He felt like he was being watched and decided to go outside. When he strolled around the house, a cool breeze caressed his face and eased his tension. He swiped a hand across his mustache and studied the sky. No clouds were visible and it appeared the night would be clear. An almost full moon would give plenty of light to the grounds. He had a feeling, tonight sleep would evade him.

He heard Jennifer call his name from the front door.

"Yes."

"You have a call from Ray Skokie."

Hawkman hurried inside and picked up the phone. "Hello, Ray."

After jotting down a few items on a notepad, he hung up. Jennifer sat on one of the kitchen stools opposite him, her elbows perched on the counter and her chin resting on her fingers.

"When will he be here?" she asked.

"Early tomorrow afternoon. I'm to pick him up at the Medford airport."

She sighed. "Good. Maybe Jack will listen to his son, and leave us alone."

Hawkman focused on her face. "Don't get your hopes up. Ray's talked numerous times to his dad and it hasn't done a bit of good. This is his last chance, because Detective Williams will arrest Hargrove for auto theft along with the hit and run charge Rita filed."

She let out an exasperated sigh. "We'll at least get him out of our hair, one way or the other."

Hawkman rose and walked toward the sliding glass door in the dining room. "We still have tonight to face."

CHAPTER TWENTY-TWO

Hawkman tossed and turned most of the night. He arose several times and peeked out the window above his head. Nothing seemed amiss and he could see the silhouette of Pretty Girl through the pickup windshield. She apparently didn't mind sleeping in the cab, probably because the close quarters made her feel secure.

Miss Marple nestled as close to Hawkman as she could and every time he got up, she rose on her haunches and gave him a disgusted glare. After about the third time, the cat moved closer to Jennifer.

"About time; after all, she's your mistress," he muttered,

When the morning's light filtered through the window, Hawkman decided to return the falcon to the cage. The truck would get too warm for her if he waited much longer. He slipped on a pair of jeans, pulled on his boots and snuck out of the room, closing the door behind him. When he stepped out the dining room sliding glass door onto the deck, he took notice of the fishing line positioned across the opening of the stairs and the outdoor electrical outlet. Nothing had been disturbed.

After returning Pretty Girl to her perch and securing the cage, he removed the trap from the post. The invisibility of the string would make it easy to stumble over, and he sure didn't want to find Jennifer at the bottom of the stairs with a broken ankle or leg. He left the rest attached to the post nearest the window. He'd probably tighten it back up tonight, even though Ray Skokie would be here.

Hawkman prepared to head for Medford Airport after breakfast.

"I'll have the guest room ready for him by the time you two return," Jennifer said, as she wiped off the counter. "Shouldn't you let the Bronsons know Ray is arriving today?"

"Why don't you give Peggy a call? Be sure you keep the place under secure lockup and your gun handy. Hopefully, there won't be any incidents. Oh, by the way, if Detective Williams calls, give him the scoop about Skokie."

"Okay, but hurry back. Even with Peggy out there, it makes me nervous knowing Hargrove is so close and watching the house."

"I'll return as soon as I can."

Hawkman had no trouble spotting Ray in front of the baggage area. He appeared shorter than what he remembered, probably due to the leg injury. His square jaw, sparkling blue eyes, and prominent nose, reminded Hawkman of a Greek god. Ray's dark hair had grayed at the temples, but even the slight sign of aging made him look distinguished.

He pulled to the curb, hopped out and opened the rear of the SUV. Ray swung his suitcase into the compartment behind the seat and closed the door. The two men shook hands, then climbed into the 4X4. Hawkman noticed Skokie had no trouble getting into the vehicle. Jennifer might be right. The man had acclimated to his disability after all these years.

As they drove toward Copco Lake, Hawkman told Ray about the incidents involving his father and how he'd discovered his hideout.

"Do you think Dad will still be in the same place?"

"I see no reason for him to move on, as he doesn't know I've found him. So unless an official ordered him off the property, he'll more than likely stay there as long as he can. He's in a little shack and protected from predators, and well hidden from the road."

"How come the police haven't arrested him yet?"

"I have a little clout with the authorities and have asked them to give you a chance to talk with him. But if he doesn't cooperate, they'll come and get him."

Ray exhaled loudly. "From what you've told me, it sounds like he's gone over the edge."

"He's definitely teetering."

Jennifer greeted the men at the door, and after introductions, she showed Ray the guest room and pointed out where he could freshen up from the trip. Hawkman noticed Miss Marple backed up and peeked around the edge of the chair as she watched Ray move across the room. Skokie's hard limp, and swaying body must have frightened her.

Coming from the back of the house, Jennifer went into the kitchen and removed a platter of hors d'oeuvres from the refrigerator. She placed them on the coffee table in the living room, along with napkins and small paper plates.

"Those look delicious," Hawkman said.

"Thank you, kind sir, I whipped them up while you were gone. Figured it would suffice for a late lunch. Then we can have dinner whenever you guys are ready. I have no idea what your plans are. Are you taking Ray to see where his dad is staying tonight?"

"Not sure. I'll play it by ear. It depends on what he wants to do."

Their guest soon emerged from the bathroom with a smile on his lips. "Nice place you have. And thank you both for inviting me to share your home. I really appreciate it."

"You're more than welcome," Hawkman said. "Have a seat and relax; I'm sure the long flight has worn you out."

Ray eased down on the leather couch and noticed the food on the table. "These sandwiches look wonderful."

"Help yourself," Jennifer said. "I'm sure they didn't feed you much on the plane."

"Very true," he chuckled. "A bag of nuts doesn't last long."

"What would you like to drink?"

His blue eyes twinkled. "I hope you're not teetotalers, because I'd love a Scotch and water."

Hawkman laughed. "No problem, I'll fix you up pronto."

As they conversed in the living room, Miss Marple crept around to the foot of Jennifer's chair and sat at her feet.

"What a beautiful animal," Ray said.

Jennifer picked her up. "Meet Miss Marple. She's a fairly new addition to our family."

"I'm not much of a cat person, but I must say she's a fine looking specimen."

"She's from the 'Ragdoll' breed. Supposedly, very gentle and cuddly."

"How'd you come up with the name, Miss Marple? Isn't that the handle of one of Agatha Christie's characters?"

Hawkman intervened. "Jennifer's a mystery writer. So the name fits."

"Ah, ha," Ray laughed. "That explains it. So you're a writer?"

She blushed. "I love writing suspenseful novels and work very hard at it."

"I'd like to purchase one of your books before I leave. I've always enjoyed a good brain teaser."

"Sure. I'll give you a run down on them later. Right now, I'm sure you have more on your mind than reading."

Ray turned toward Hawkman. "Yes, but before we get into any serious discussion about my father, I'd like to know what to call you. I knew you as Jim years ago, but since then your name has been changed to Tom Casey, yet I heard your wife call you Hawkman. So needless to say, I'm a bit confused."

"Call me Tom. Hawkman is a nickname bestowed upon me by the Copco Lake residents."

"How'd that come about?"

Hawkman pointed out the picture window toward the aviary. "I guess because I've always had a falcon, except for a short period of time after my original pet passed away of old age."

"He's also saved many birds from dying by taking them in and healing their injuries." Jennifer said. "And most were hawks; therefore, the name, Hawkman."

"I hate to be personal, but when you left the Agency, rumor had it you'd received an eye injury while searching for the murderers of your first wife. I'm assuming the eye-patch is the result. Are you blind in that eye?"

"No, just very sensitive to light. Maybe one of these days the doctors will figure out a way to fix it."

Ray stood, and moved toward the window to take a closer look at the falcon. When he inched toward Miss Marple, she scooted around to the side of the chair and watched him with interest.

Jennifer picked her up. "Looks like our little pet is a bit shy."

Ray waved her off. "I'm a stranger in her domain. She hasn't had a chance to warm up to me. Just give her time. We'll probably be the best of friends before I leave."

CHAPTER TWENTY-THREE

Hawkman took his guest out on the deck and introduced him to Pretty Girl. He told Ray how he'd discovered his dad had sneaked upon his porch at night and used the outside electric plug to charge his cell phone. "He doesn't know I've spotted him."

Ray glanced down at the outlet and shook his head. "It's hard to believe Dad would stoop so low."

"I've got a plan to catch him, but I might have second thoughts." Hawkman explained what he'd rigged up across the porch steps.

"It seems rather humiliating. Don't you think?"

"If it makes you uncomfortable, I won't proceed."

"Thanks. If I can't talk him out of pulling his stunts, then I won't care what you do after I leave."

"Fair enough." Hawkman motioned to the chairs on the deck. "Want to stay out here for a little while?"

"Yes," Ray said, sitting down. "What a beautiful view of the lake."

"We really enjoy it. Very relaxing."

"How far is my Dad camped from here?"

Hawkman pointed up the road toward Topsy Grade. "A couple or so miles. There are ruins of an old hotel and spa. Behind them, in a wooded area, are several workmen's shanties that have survived years of weathering. He's settled in one of those."

"Maybe we should go up there tonight, since I only have a couple of days before I have to get back to work."

"If you feel up to it after the long flight. We can go right now."

Ray rubbed a hand across his forehead. "I don't look forward to this encounter. But I might as well get it over with as soon as possible."

Hawkman stood. "You'll probably want to change out of your good clothes. It's pretty rugged country. I'm sure my 4X4 can make it to his front door. If not, we'll have to walk a short distance."

Ray looked out over the lake, his arms resting on his thighs. "I've been thinking about this. Maybe I should go in alone. Drop me off far enough away from the place so Dad can't see your vehicle and I'll hike in. We'll set a time for you to pick me up."

Hawkman studied the man's posture. "Are you sure you want to handle it this way? Your dad's mind is not stable. He's liable to shoot you."

"I doubt it, since I'm the reason for this whole mess."

"The only problem is, I won't know if Jack's there when I drop you off, since you can't see the shack from the road."

"Drive by about thirty minutes from the time you let me out. I'll be back at the road if he's not there."

Ray rose from his chair and turned to go into the house. "I'll go change and we'll get on our way."

When Ray stepped inside, Miss Marple scampered off Jennifer's lap and hid behind the chair. Hawkman figured since Ray was a stranger and had a lumbering gait, she'd really gotten spooked.

Jennifer closed her magazine and placed it on the coffee table. "So what are the plans?"

Hawkman sat down on the couch opposite her. "I'm taking him to his dad's campsite. But I'm not going in with him."

She frowned. "Couldn't it be dangerous?"

"He doesn't seem to think so."

She shook her head. "I don't like the sound of it."

"Me, either, but he's calling the shots."

"If he had to get out in a hurry, he'd have a difficult time," she whispered, glancing toward the guest room.

"I agree," he said in a low voice. He reached down and stroked Miss Marple's head while she rubbed against his cowboy boots.

Ray Skokie limped into the room, clad in camouflage pants, shirt and combat boots. "Hope my attire will do the trick."

Miss Marple slithered behind the chair, leaving Hawkman's hand suspended in air.

Hawkman rose. "It should do fine," he said, studying the man's garb and figuring there were several weapons hidden underneath. "You got a flashlight hidden in those pockets?"

Skokie snapped his fingers. "Dang, the one thing I forgot."

Hawkman crossed over to the coat closet. "It's going to be dark soon, and if there's any clouds obscuring the moon, that area will get so black you can't see your hand in front of your face." He handed him a powerful Dorcy.

"Good idea. Thanks."

The two men left the house and climbed into the SUV. When they reached the area, Hawkman turned off the road and pointed toward the grove of trees. "Can you see what looks like an old road?"

"Yes."

"Follow it into the forest. About twenty to thirty yards off to your right, you'll see a structure resembling a large outhouse. That's where your dad has set up housekeeping. If he's there, an old red Willys Jeep should be parked nearby."

"Got it. Give me a few minutes to get into the area. If he's not there, I'll be back at this spot within thirty minutes. If I'm not here, give me at least an hour and a half before getting worried. It might take me awhile to get him to talk."

Jack Hargrove sat on the boulder he'd used the day before, and found it afforded an excellent view of Casey's house. His binoculars were focused on Hawkman's SUV as it came across the bridge, and pulled into the driveway. Jack yanked the glasses away from his face as the sun hit the windshield causing a flash of light to hit him in the eyes. By the time he placed them back to view the scene, a man had climbed out of the passenger side. Jack jerked to his feet. "What the hell's Ray doing here? Damn Casey or Hawk Man, whatever he calls himself, has obviously tracked me down and notified my son."

Grumbling, he picked up his backpack, threw the strap over his shoulder and took out in a run across the field. Once he reached his little home, he immediately, packed up his belongings. When he opened the back door of the jeep, he stopped abruptly.

"Something doesn't look right," he grumbled. "Why's there so much room?"

It appeared someone had moved stuff to the sides. He quickly took an inventory and found nothing missing. "Must have jiggled around when I drove out of here the other night," he mumbled, stuffing his bedroll inside. "I can't worry about it now, I don't have time. They could come bursting in here any minute. I gotta get going." He poured the last of the gasoline into the tank and strapped the empty container to the back.

He then loaded the rest of the items from the hut, hopped in the jeep, twisted the key in the ignition, and smiled when the engine turned over. "It hums like a baby. I definitely picked the right vehicle," he muttered.

Turning the jeep around, he headed out of the cover of the forest and onto the road. He turned east toward Topsy Grade and the Oregon border.

⁂

Ray took a deep breath when he reached the edge of the trees, then plunged into the shadowed area. When he reached the small shack, he could see fresh tracks and oil drips where a vehicle had parked. The door of the hut stood open and he peeked inside. He directed the beam of the flashlight around the one room shanty. A potty bucket stood in one corner, but nothing else gave any indication anyone had lived there. But when he stepped inside, he could smell kerosene and noticed a couple of crackers on the floor. The place had been recently vacated; no animal would have left those tidbits there for long. He slapped a hand against his thigh, walked out and headed back toward the open field.

The sun had set, and a few wispy clouds floated across the sky. He felt disappointed he'd missed his Dad and it might be his last chance. Unless they could figure out where he might have gone. Ray reached the road just as Hawkman's SUV pulled into the opening. He climbed into the passenger side.

"He's moved out."

"Are you sure you found the right place?" Hawkman asked, in disbelief.

"Yes. It'd been stripped. There were fresh oil spots where I'm assuming he parked the jeep, and tire marks where he'd turned around. I could smell kerosene inside the little shack and there were remnants of food on the floor. I'd say from the looks of things, he's only been gone two, maybe three hours."

Hawkman looked pensive. "I bet I know what caused him to flee."

"Give me a clue."

"He's been spying on our house from a hidden vantage point. It wouldn't surprise me a bit if he didn't spot you when we came in from the airport. The timing sounds about right."

"Do you think we can find him?"

"We can try. I'd have spotted the Willys if he passed the lake, so I don't think he went west. He's probably headed toward the Oregon border, and might use some back roads to camp at night. I don't expect him to stray far from the jeep, but he'll keep the vehicle hidden from view because it's stolen."

"Wonder how much fuel he's got?"

"Good question. It wouldn't be hard for him to steal a gallon here and there, as there are all kinds of vehicles around these ranches, along with storage tanks. That's probably what he figures on doing."

"Is there a campground nearby?" Ray asked.

"Access six. It's before you get to Topsy Grade. It has tables, benches and a place to build a fire. I doubt he'd stay there, he doesn't want to be seen. And since fire season's started, you can't build a fire."

Ray guffawed. "You think that'll stop my Dad?"

Hawkman shrugged. "You got a point."

"I'd like to start looking for him tonight. Maybe we can spot his campfire."

"Okay, but let's head back to the house, and I'll pick up my gear and change boots. We better pack some food, as this could take awhile."

CHAPTER TWENTY-FOUR

Hawkman hurried back to the bedroom to change into his hiking boots. Jennifer followed and softly pushed the door shut. He explained to her about Jack's disappearance. "We're going to scout the area and see if we can find him."

"Do you want me to drop you off?" she asked.

"No, we'll just take my vehicle."

She lowered her voice. "Do you think Ray can hike through that rough terrain without running into a problem?"

"I doubt he'll have any trouble. You were right; he seems very strong."

"Be sure and carry the walkie-talkie in case something happens. I contacted Peggy and told her Ray had arrived; she's very wary about the whole situation."

"I can understand her concern." Going into his closet, he pulled out the backpack he'd carried the night he searched for Jack. Thankful he'd left everything intact, he placed it on the bed.

Jennifer moved to the door. She turned with her hand on the knob. "You want me to make you guys some sandwiches?"

"That'd be great."

Hawkman rummaged through his possessions until he found another pack, brought it into the living room and dropped it on the couch next to Ray. "I'll get you a bedroll, and Jennifer's going to fix us some food to carry with us."

"This is great, thanks." He picked it up and adjusted the straps so it slipped easily over his broad shoulders.

Hawkman disappeared into his office and found Miss Marple rolled into a ball on his swivel chair. "What the heck are you doing in here?" he asked, as he searched the shelves in the closet. Finding the rolled blanket, he left the cat undisturbed.

Handing the bedding to Skokie, he moved into the kitchen and helped Jennifer with the food. "Thanks, hon. Appreciate your doing this." He stuffed the last sandwich into a paper sack and patted her on the shoulder. He leaned toward her ear and whispered, "Oh, by the way, Miss Marple's in my office. I don't think we have a very social pet."

She grinned. "I'm afraid I agree." Jennifer stuck a couple of bottled waters and an apple into each of their knapsacks. "That should be enough food to carry you guys until tomorrow."

She touched Ray's arm. "I hope your dad will listen."

He nodded. "Thanks. Me, too."

Hawkman glanced at Skokie. "Where's the flashlight I gave you?"

"I left it in your vehicle."

"Be sure and stick it into your pack. I'll grab another one."

The two men climbed into the 4X4, and headed east on Ager Beswick Rd. In the dim light of the evening, Hawkman drove cautiously, watching for deer and any signs of a red Willys Jeep.

Glancing at Ray's feet, Hawkman noticed one seemed larger than the other, "Are you able to walk any distance?"

"Absolutely. I stay in good shape. Even though I have a bad limp, my legs are stronger than they look."

"Excellent." Hawkman said. "As soon as we reach the Oregon border, I'd like to park this vehicle and hike the rest of the way. Jack might spot the headlights and flee even farther."

When they reached access six, Hawkman pulled into the campsite. "I doubt we'll find your dad here, but we can take a look, just in case."

A couple of young men were roasting hot dogs over a small camp stove. Hawkman poked his head out the window. "Hi, having a good time?"

They nodded, their mouths full.

"Have you by any chance seen a red Willys jeep in the area? We've lost our camping buddies and can't figure out where they went."

"No, sorry, can't help you."

"Thanks."

Hawkman turned the SUV around and they continued their journey toward the Oregon border. Soon after they hit Topsy Grade and started downhill, he turned off on a side road which looked more like a cattle trail. "If my memory serves me right, there's a small grove of good sized trees up the way. I think I can conceal the 4X4 in the midst of them."

"Man, it would take me forever to learn this area. Where does this path lead?"

"Years ago it used to be a lumber road. Big logs were taken to the river and floated downstream to a saw mill which later burned down."

He soon spotted the cluster of oaks. As he eased deep into their midst, a few branches rubbed the top of the SUV. Glancing into his rearview mirror he could tell the vehicle would pretty much be hidden from view. "Okay, that should do it," he said, as he opened the door and dropped his feet to the ground.

Both men readjusted their packs and Hawkman slid the stun gun into a zippered pocket in his jacket. He checked his shoulder holster, and released the flap over the gun. By the time they started hiking down the hill into the dense trees, darkness had set in. With a clear sky above, the moon cast strange shadows across the ground as a slight breeze rustled through the trees.

"I'm hoping your dad has a small fire going. It would definitely help us spot him," Hawkman said in a low voice.

"Are we heading for any particular destination?"

"Yes. I'm pretty familiar with this area. My son and I used to hike it a lot. There are several old logging roads that dead end before reaching the river and are seldom used. I'm thinking your dad might find those very enticing and head down one. So I thought we'd stay north of the road going into Oregon. I could be all wrong, but it's worth a first try. If we don't find him, we'll opt for going back up the south side."

"Sounds like a good plan. I'm glad you know where you're going."

Hawkman chuckled. "I didn't learn overnight."

The men continued in silence, their gazes searching the landscape for any sort of glow which might indicate a campfire. They trudged onward for another hour before Hawkman stopped near the edge of some trees and plopped down on a large boulder. "I think it's time for a rest and a bite to eat."

"I'm with you there."

They ate a sandwich, and washed it down with water. Hawkman then pulled out his night binoculars and put them to his eyes. He scanned the area for several minutes, then focused on a darkened unleveled stretch of land. He couldn't make out if the uneven lines were buildings or shadows. He handed the binoculars to Skokie and pointed. "Take a look and tell me what you see."

Ray looked through the glasses and studied the terrain where Hawkman indicated. "Hmm, hard to say. It could be some type of structure. Yet on the other hand, it might be no more than a sunken area surrounded by a bunch of bushes."

"I say we go canvass the place and find out."

He handed the binoculars back to Hawkman. "Definitely looks like a good place to hide."

They hoisted their packs to their backs and hiked across a short stretch of meadow. As they neared the tract, they moved toward a row of oaks and hid in the shadows.

"What do you make of it?" Hawkman whispered.

"Appears to be a building of some sort tucked within a growth of bushes."

"Stay here and I'll go see what it is. I'll come back and get you if it looks promising."

Ray gave him the go sign and scooted behind the trunk of a tree.

Hawkman stayed hidden as he wound around the enclosure. When he got to what he suspected to be the front, he hunched behind a large rock and peered around the edge. Between two small structures sat the Willys jeep. *Now where was Hargrove?* Just as the thought passed through his mind, Jack walked out from an opening in one of the buildings. He had a flashlight and threw the beam on the ground as if looking for something. Hawkman ducked as the ray came closer. He could hear the man mumbling, but couldn't make out the words. Soon, he heard, 'Ah ha, there it is.'

When it grew quiet, Hawkman decided to take a chance and stole a glance around the boulder. Jack had returned to the wooden structure and a glow showed through the wall cracks. He eased away and headed back where Ray waited.

"Your dad's there with the jeep."

Ray took Hawkman's arm. "I want to go in first. Maybe I can talk some sense into his thick head. I'm afraid if he sees you, he'll just pull a gun and I might not be able to stop him from shooting."

"It's going to be risky, regardless. He might gun down anyone who surprises him."

"I'll let him know who it is."

"If you're sure that's the way you want to handle it. I'll follow close behind, but stay out of sight. At least I can cover you."

He nodded. "Sounds good."

Hawkman gave him a quick description of how things were set up at his dad's campsite.

Ray took a deep breath and exhaled. "Okay, here goes."

Skokie set out and Hawkman followed. Whey they reached the hideout, Hawkman, his gun poised, crouched behind the boulder he'd used earlier.

He watched Ray walk right up the middle of the small opening, set his body in an awkward straddle legged stance, then he reared back his head and yelled. "Dad, are you in there?"

CHAPTER TWENTY-FIVE

Jack Hargrove jerked up his head. He reached over and grabbed the pistol lying on the cot. Turning down the kerosene lamp, he inched toward the opening. "Who's there?" he called.

"It's me, Dad, Ray."

Yanking the flashlight from his back pocket, Jack stepped outside and guided the beam toward the voice. Ray flinched when it met his eyes.

"What the hell are you doing here?" Jack asked.

"I need to talk to you."

Hargrove swung the light across the ground and over the boulder where Hawkman was hidden. "You alone?"

"Yes."

"I don't believe it. You don't know this area. And I saw you getting out of the car at the ex-agent's house."

"You're in trouble, Dad. I want to help."

"How'd you find me?"

"Spotted the stolen jeep."

"Who told you about it?"

"I spoke with Bill Broadwell, he found out from Tom Casey. After I heard the story, I flew out here in hopes of finding you before you got yourself in deeper."

"Where you staying?"

"At Casey's place."

Jack stood rigid with the flashlight trained on his son's face. "I can't believe you walked all the way from the bridge."

Ray shielded his eyes with his hand. "Dad, move the damn light. You're blinding me. I need to sit down, my legs are tired."

Hargrove's hand twitched as he let the beam drop to the ground. "Sorry, son. Come on in and rest on my cot."

Once Ray shuffled inside, Hawkman crept to the back of the encampment. Even though he didn't think Jack would harm his son, he didn't trust the man. Edging closer to the building, he watched his footing and tried to be as quiet as possible. The shrub, a bramble type, kept catching on his jacket and jeans. He had to remove each individual vine carefully as not to make any noise. Finally, he made it to a very small window where he could hear the two men talking. Afraid to lean on the rotted wood, he crouched below the opening.

What Hawkman heard made his skin crawl. After listening for close to ten minutes, he decided to get out of there. He climbed swiftly out of the sticky bush and jogged back to his 4X4. He jumped into the cab and gunned down the dirt trail onto Ager Beswick Road, then aimed toward home.

When he crossed the bridge, he noticed a glow through the living room drapes. Jennifer must have had a surge of ideas and remained working at the computer or had found a good movie on the television.

He pulled into the driveway and hit the garage door button on the visor. Once he'd parked, he dashed to the front door and almost forgot about the alarm, but caught himself in time to quickly punch in the code.

Jennifer sat on the couch with Miss Marple curled in her lap. The minute he stepped into the living room, the cat jumped down and made a beeline toward him, but immediately backed away as soon as she smelled his footwear. Jennifer flipped off the television and looked confused.

"Where's Ray?"

"He won't be back."

"Why?" she asked, frowning.

"He and his dad are in cahoots."

She jumped up. "What!"

He flopped down on the couch and unlaced his boots. "They're in this mess together and tried to play me for a fool. But I overhead their conversation and got the hell out of there before they both came gunning for me."

Jennifer put a hand to her throat and fear crossed her face. "I don't understand."

"Neither do I, but I think Ray played his father into thinking it was all my fault for his accident. He hoped to get his dad so worked up he'd do the dirty work of killing me. I gather he slyly seeded his dad's mind with tidbits of bitterness. Then when Jack disappeared, Ray knew where he'd gone and somehow kept track of his movements. When things didn't happen quickly, and Jack seemed to get in more and more trouble, Ray wormed his way into coming out here. Bill and I both fell for his line."

"How did you find out all this?" She asked, dropping back down on the couch and giving him her undivided attention.

"Using my sleuthing technique of eavesdropping."

She wrinkled her forehead. "You've lost me. Please, explain."

Hawkman told her about finding Jack and what had transpired. "I don't think Ray counted on my overhearing their conversation. He's going to come out of there thinking I'm still waiting."

"Do you think he planned on shooting you right then and there?"

"It would've been as good a place as any. Far out in the country, no one around to hear the shot. They could have buried me in that old building and taken off in my 4X4." He glanced at her. "And think about it. You had no idea how long we might be in those hills, so you probably wouldn't have called for help before a couple of days. By then, they'd have been long gone."

Jennifer hugged herself. "Oh, my, the thought of it gives me the willies."

He smiled, reached over and patted her leg. "It didn't happen. A bigger force is watching over me."

"So what are we going to do now?"

"First of all, I'm going to go search his stuff and see if I can get more clues as to what he has in mind. Then I'm contacting Ken." He stood and ambled toward the guest room. "I doubt I'll find any weapons. I could see the outline of several under the outfit Skokie wore."

Jennifer followed close at his heels with Miss Marple bringing up the rear. As they entered the room, the kitten stood back and meowed.

"She doesn't even want to come in here," Jennifer said.

Hawkman chuckled. "One smart feline, if you ask me."

He picked up Ray's suitcase, tossed it on the bed and tried to open it. "Strange, why would he lock it?" Suddenly, he snatched it off the bed, ran out the front door, and threw it into the lot beside the house. He stood back and watched it explode when it hit the ground, then burst into flames.

When he turned, Jennifer stood in the doorway with hands over her ears. "Oh my God! I could have been blown to bits if I'd gone in there with the vacuum and moved his bag?"

"I'm not sure. Depends on how he had it rigged. I jiggled the latch and thought I heard something." Hawkman picked up the hose and turned on the water. He sprayed the burning area until he'd drowned all signs of fire. "When it gets light I'll collect what's left for Bill to send to the lab."

Just as he turned off the water, the Sheriff's white wagon screeched into the drive. "We heard an explosion," Ken said, as he jumped out of the truck.

Peggy hopped out of the passenger side. "I smell smoke. Everyone okay?"

Hawkman pointed toward the debris. "Yeah, had a close call. Come on in and I'll clue you in."

Once they were gathered in the living room, Hawkman recounted the events of the evening. "I feel like I've been taken for a fool."

"I knew something didn't fit about the stepson," Peggy said.

Jennifer rubbed her hands over her cheeks. "It still gives me the shakes to think we had a bomb in the house. I wonder if he planned on using it on us, or just hoped by chance we'd be snoopy and try to open the bag?"

Ken scrubbed his fingers across the day old stubble on his chin. "We may never know, but at least you're safe." He hooked a thumb toward the back of the house. "Let's take another look at the guest room."

The two men gave the room a thorough search and found nothing. Hawkman emptied Ray's shaving kit onto the dresser top and only found a razor, toothpaste, toothbrush, aspirin and a comb. He felt around the outside of the small bag, but found it void of hidden compartments. Tossing the items back inside, he picked up the shirt Skokie had worn on the plane and ran his fingers through the pockets. He pulled out an airline ticket and read through the information. Raising his brows, he handed it to Ken.

CHAPTER TWENTY-SIX

Jack quickly turned up the lantern as Ray hobbled into the small room. He waved an arm toward the cot. "Have a seat."

Not sure it would hold his weight, Ray eased down on the rickety makeshift bed, and stared at his father. "How are you doing, Dad."

Jack nodded as he straddled the three legged milk stool. "I'm fine. But tell me how you got here?"

"Casey and I drove around the area in search of you. We noticed this shadowed area from the road, left his vehicle and hiked in to examine it. When Casey spotted the jeep, I told him to go back to the 4X4 and wait for me, as I wanted to talk to you alone."

"Okay, talk. You say, I'm in trouble. But you know that doesn't bother me. I've been in worse situations and gotten out. My goal is to get Casey for what he did to you."

Ray looked his dad in the eye. "And I'm going to help you."

And expression of surprise crossed Jack's face. "I don't understand; I figured you were here to stop me. I didn't think you approved of my plan of going after the sorry son-of-a-bitch. You never gave me any indication you blamed him."

Chuckling, Ray placed his elbows on his knees. "How do you think you came to hate him so much?"

"Just watching your agony. I had dreams of you being a super spy. Then after the accident, I knew it could never happen."

"You don't remember me telling you how I hated him?"

Jack shook his head. "No. I always had the impression you were thrilled to work with Jim Anderson. You tried to discourage me from disliking him. The only negative thing I ever remember you saying, was while you were recovering and in quite a bit of pain. You told me you shouldn't have been on that mission. But you never explained why."

"It's really not important. The fact is, the man ruined my life."

In the flickering light of the lantern, Jack studied the peculiar expression on his son's face, and noticed a tic below his jaw. "How come?"

Ray glanced at his father. "How come what?"

"That it's insignificant for me to know the reason you were there."

"Because the damage is done. Now, we have to make him pay."

Jack picked up the flashlight and pistol, then walked outside. He threw the beam behind the boulder and down the road as far as he could see. Spotting a backpack resting against a tree, he carried it inside. "Is this yours?"

"Yeah, thanks."

"Looks like the big man is nowhere in sight. He must have taken you for your word. How long will he wait before he comes looking for you?"

"I'll go find him, after we've formed a plan. I can't let him go back to his house without me."

Jack gave him a suspicious look. "Why?"

Ray raised an eyebrow. "Because if he has a nosey wife, he'll find her dead, and I want to see his face when he turns around to my gun pointed at his heart."

"She didn't do anything to you," Jack said, glaring at his son. "There's no need to hurt her."

"Yeah, but she's a part of his life, and I understand you left threatening messages on the phone about her."

"Those were empty. I don't like to hurt women. I just wanted to scare him."

"What about the gal you ran off the road?"

"How'd you know about her?"

"I've been keeping a close account of your doings."

"She had nothing to do with me going after Casey. She spurned me."

Ray threw back his head and laughed. "Sorry. It just sounded funny for you to say that at your age."

"Hey, I'm not dead. I still like pretty women. And I thought she'd taken a fancy to me. Figured I could have a little fun on the side. But it didn't work out."

"You can quit worrying about Casey's wife. Nothing will happen unless she tries to open my suitcase."

"You've changed, Son." Jack shook his head. "What happened to the kind man I used to know? Your mother always said you had a heart."

Ray took a deep breath and stared at his dad. "Time and agony. We can go into this at a later date. Right now, we've got to set up our strategy. Casey may start worrying and drive down this way."

After they'd discussed what Ray had in mind, he stood, took the flashlight from the backpack, then slipped the straps over his shoulders. "I'll meet you on the main road tomorrow morning."

Jack strolled outside with his son and watched him walk off into the darkness.

After Ray had gone some distance, he figured Tom would step up to his side, but he never appeared. Finally, he called in a low voice. "Casey, where the hell are you?" When no response came and he saw no sign of the ex-agent, he headed in the direction they'd parked the SUV. When he reached the spot and found the vehicle missing, he knew something had gone awry. Had Casey overheard him talking to his dad? He remembered hearing some noise outside the hut window, but assumed an animal had rustled through the underbrush. Maybe the varmint was Tom Casey.

He immediately turned and hobbled quickly back toward his dad's hideout. His legs were definitely feeling the strain. Even with the flashlight, he stumbled and fell several times, but soon could see the deep shadowed hole. He made his way around the boulder, then flashed the beam onto the hut. To his horror, he discovered the jeep had disappeared. He hurried to the door and shined the light around the empty hull.

Staggering back outside, he stood in the front of the shanty with his fists on his hips. He reared back his head and his voice echoed through the hills. "Dad, where are you?"

CHAPTER TWENTY-SEVEN

Hawkman carried the ticket into the living room with Bronson at his heels. He glanced up at the wall clock. "Too late to call Detective Williams. I'll wait until morning."

Jennifer stood beside him with Miss Marple in her arms. She pointed at the paper. "That looks like a plane ticket."

"It is. And a very odd one."

"Why?"

"Ray told me he only had a couple more days before he had to get back to work. However, this ticket shows his return flight isn't for two weeks."

Jennifer cocked her head. "He'll have a little trouble retrieving it now."

"I don't know how he figures on using it. It won't be long before the whole country will be looking for him and his dad," Ken said.

"Maybe he thinks he can escape another way." Jennifer shivered. "Every time I think about that suitcase exploding, chills go down my spine. After what I've heard, there's no telling how the man's mind works. He's scary."

Hawkman put his arm around her shoulders and gave a squeeze. "Don't worry honey, the catch had to be tampered with, which activated a timer. When I heard it ticking, I ran outside. It might have gone off prematurely when it hit the ground. We'll probably never know. Ray probably thought he could make our deaths look accidental. I'm afraid he's more evil than his father."

"I think we better do a little brain storming," Ken said.

The four sat down in the living room.

"You obviously didn't hang around the hideout long enough to hear what they planned," Peggy said,

"No, I'd be out of luck. Dealing with two Agent men, the chances of surviving their onslaught were nil. My best bet was to get out of there as fast as I could. By now Ray knows I didn't hang around. He'll put it together and figure I overheard him talking to his dad."

Jennifer looked at her husband with concern. "So what's the plan?"

"First thing in the morning, I'm going to contact Detective Williams, then call Bill and let him know what I've learned. I think the news is going to shock them."

"All fine and dandy, but what about the rest of tonight?" Peggy asked

"We could call in a couple of back ups, and keep the house under a tight surveillance," Ken said.

Hawkman waved a hand. "I don't think it's necessary. We can pretty much barricade ourselves inside. I'll activate the alarm system and we're both armed." He shifted his position and rubbed a hand across his chin. "Ray probably did a lot of walking tonight, and will do more, when he discovers I'm not there. He's going to be very tired and will need some rest before they pursue any plan. I don't expect any action before tomorrow. So I think our best bet is to get rested up so we'll be alert for anything they might throw at us."

Ken stood. "Peggy, I think the man knows what he's talking about. Let's get home and we'll see you two first thing in the morning. If anything unusual happens, give us a call."

Hawkman and Jennifer walked them to the door. After they left, Hawkman moved toward the deck. "I think I'll bring Pretty Girl into the living room. We can put some old sheets on the floor. We've done it before." Hawkman eyed Miss Marple. "To keep the nervous factor down in both our pets, we better separate them. Put the kitty in our bathroom and shut the door. I'll want our bedroom open so I can hear any noises."

Jennifer nodded. "No problem."

Hawkman hurried out to the garage, retrieved one of the portable perches, and dusted it off. Jennifer draped the floor on one side of the fireplace.

"You think she'll like this corner okay."

"Perfect." He set up the contraption and checked it for stability. "That should work fine. I'll go get her."

He came back in with Pretty Girl resting on his protected arm. When he placed her on the top rod, she let out a squawk and batted him with her wings.

"It's okay, girl, it's just for tonight."

Once the falcon settled, Hawkman tethered her to the perch, then slid a water and food container on the extended rod. "There you go girl, you'll be just fine until morning."

Jennifer had put Miss Marple to bed and secured the doors and windows. "Are you through going out for the night?"

"Yes."

"Okay, I'm setting the alarm."

Jennifer threw all the switches, even the one connected to the garage, and watched all the lights turn green. She then flopped down on the couch. "If someone even so much as touches this house, the alarm will go off and wake the whole community."

Hawkman chuckled. "It's better than being dead." He disappeared into his office and within a few minutes came back with several pistols. "Watch where I'm putting these. They're all loaded and ready to fire." He placed one in the drawer between the two chairs, one on Jennifer's desk in front of her computer, but out of sight and one in the kitchen drawer nearest the front door. Then glanced at her. "Got it?"

"Yes. I also have on my fanny pack."

"Good. Hopefully, we won't have to use any of them. But better to be safe than sorry." He took her hand and led her toward the bedroom. "Come on, hon, let's try to get a few hours rest."

"Are we leaving the kitchen light on for a reason?"

"Yes. I want it to look like someone is still up. It might deter Ray or Jack."

She sighed. "I don't know if I'll be able to sleep."

Shortly after climbing into bed, Hawkman lay there staring into the darkness. Suddenly, he sat up. In the stillness of the night, he could hear the distant low rumbling of a vehicle. He threw his legs over the side of the bed, grabbed his jeans from the floor and hopped into them as he made his way to the sliding glass door and peered out. If he slid it open, he'd set off the alarm, but he couldn't see around the aviary. He sat on the edge of the bed, quickly slipped on his boots and a tee shirt, then pulled the gun from the shoulder holster draped over the chair next to the bed. Leaving his eye-patch on the table, since he didn't need it in the dark, he snatched the night binoculars from his office and made his way to the living room. Pretty Girl squawked as he turned off the alarm and lights. "Hush, girl. I don't need any distractions." He then marched onto the deck. Sticking the pistol into the waistband of his jeans, he put the binoculars to his eyes. He could make out the faint glow of headlights shining into the sky as a vehicle bobbed across the rough road coming from Topsy Grade.

"Can you see anything?" Jennifer said, moving to his side, clutching her Beretta.

"Sorry, didn't mean to wake you?"

"You didn't. I couldn't sleep. Noises tend to travel a long ways in the still of the night, especially here at the lake. I thought I heard the grumbling of an engine."

"Me, too." He pointed east. "If you'll watch where the road goes, several miles up, you can see the glow of headlights. If my hunch is right, we'll have visitors in about fifteen minutes."

She clutched his arm. "Now what?"

"Let's see who it is before we panic. Ken and Peggy are just up the road. If the vehicle turns out to be the jeep and crosses the bridge, we'll take action. You call the Bronsons, if things get hot. They can radio for back up."

"How do we get ourselves into these life or death messes?" Jennifer mumbled as she went back into the house and headed toward the bedroom. As she passed the falcon, the bird ruffled her feathers and let out another squawk. "Shush, Pretty Girl, I don't need you butting in." In the darkened room, she donned a pair of jeans and shirt, then fastened her fanny pack around her waist.

She eased open the bathroom door and by the soft glow of the night light made out the silhouette of Miss Marple curled up in the box of tissue paper. She grinned and shook her head. "At least I can smile," she whispered, and shut the door.

Hurrying back out to the deck where Hawkman stood looking through the glasses, she stared at the area where he had them trained. "I don't see anything. Maybe it was just a rancher going after a bear or mountain lion."

"Nice thought. But they might be going downhill. It's when they're going up, I can see the lights against the sky and tree tops."

Jennifer plopped down on the deck chair and put her head in her hands. "Tell me when you see anything."

Hawkman changed his stance. "Whoever it is, they're still coming and getting closer."

Jennifer got up and moved next to him, her gaze focused on the road. "Yes, I see the lights."

Within a few minutes, he dropped the glasses from his face. "It's the red jeep and he's turning on the bridge." He gently shoved her toward the door. "Let's get inside."

Jennifer headed for the phone.

"No, wait."

The Willys jeep turned into the driveway throwing its head light beams through the window sending a flash across the kitchen walls. Hawkman motioned for Jennifer to duck behind the bar as he stood next to the front door.

The low rumbling of the jeep engine held steady and then a loud voice echoed through the air. "Tom Casey, I need to talk to you."

Hawkman poised his gun, flipped on the porch light, then opened the door a crack. He found himself looking at the hairy face of a mountain man holding a tire iron out the window of the jeep and tapping it against the side. Except for the reflection of the porch light on the narrowed green eyes, Hawkman would never have recognized Jack Hargrove.

CHAPTER TWENTY-EIGHT

Hawkman raised his gun so it pointed straight at Jack's head. "Don't try anything stupid."

Jack tossed the pipe onto the gravel. "I came to talk. Where's Ray?"

"Haven't seen him."

"I thought he'd be here." He frowned. "Didn't you pick him up on the road?"

"Not after I overheard you two talking about my demise. As far as I'm concerned, I hope never to see him again. And I'm not too happy about your appearance."

Jack scratched his sideburn. "I've come to the conclusion my son's lost his ability to think straight."

Hawkman knitted his brows. "I see."

"I guess I better go find him. But he's not going to be happy when I tell him I won't be part of his game." Jack gunned the jeep and started backing up.

Hawkman stepped out on the landing. "Hold on, Hargrove. What do you mean?"

He stepped on the brake and glanced up with a sad expression. "I've been betrayed and used."

"I'm not following you."

Jack leaned his head out the window of the Willys. "I thought you were a mean bastard. Didn't care anything about others. After my wife died, I went downhill. My son took advantage of my situation and planted seeds of resentment about you in my mind without me even realizing it. So I concentrated on getting revenge for what I thought you'd done to Ray. I've made a terrible mistake."

Hawkman moved toward the jeep, but Jack threw it into reverse and kicked up gravel as he backed up. When he hit the asphalt, the smell of rubber wafted through the air as he sped away. Picking up the tire iron, Hawkman held it by the end so he wouldn't disturb any fingerprints and headed back to the house.

Jennifer quickly turned off the porch light. "Get inside, you're a nice target standing out there."

He stepped into the kitchen as she shut the door. "Did you hear what he said?"

"Yes. It's a little hard to believe after all the things he's done."

He placed the pipe in a paper grocery bag.

She pointed at the sack. "What'd you just put in there?"

"I have a suspicion it's the weapon used on my head."

"I thought we were going to call the Bronsons."

"If he'd seen their vehicle, he wouldn't have stopped. He knew he had a chance of getting away, If he just had to face me and Ray." Hawkman glanced out the kitchen window. "I'm not sure if this visit is part of a plan he and Ray contrived or if the old man has actually had a change of heart."

Jennifer grabbed his arm. "Don't go soft. Didn't you say you got out of there because you heard them talking about killing you?"

"Yes. That's why I don't understand how he could think Skokie was here."

"Maybe Ray thought you were still waiting for him and left his dad at the hideout."

"Possible. But somehow the pieces of this puzzle are not fitting together."

She rubbed her arms and gave a little shiver. "It sounds mighty fishy to me. I don't trust either of them."

"Me either." He turned on the alarm. "I don't think we better let our guard down. It may be exactly what they're wanting."

She snapped her fingers. "You know, he might have been checking on whether the suitcase blew up in the house."

"Good point. He figured he'd have won half the battle, if something had happened to you."

"I'm sure he saw me standing in the doorway. So he knows I'm okay."

"And it's too dark outside for him to have noticed the burned debris in the yard. He could very well be checking, and then report to Ray."

Jennifer rubbed her eyes and stifled a yawn. "It looks like a night of little sleep."

"Go ahead and get to bed. I'll stand guard. Once you're rested, I'll catch a few winks."

❧

Jack clicked the headlights onto bright, then drove east on Ager Beswick. He wondered if Ray had gone back to the hideout and discovered him gone. Would his son risk staying at the shack for a few hours to rest or would he be hiking toward the lake?

He reached the cutoff and drove toward the hideout. Stopping in front of the shadowed area, he took the flashlight from under the seat and shined the beam at the shanty. "Ray, are you in there?" he called.

Several seconds passed before his son stumbled out of the opening with his hand shading his eyes. "Get the damn light off my face."

Jack lowered the beam to the ground as Ray made his way to the side of the jeep.

"Dad, where the hell did you go?

"I thought I better get out of here before someone discovered me. I took a chance and drove up to Casey's place thinking you'd be there. When I didn't see any cops around, I called him out."

"You talked to him?"

Jack nodded. "Yeah. That's when I found out he'd left you, so I figured I'd better do a little searching."

"I thought you'd deserted me and I sure didn't cherish the thought of walking all the way back to the lake."

"A confrontation with Casey would have been dangerous. He overheard us talking and wouldn't be very receptive at seeing you."

"How come he let you leave?"

"I didn't let him get close and then I gave him a song and dance about how I'd made a big mistake about going along with your plan, and wanted to tell you."

"He believed it?"

Jack shrugged. "He didn't shoot me."

Ray rubbed the hair growth on his chin. "He'll probably have the cops swarming these hills before long."

"I think we should go to Klamath Falls. It'll be a rough ride, but I think we can make it in the jeep. The farther we get away from here, the safer it'll be."

Ray glared at his dad. "No. I didn't come all the way back here to turn tail and run. I came to help you complete a mission, and we're not leaving until it's done. But before we find another hiding spot, I'd like to get some items I left at Casey's place."

Jack shook his head. "As I said, I don't think it's a good idea. He's armed his household to the hilt."

"How do you know?"

"He met me at the door with a .45 pointed at my head. And I could see his wife standing behind him and she had a gun in her hand. I've also spotted police vehicles parked around their place."

"Doesn't sound like they've fooled with my suitcase."

"I couldn't tell you. But I didn't see any holes in the walls."

Ray shifted his position. "If our agent overhead our conversation, I'm surprised he hasn't gone through my things."

"I have no idea, but I think we're wasting time here. The longer we stand around shooting the breeze, the sooner daylight will be upon us." He patted the steering wheel. "And this little baby stands out like a sore thumb."

"Okay, let me gather up my stuff and I'll be right with you."

Ray hoisted the backpack into the jeep and climbed onto

the seat. "Okay, let's go. Any idea where we can hide for a couple of days?"

"I spotted an old deserted barn past the ranch. No houses near it. We might be safe in there for a while. You got any food in that pack?"

Ray opened it and pulled out several items. "Yeah, a couple of sandwiches. Some water, an apple, and a can of beans with a pull-top. Probably should eat these sandwiches before they go bad."

"Sounds good to me. It's been a long night and I'm hungry."

The two men munched as they drove along. Soon, Jack pointed to a big building off the road. "There it is. I think we can sneak in without being detected."

He moved along slowly as he searched for an opening. Finding the gate, he hopped out, fiddled with the chain and pushed it open. He drove through, then went back and hooked the padlock so it appeared locked. Driving toward the doorless structure, he noted a horse trailer occupied the middle of the barn floor. "This is perfect; if I park in front of the trailer, it will hide the jeep from the road." Jack drove deep into the darkened area and turned off the lights.

"Man, it's pitch dark in here," Ray said, flipping on the flashlight and scouring the walls.

"Our eyes will get accustomed to it soon," Jack said, as his light focused on the other side. "Let's make sure there isn't a nest of rattlers in here."

"Nice thought, Dad. Think I'll wait until daylight before I put my bedroll down on the ground."

Jack chuckled. "Don't blame you. However, it might be a bit more comfortable to sleep in the trailer."

"Great idea. Let's check it out."

They inspected the inside, and found it reasonably clean. Spreading out their bedrolls, they scooted between the covers and before long both men were snoring.

CHAPTER TWENTY-NINE

Jack awoke first, and rolled up his bedding. "Sure don't want any varmints crawling into it", he mumbled, propping it on the inside wall of the trailer. He scooted out of the enclosure, and went to the jeep. He rummaged through the gear until he found a couple of canteens and a small bucket. He stood in the shadow, behind the opened barn door, and scanned the region. Not seeing any vehicles or movements, he hunkered down behind the brush and scurried toward Shovel Creek, a small stream he'd spotted earlier, not more than a hundred yards from the building. While keeping an eye peeled, he kneeled down to fill the containers with water, and almost fell in when a doe crashed out of the bush. Catching his breath, he watched the deer scamper away, then tried again. Once he'd filled the canteens to the brim, he screwed on the lids, then rinsed out the bucket and dipped it into the stream. Hurrying back to the barn, he placed the water pail under the jeep and covered it with a board.

The wall of the barn had several timbers missing and lots of rotted wood lay on the ground. He rubbed a hand down his beard as he stared out one of the slots. "Sure wish I knew the territory better," he mumbled. He turned and walked back toward the jeep. "Wonder if I should build a fire and make some coffee?" he said aloud.

"Sounds like a great idea."

Jack whirled around as Ray stumbled out of the trailer.

"Good Lord, don't scare me like that."

"Sorry, didn't intend to."

"I've noticed signs along the road saying no fires permitted. Smoke in broad daylight would draw attention. We'd be better off to build one at night. We'll find a protected spot where the flames can't be seen and the wind is right."

"We for sure don't want any firemen up here." Ray massaged his thigh. "But boy, a cup of coffee would taste good." He pointed toward the Willys. "You wouldn't by chance have a camp stove tucked away?"

"Nope. Things moved too fast and I had to get out of town. Have very few supplies, but I do have coffee. You like it cold?"

"Naw." Ray moved to the rear of the jeep and peered inside. "We're going to have to eat. What sort of food stuffs do you have?"

Jack rummaged through a sack. "Here's a couple of wieners and some hot dog buns. We can eat these raw. In fact, we better devour them now or they'll go bad. Even have some mustard and catsup."

Grinning, Ray took a bun from the wrapper and plastered it with catsup. "I can hardly wait to sink my teeth into this."

"Call it gourmet dining," Jack said, laughing and handed him one of the canteens. "Here's fresh stream water to wash it down."

Munching on his cold food, Ray walked to the entrance of the barn and looked out. "How far are we from the nearest farm house?"

"I'd say about half a mile. Why?"

"Might just have to make a little raid on someone's kitchen."

Jack found a bag of crushed potato chips in the bottom of the sack. "Want some chips," he said, walking toward Ray.

He dug in and pulled out a handful of broken pieces. "Better than nothing."

"Might be a little risky to break into a house with farm hands around."

"We'll wait until the wife's gone into town and the men are in the field. It'll probably be a piece of cake, as I doubt they lock their doors."

While his son talked, Jack strolled around the barn looking into each corner and noticed a red can attached to the front of the horse trailer. He unscrewed the lid and gave it a sniff, then lifted it from its spot. "Ah, ha. Found just what we needed."

Ray turned his head and looked at his dad. "What?"

Jack held up the can. "A gallon of gas. This will get us a long way in the jeep."

"I think we better hoof it to the farm houses. The Willys would draw too much attention."

"True, but we'll need this later."

The two men prepared for their hike.

Hawkman turned off the lamp, opened the drapes and sat in his chair by the picture window overlooking the lake. He watched the road for any headlights but knew Pretty Girl, resting on the perch nearby, would make a noise if anyone came around. Soon, he drifted into sleep.

The light of a new day perked up the outside and a large flock of Canadian geese flew over the house, vibrating the tiles on the roof with their loud honking. Hawkman yawned, stood up and stretched.

"Pretty Girl, I think it's safe to take you back to the aviary." He slipped on the long leather glove and untied her tether. She stepped onto his arm without hesitation and he carried her out to the deck. After cleaning out the bottom of the enclosure, filling the water tin and checking her food supply, he secured the cage, then stood for a moment taking in the beautiful morning.

Back inside, he folded and draped the sheet over the perch. Might need to put her in again tonight, he thought, as he moved the contraption deeper into the corner. He put on a pot of coffee and ate a bowl of dry cereal.

Jennifer came around the corner with Miss Marple draped over her shoulder. "Okay, time for you to grab a few winks of sleep."

"I already did. Pretty Girl turned out to be the guard. I'm going to go see if I can find Jack."

She glanced toward the perch, and seeing the falcon had been returned to the aviary, placed the cat on the floor. "Did you call Ken?"

"No. I'm debating if I should."

Jennifer put a hand on her hip. "You can't go alone. They've had time to find another hiding spot and it's a huge area out there. You'll be like a big target with cross hairs painted on your chest. If you're so set on this mission, I'll go with you. Another set of eyes can only help."

He poured them some coffee, then looked at her with a scowl. "Are you crazy?"

She glared at him. "No more than you wanting to go hunt down two ex-agents, who know the ropes as well as you, if not better."

"I'm not going to risk you getting shot."

"That goes both ways."

"This is my job, not yours."

"Weak excuses don't hold water."

"Well, you're not going and that's final."

"I hate to tell you this, Mr. Tom Casey, but don't try to leave without me, or I'll take my own car and seek them out. Now, do you want me to go by myself or with you?"

"What's with the 'Mr. Tom Casey' bit?"

She slapped a fist on the counter. "Because you make me so angry."

"I guess I don't have a choice." He glanced down at her bare feet. "You better get on some boots, make sure your gun is loaded and you have extra shells."

Jennifer dashed to the bedroom, threw on her jeans, hiking boots and a long sleeved cotton shirt. She grabbed a wind breaker from the closet and ran back to the kitchen, fastening her fanny pack and gun around her waist. "Okay," she panted. "I'm ready."

Miss Marple sat in the middle of the living room watching, her head twisting from side to side. She seemed to know better than to get in her mistress' way.

Hawkman studied his pretty wife. "Settle down. I promise I won't go off without you. I certainly don't want you out there roaming around alone."

She grabbed a yogurt out of the refrigerator. "Want one? Guess we should eat something."

He nodded and slid onto the bar stool. "Already had a bowl of cereal, but I could eat a piece of toast."

Jennifer threw a couple slices of bread into the toaster. "I'm going to call Peggy and tell her what we're planning to do."

Hawkman let out a sigh. "Well, if you insist. But all we're going to do is look around. I don't think we're going to need any help." He stood and pointed at her binoculars on the counter. "Be sure and take those."

"And my camera", she said, grabbing if off the computer table.

The morning felt crisp and clean as they climbed into Hawkman's 4X4.

Jennifer adjusted her seat and rolled down the window. She put the glasses to her eyes as soon as they turned onto Ager Beswick Road.

CHAPTER THIRTY

The cool morning breeze rippled through Jennifer's hair as she peered through the binoculars. When they approached an old deserted house, she examined the grounds, and took some pictures. "This place would be a perfect hideout, but I don't see any sign of the jeep."

"They wouldn't want to be this close to the road."

"Is there any way we could look into those outbuildings. You could conceal a vehicle in one quite easily."

Hawkman pulled off to the side and parked. He craned his neck to look around her. "You might have a point. I'll go take a gander." He jumped out, opened the back door and rummaged through the duffel bag until he found a pair of heavy work gloves.

Jennifer watched him pull them on as he walked down the barb wire fence surrounding the property. He finally found a spot where the wires hung loosely, and cautiously pushed down the top strand, and threw his leg over to the other side. As he strolled toward the house through the overgrown weeds, a covey of quail, chattering their warning signal, dashed from under the porch, raced across the field and flew into a nearby tree. Hawkman continued his search and disappeared behind one of the buildings. Jennifer snapped some more shots while waiting, and within a few minutes, he reappeared on the other side. Soon, he headed back toward the road, hopped over the barricade, and climbed into the SUV.

"Nope, there's not a sign of a jeep, tractor or any mechanical machine. In fact, it doesn't look like a human has been on this property for a long time."

"Doesn't hurt to make sure."

They next passed an ancient homestead where the house had fallen down long ago and only two rickety structures stood. You could see daylight through the missing planks in the wall.

"How in the world do those old buildings stand up against the winds we get here?" Jennifer asked.

"The old timers built things mighty sturdy and able to withstand the rigors of weather. Doesn't look like this place warrants a closer look."

When they approached the Hill's ranch, they spotted Sue in her car waiting at the road's edge for them to pass. Her two young boys were in the back seat, along with their big brown mutt, whose wagging tail slapped the youngsters in the face as he barked a loud greeting. Hawkman put on the brake and poked his head out the window. "How's it going, Sue?"

She smiled. "Fine, and how are you two? You're sure out early this morning."

"We're looking for a couple of guys in a red Willys jeep. Have you seen such a vehicle drive through here?"

"No. But I haven't really been very observant. Is there a problem?"

"Checking out a stolen auto report."

"Bill's more aware of strange cars going down the road than I am, but he's already gone into town for supplies. I'll ask him tonight and have him give you a call if he's seen anything."

"Thanks, appreciate it." Hawkman gave a wave and headed up the hill.

They soon approached a big deserted barn, and as Jennifer held the binoculars to her eyes, the sun's beams hit the chrome on the horse trailer reflecting a flash of light right into her eyes. Dropping the glasses to her chest, she picked up the camera off the dashboard and shaded it with her hand as she snapped a couple of pictures. "Geez, the sun's bright this morning. I'm not sure these will turn out." She put the camera aside. "Looks like someone's using this place for storage. I'd be afraid some of the planks would fall off the roof and crush my trailer."

Hawkman chuckled. "Like I said, a lot of these old barns and houses will probably be standing for another fifty years." He drove slowly as they neared the decaying hotel and saloon. Stopping at the side of the road, he scanned both sides. "Now there's a possibility Jack and Ray are in this neck of the woods." He pulled into a smoothed off parking area near the weathered inn. "I'm going to walk over to the tavern and check it out." He swung an arm encompassing the whole area to his right. "You can sit in your seat and search the lodge site with your glasses."

Jennifer raised a brow. "May I ask, why you insisted I wear my boots if I'm not allowed to get out?"

He shrugged. "I didn't say you couldn't get out. Just thought it might be easier."

She curled her mouth in disgust and opened the passenger side door. "I'll check the boarding house; you go over to the pub. I'll meet you back here in about fifteen minutes."

He studied her with concern. "Maybe we should do this together."

"Hawkman, I have my gun." Exhaling loudly, she jumped out and set off toward the building.

He watched her for a few moments. "Stubborn woman," he mumbled as he climbed out of the SUV and stomped across the gravel.

Jennifer, with Beretta in hand, traipsed gingerly, keeping a wary eye for snakes or other creatures in the tall grasses surrounding the hotel. When she stepped inside one of the units, she gasped as she lifted her weapon and pulled the trigger twice.

The echo bounced off the hillsides, sending birds in scared flight to surrounding trees. Hawkman had just entered the saloon when he heard the shots. He whirled around, raced out the door and dashed across the road.

Jack and Ray lay stretched out on their bellies on the peak of a small knoll across the road from the Hill's ranch. Protected by tall grass, Jack put the binoculars to his eyes as he watched a woman, two boys and a big dog climb into the car. "Okay, she'll be leaving in a few minutes. The husband left about half hour ago, so we should find ample food in that kitchen. She looks like a good cook," he said in a harsh whisper.

Ray chuckled under his breath. "Since when could you tell a good cook by her appearance?"

About that time, a beige SUV stopped in front of the house. Jack reached over and poked his son. "Appears we've got company."

Ray jerked his head in the direction his dad pointed. "Give me those glasses." He put them to his eyes. "Damn, that's Tom Casey and his wife."

The two men crunched closer to the ground and waited silently until both vehicles drove off in opposite directions.

Ray climbed to his feet. "Okay, let's get into that pantry before anyone returns. My gut tells me the woman won't be gone long since she took the dog."

"Let's go in the back way, in case we have to run for it," Jack said.

The two scampered across the road, then cut between the house and barn. They stood for a moment, leaning against a parked trailer, and caught their breath as they surveyed the grounds. Hurrying to the back door, they found it unlocked as suspected. They stepped into the kitchen and immediately started opening cabinet doors. Ray found a couple of grocery sacks and started loading them with bread, peanut butter, chips, canned goods and whatever he could find available that didn't need refrigeration or cooking.

"We'll eat these tonight," Jack said, as he threw in lunch meat, a couple of cold beers, and some pieces of fruit. Then his eyes glistened as he pulled out a round tin from the refrigerator. "Would you look here, a blackberry pie."

"Grab it." After checking their bags, Ray put one under his arm. "I think we've got enough to last a few days. Hope you've got a can opener."

"I have a Swiss knife that'll do the job."

"Let's haul ass out of here."

The men had no more exited the door when they heard a vehicle pull across the gravel at the front of the house. Lugging the heavy bags, they ran past the barn and into the field. When they were far enough away, they paused and glanced back. The dog was running around the yard barking furiously.

Ray let out a laugh. "I wish I could see that woman's face when she walks into the kitchen and discovers her pantry's been raided."

Jack pushed ahead. "We need to put more distance between us and the dog before he picks up our scent. He'll for sure be on our heels within moments."

"He's nothing but a mutt, and will lose our trail the minute he gets into the tall grass. But we need to get back to the barn, before she calls and reports the burglary. We don't want to be caught out here in the field with the goods."

Suddenly, the sound of gun shots burst through the air. Ray and Jack, dived for cover.

"What the hell?" Jack said, looking over his shoulder. "There's no one behind us."

"It's hard to tell where it came from with the sound bouncing off these hills." Ray pointed east. "But I think it came from farther up the road. Maybe some kid shooting at ground squirrels."

Jack picked himself up and brushed the dirt from his pant's leg, then checked the sack of groceries. "Thank goodness, I didn't smash the pie. Let's get our butts outta here."

CHAPTER THIRTY-ONE

Hawkman crashed through the brush yelling Jennifer's name. Then another blast echoed through the air.

"I'm in here," she called, backing out of a doorway, holding her small smoking pistol. "I think I've disturbed a rattlesnake den. I just killed three of them."

He grabbed her arm and pulled her away from the scene. "No telling how many more are around. Let's get to safety. Obviously, Jack and Ray aren't here."

They hurried to the SUV and climbed inside.

"You're lucky you didn't get bit."

"I always watch for signs of those serpents."

"When I heard those shots, it scared me. I immediately thought Jack or Ray were firing at you."

"Sorry, but I certainly couldn't let the rattlers strike, or you might have found me in bad shape."

"You did the right thing. Doesn't appear you've lost the skill to hit a bulls eye."

She smiled. "Thanks."

They moved up the road to Lawbacker's ranch. Hawkman parked in front, jumped out and knocked on the door. The ranch hand and his wife didn't appear to be home. Hawkman ambled down the driveway to the bunkhouse and peeked inside. Seeing nothing suspicious, he stood for a moment and viewed the out buildings, noting most of their doors were wide open and could be viewed straight through. He saw nothing resembling a red Willys jeep.

They drove up to access six, which consisted of the camp ground with tables and a place to build a fire. They found it empty and no evidence anyone had been there for some time. Hawkman slapped his hands on the steering wheel. "Well, we didn't luck out. It's possible Ray and Jack have fled into Oregon. They've had plenty of time to put many miles behind them."

"Where in the world would they get gas?"

"Siphon it out of farm machinery, or steal a can out of someone's barn. All these ranchers have extra fuel around."

"What about their goal to get you?"

"That's what bothers me. Since neither of them know this territory, I might be searching too far out. They could be hiding right under our noses."

"Also, there's the problem of eating."

Hawkman shrugged. "You only need water. And there are plenty of streams around. Jack probably had some food he'd stored before his son got here. Also, Ray had those sandwiches you made when we went out looking for Jack. So they've only been maybe a day without any. You can survive a long time without nourishment."

"They could easily be seeking shelter in one of the homes where people only come two or three weeks out of the year."

"That's another option to keep in mind. I think we'll do more searching closer to our place."

Hawkman turned around and headed toward the lake. As they approached the Hill's place, Jennifer scooted to the edge of her seat.

"I think we'd better stop. Something's happened. Peggy and Ken's police cars are parked in front."

Hawkman came to a halt on the side of the road and they both hopped out. Just as they reached the front porch, Sue, Peggy, and Ken came out the door.

"Sue, is everything okay?" Jennifer asked.

"It's the craziest event I've ever had happen. Would you believe someone raided my kitchen?"

"What?"

"Yes, they only took food. Even the blackberry pie I'd made last night with several pieces gone."

Hawkman put a hand on Jennifer's shoulder. "Well, now you know how they've supplied themselves with grub."

Peggy looked at him with a question. "Who?"

"Jack and Ray."

"You found their hideout?" Ken asked.

Hawkman shook his head. "No, not a sign of them anywhere. But they're obviously nearby. I'd bet my bottom dollar they're the ones who raided her refrigerator."

Sue put her hands on her hips. "And to think I've always had this false sense of security up here and never locked my doors. Well, that's about to change. And I'm going to leave my dog, King, home too. He might be harmless but he has a mean bark. And those guys must have been close by, because he headed for the back and circled the yard with his nose to the ground, carrying on like crazy. I didn't think much about it at the time; figured some critter had been snooping around."

Ken turned to her. "I'll write up the report and get a copy to you in the next day or two."

"Thanks, Ken."

Everyone left and returned to the lake. When Jennifer and Hawkman arrived home, she jumped out, deactivated the alarm, and went inside while Hawkman moved the sprinkler to a dry spot on the lawn. She opened all the drapes, placed her camera beside the computer, then went to the bedroom to change her footwear. Miss Marple lay stretched out on Hawkman's pillow. Jennifer grinned and sat on the edge of the mattress to remove one of her boots, the kitten immediately reared on her haunches and hissed.

"Oh, don't tell me you don't like mine either." She teasingly put one near the cat. Miss Marple struck it with an extended paw, leaving a nice scratch mark on the leather. Jennifer laughed. "Boy, I have to agree with Hawkman, you're an indoor kitty. You definitely don't like outdoor scents."

She removed her gun from the fanny pack and took it into the kitchen where she placed it on an old newspaper on the counter, then took out her gun cleaning kit. After running a swab down the barrel and cleaning the chamber, she left it to air while she fixed some lunch.

Hawkman walked in about the time she had the makings on the cutting board.

"Man, my stomach yelled, food, food. You must have heard it clear in here."

"Oh, yes, it rang in my ears and I knew I had to do something to shut it down."

While eating their sandwiches, they discussed Ray and Jack.

Hawkman swallowed. "They must have been casing Sue's house and knew when she left. So they probably saw us too. Once the coast was clear, they made the hit on her kitchen."

"They could have been in the barn, but where in the world would they have hidden the jeep? We looked at all the vacant buildings from here to the Oregon border."

"Anywhere back in the hills. Behind a knoll, in a cluster of thick trees or bushes. It wouldn't be hard.

"If we had a helicopter at our disposal, we could scout the area and probably spot it."

"That's out of the question right now." Hawkman said. He pointed a finger at her. "But remember, if they kill me, you demand one of those little babies to search for those murderers."

She scowled. "Don't talk like that. By the way, did you activate the alarm?"

"No, but I will as soon as I finish eating. I noticed Peggy's car out near the mailbox. She's certainly kept her word about keeping an eye on the place."

"I'm sure she thinks of us as very difficult, because she grumbled when I called and told her we were heading up to Topsy Grade alone."

"Probably a good thing, as it turned out Sue needed them."

Jennifer retreated to her computer and set up her camera. Combing through the prints, she suddenly stopped and studied one of the pictures. She made the photo larger and let out a gasp. "Hawkman, come here a minute. I want you to see something."

When she didn't get a response, she peeked over the monitor into the living room, but didn't see him or the kitten. Spotting a sliver of light coming from under his office door, she jumped up and hurried down the hallway. When she entered, she burst out in laughter. "I wish I had a picture of this."

Miss Marple sat on Hawkman's lap, her front paws perched on the keyboard. They were both staring at the screen.

A grin danced across his lips. "I'm teaching her how to use the computer."

"Dismiss class. I have something to show you."

He carried the cat into the living room and placed her on the floor beside some of the toys.

"Remember when I took those pictures of the barn and said, I'm not sure they'll turn out because of the sun's glare."

"Yeah."

She walked around to the front of her computer and pointed. "Well, look at this."

Hawkman inspected the image. "Okay, we got 'em. Leave this picture up. Get Peggy and Ken over here pronto."

CHAPTER THIRTY-TWO

Jennifer quickly crossed to the kitchen bar and grabbed the receiver of the landline. She dialed the Bronson's number, and left a message for Peggy or Ken to call as soon as possible. After hanging up, she turned to Hawkman. "They're not home."

"Give the cell phone a try."

Punching in the digits, she shook her head. "No signal." Moving to the dining room window, she gazed out and pointed. "Peggy's parked near the bridge. I'll run over and talk to her."

Hawkman assessed the surrounding area. "I'm not sure I want you in the open. We don't know where Jack has his vantage point, but he's probably watching the house. I'm sure he's got a rifle and could pick you off in a second."

"What if I run close to the blackberry bushes? He might not be able to see me. Otherwise, we're not going to be able to reach Peggy or Ken until one of them checks their answering machine at home. Unless you want me to contact the police dispatch; then they can reach them through their radio."

"No, this isn't an emergency yet. I'll run the route and talk to her."

She touched his arm. "They're after you, not me. You'd be in more danger. It'll only take a few minutes. And Peggy will bring me back in her shielded vehicle."

He pondered for a moment, then patted her shoulder. "Promise you'll stay close to the brush."

Jennifer nodded, then took off down the deck stairs and practically hugged the bushes as she ran toward the police carrier. About half way between the house and the road, a shot rang out, ricocheting off the trunk of the oak tree. She dropped to the ground and rolled under the thorny vines.

Hawkman leaped out on the deck with his gun drawn and dashed forward where his wife had fallen.

"Are you all right," he yelled.

"Yes, get down," she screamed.

He quickly darted behind the trunk of the tree.

Peggy had jumped out of her vehicle and crouched at the front end, her gun aimed southeast. For several minutes, no one moved. Then Hawkman called out to the officer.

"Do you see anything?"

"No. I'm not sure whether we're dealing with a stray bullet, or someone aiming at Jennifer. I've put a call in for Ken to come immediately. You two get back inside. I'll be over in a second."

Hawkman crouched and moved to where Jennifer lay curled in a fetal position. He grabbed her around the waist, lifted her off the ground, and held her within the curve of his body, as he hurried toward the deck. "Keep your head down."

Once inside, he pushed her forward. "Get in the kitchen. It's the safest room in the house. Stay behind the bar and below the window." He dashed out the front door, moved along the wall until he reached the corner of the house, then dropped to his haunches and studied the landscape for a glint of metal, or some clue telling him where the shot had originated.

Peggy drove her vehicle into the driveway and joined him. "Spot anything?"

"No, but I'm going to go search. You stay here with Jennifer."

"Ken isn't far away and will be here in a matter of minutes. Wait for him."

❧

Jack hit the barrel of the gun upward as Ray pulled the trigger. "What the hell are you doing? We're supposed to be just watching."

Ray glanced at his father's blazing green eyes. "Just having a little fun."

"You were trying to hit his wife. She's done nothing to you. I told you, we're not going to harm her. Now you've alerted the policewoman, and she's probably contacted the whole department. The place will be crawling with cops in a matter of a couple of hours." He turned away and headed east in a fast jog. "Let's get the hell out of here," he called over his shoulder.

Despite Ray's handicap, he caught up with Jack as they made their way back to the barn. When they finally reached their hideout, both were winded and leaned against the fender of the jeep. Catching his breath, Jack glared at his son.

"You did a stupid thing. They'll find us for sure now. We're going to have to pack up and head out."

"Ease up. They have no idea it was us. Could have been a stray bullet."

"They're not fools," Jack spat. "Don't you realize I've caused a lot of havoc around here? They're bound to have a warrant out for my arrest. Jim, Tom Casey, or whatever he goes by, knows we've joined forces against him." He flung his arm up in disgust. "Also we're traveling in a stolen jeep. It's like a red cape in front of a bull."

Ray shrugged. "Okay, so let's find another vehicle."

Jack looked at him in disbelief. "Are you kidding?"

"No. It seems everyone up here has a four-wheel drive." Ray gestured toward the road. "I've seen several heavy duty pickups pass here, so there's bound to be another ranch up the way. I've also noticed extra vehicles parked around the corrals and barns. We both know how to hot wire them. So let's grab our food and hike outta here. We'll leave the jeep for the police to find. Hell, by the time they get here, we'll be long gone." He scratched at his scraggy beard.

"Yeah, I remember a pretty big spread east of here." Jack narrowed his eyes. "So after we steal another form of transportation, then what do we do?"

"I've been thinking. Why don't we hike up into the hills, lay low for a few days, and let the heat pass." He pointed to the bags of food. "We've got plenty to eat for several days. We can stay close to the stream so we'll have water. Then when people figure we're long gone, they'll let down their guard. We'll meander back, swipe a vehicle and kill Tom Casey."

"I don't know this area, but if we stay near a stream, we shouldn't have any problems."

"We better get moving."

The two men quickly loaded food into their backpacks. Jack hid the can of gas in the barn behind some fallen lumber.

Ray raised a brow. "What are you doing?"

"Mark my word, we'll need it later." Jack pulled a rifle out from under the seat of the jeep, then removed a pistol from his duffel bag and slipped it into his waist band.

Ray eyed him with a sly grin. "I wondered if you had any weapons."

Jack smiled. "You think I'd be out here without them? Remember, I'm on a mission."

The two men left through the back of the barn and disappeared into the trees.

☙

When Ken arrived, and before Hawkman could lead him off to search the nearby hills, Jennifer insisted he come inside. She led him and Peggy to the computer where they all huddled around the monitor as she enlarged the picture.

"Can you see the small corner of red behind the trailer?" she asked.

Peggy squinted. "It appears to be another vehicle."

"The glare from the sun hitting the chrome made it impossible to see with the naked eye, but I caught it with the camera. Want to bet it's the Willys jeep?"

Ken smacked Hawkman on the shoulder. "Let's go check it out."

Peggy glanced at the two men. "Not without Jennifer and me. We're the ones who got caught in this little sniper game this afternoon. We'll follow you guys in my Tahoe."

Jennifer checked her gun and ammunition, then made sure Miss Marple had plenty of food and water. "You be good while we're gone," she said, giving the kitten a rub down her back.

Hawkman set the alarm and the four hopped into the patrol cars.

Peggy called the dispatch and let them know what was going down. She'd report back with their findings.

When they were almost to the barn, Ken pulled to the side of the road. "We'll go the rest of the way on foot, I think it'd be safer."

They all piled out, their guns drawn, and climbed the fence along the west side of the barn. Ken led the way, Hawkman close behind, with the women trailing. He marched them through the trees until they were several yards from the large structure. "Let's approach cautiously in case they've spotted us. You gals stay here and cover our backs."

Peggy nodded and crouched down behind some bushes. Jennifer scooted in beside her.

Ken and Hawkman, their weapons poised, eased their bodies along the wooden wall as they approached the front opening. When they reached the edge of the big barn door, Ken hollered. "Police. Come out with your hands up."

No response came from the inside, and again Ken yelled. "We're coming in."

He stepped out, and Hawkman followed. Nothing happened. The men charged into the barn, weaving from side to side. After a quick search, they called for the women.

"You were right, Jennifer, here's the jeep hidden behind the horse trailer." Ken hooked his thumbs in his pockets and glanced around the walls. "But since there's no sign of them or their belongings, I believe they've taken off." He motioned toward the jeep. "And they left this, because they'd be spotted a mile away."

Ken left the group after warning them not to touch anything, and jogged to his vehicle, where he reported over the radio what they'd found. He requested a tow truck to remove the stolen Willys. After dispatching the information, he drove back to the barn and stopped at the gate. When he discovered the padlock broken, he pushed it open and drove up to the building.

Jennifer followed Hawkman out to the back of the barn. "You look worried."

He pointed to some crushed grass, like a small trail leading toward Shovel Creek.

"They haven't been gone long. The weeds haven't even had time to right themselves."

She grabbed his arm. "Are you going after them?"

He stared across the pasture and exhaled. "No. They'll be back."

Jennifer studied her husband's solemn face. "How can you be so sure? Maybe they've given up and are going into hiding."

He grimaced. "And leave me alive? I don't think so."

CHAPTER THIRTY-THREE

Hawkman and Ken took a swing around the barn and figured the two fugitives had taken off; probably following the stream deeper into the hills. They strolled back into the big structure and Hawkman slipped his gun into the shoulder holster, then circled the Willys. "Nice vehicle. Someone's put a lot of work into restoring it, and he's sure going to be pleased to get it back in one piece."

Ken eyed the interior. "Yeah, Detective Williams told me it belongs to a kid who's worked on it for the past year, getting it ready to take to college. He's called the station every day, wanting to know if it'd been found. He'll be one happy fellow when they let him know it's still in its original condition."

"At least it's a bright ending for him." Hawkman took a deep breath. "Now to catch the guy who took it."

"We should be able to get some fingerprints off the steering wheel and body, verifying Jack Hargrove is the culprit." Ken pointed out toward the field. "The trail out there indicates they haven't been gone long. Wonder if we should send out a scouting party?"

"Probably won't be necessary. They'll be back. They haven't completed their mission. So there's no sense in trying to track them in the wilderness. I say we just regroup and wait for their return."

"Peggy thinks the shot fired earlier might have been a stray."

"My gut tells me it was Ray or Jack. They figured they'd made a mistake and the police would come down on them in droves." Hawkman pointed at the jeep. "They didn't want to risk driving that little bugger any longer as it stands out like a sore thumb, so they decided to abandon it and take off for the hills. Both men know how to survive in the wilds. Their downfall will be not knowing the territory, but they'll camp near the stream for a few days and do nicely with the food they stole from Sue. Then they'll be back, and more than likely steal another vehicle and raid someone else's kitchen. It might be good to warn the community to contact you immediately, if anything's stolen."

"Good idea. Peggy and I'll make a few house calls."

The four strolled around searching for clues while waiting for the tow truck. They found an empty potato chip bag and wiener wrapper that indicated their villains had definitely been there recently. Ken stayed in contact with dispatch, and after a couple of hours, the big tow truck rumbled into the area. "Did you get instructions?" Ken asked, as they loaded the jeep onto the bed.

"Yeah, the chief told me to take it to the Medford Police Station. Detective Williams wants to examine the Willys before releasing it to the owner."

"That'll save time." Ken backed away, and waved to the driver as the truck pulled onto the road. He then turned and motioned. "Hop aboard, ladies, and I'll take you to Peggy's Chevy."

After he dropped them off, Peggy made a U-turn and followed him back to the lake. Once they pulled into Hawkman's driveway, Jennifer turned to Peggy. "There's no sense in your keeping the place under surveillance. Jack and Ray will probably stay low for a couple of days. Take a break. We'll know when they're back."

"Okay, but if you feel uneasy at all, you let me know."

"I will."

After deactivating the alarm, Hawkman and Jennifer entered their house, where they found Miss Marple curled up in Hawkman's chair. She raised her head and gave them a big yawn.

He laughed. "See where she is? I told you the little stinker likes me better."

"It's because your butt is bigger and the cushion has a nice hollowed place. It fits her rather nicely, especially since she's grown so much."

Hawkman eyed the cat as she stood and stretched. "You're right. She looks almost full grown. Good grief, how large will she get?"

Jennifer shrugged. "I have no idea." She placed her fanny pack on the counter. "Want something to eat? I'm starved."

"Me, too. What've we got?"

The next morning, Hawkman carried the portable phone to his chair by the window and dialed Bill Broadwell at the Agency. He punched on the speaker phone and as he talked, Miss Marple climbed into his lap. Giving her a couple of rubs, he moved her to the floor with his free hand and tossed a soft fuzzy ball toward the middle of the floor. She pounced on the toy, then knocked it close to his boot. When Jennifer entered the room, he made motions for her to get the cat out from underneath his legs.

"Yep, it's not a pretty picture, Bill. But right now, I'm interested in learning more about Ray Skokie."

"After talking with him about his dad, I'm shocked at this turn of events," Bill said.

"Yeah, me too. What's his work record been like?"

"Good. Of course, he's not allowed in the field, but he's a damn good organizer. However, one of the managers told me the other day when I was questioning him about Jack, they were keeping a close watch on Ray. I didn't pay too much attention as I was more interested in his dad."

"Oh, yeah, why are they watching him?"

"I didn't get the whole picture, but got the feeling Ray's had a couple of assignments go bad in the past year. I'm going to talk with his manager again and find out more of the story. It might give us a clue on Ray's change of character."

"Also find out how long he's on vacation. I have a strange feeling he's not coming back."

"Sure you don't want me to send some men out there? Sounds like you're the center of attention."

"No, I don't think it's necessary. I have a couple of pretty sharp police officers working with me, and they know the region."

"Okay, I'll get back to you on this thing with Ray. Sounds like we'll be hunting for a new organizer."

"Yep, cause I have a feeling this guy's through with the Agency."

He hung up and when Jennifer entered the room carrying Miss Marple, he pointed at the cat. "That little animal can be a real pest."

She waved him off. "Don't forget, even though she's big, she's still just a kitten."

"You've got to teach her some manners. When I'm on the phone with business, I don't want to be distracted."

She raised her brows. "I see. How do I do that? I don't think she understands the word, 'business'."

He picked up the newspaper and hid his grin behind the pages.

Several uneventful days passed, then one evening Hawkman came in from outside and closed the drapes. Jennifer glanced up from her computer, fear in her eyes. "What's happened?"

"Ken dropped by to tell me a report had come in from Lawbacker's ranch hand. One of their pickups is missing. Appears Jack and Ray have returned."

Her shoulders slumped. "I prayed they'd just keep on hiking and disappear. Or maybe a mountain lion would eat them."

"I don't know how they'd expect us to drop our guard when they come back into this territory and steal a truck."

"They probably figured if they hiked far enough, they'd find a vehicle no one would miss for awhile."

"Appears they discovered it's pretty desolate out there, with just a few homes scattered among the hills. I imagine they scouted out a vehicle before they left, just in case nothing showed up on their trek. They're planners. And what worries me now, is wondering what they've got in store for me."

"Did Ken give you a description?"

"Yeah. A green pickup with a small camper shell."

Jennifer stood and put a hand on her hip. "How in the heck do they figure to hide it?"

He plopped down on one of the bar stools. "I have an idea they won't be driving it much, only out of necessity. They'll park it in a secluded place and use it as their base camp."

She walked around the bar and sat down facing him. "Okay, so what are they going to do about food? You know they're bound to have used up what they stole from Sue."

Hawkman chuckled. "I forgot to tell you. Apparently, they did their job during the day while Karen was at work and Hank out in the field with the dog. They picked the lock on the back door, stole most of the food out of the pantry and stripped the refrigerator of its contents. Even though Ray and Jack are both crack shots, and there are plenty of deer, rabbit, squirrel and birds in the fields, I guess they wanted the easy way out." He raised a finger in the air. "Oh, yes, and Ken said they also stole a camp stove off the back porch. Jack and Ray now have all the accommodations of home. At least they won't set off a forest fire with abandoned embers."

Jennifer raised her hands in the air. "I can't believe these men are so bound and determined to make our life miserable."

CHAPTER THIRTY-FOUR

Jack drove up the steep hill and chugged over the crest. "Damn, I think we picked the wrong vehicle. This thing has about as much get-up-and-go as a ninety year old grandma."

Ray leaned his elbow out the window and hung on as they bounced across the barren terrain. "I agree, but at least we'll have a place to sleep other than the hard ground. Let's hope the stove works."

"There's a nice grove of trees," Jack said pointing. "It would hide the truck from anyone in the air and the creek is only a few yards away."

"Go for it."

Jack guided the truck around an upsurge of rock and avoided a good size drop-off as he wound his way down the hill. "I want to look it over first and make sure we don't end up camping under a hornets' nest or over some varmint's home." He threw the truck into park and jumped out. After surveying the inner parts of the trees, moving some fallen limbs, and kicking away some large rocks, he backed the pickup into the shadowed area. Making sure the vehicle was completely out of view, he killed the engine and removed the key. Chuckling he tossed up the ring and caught it. "Funny how people around here feel so secure, that they leave the key in the ignition."

Ray pushed open the door. "Nobody would want this pile of junk anyway. You could leave it on the streets of a busy city with the motor running and no one would take it."

They both laughed as they hopped out of the cab.

Jack walked to the rear of the truck, dropped the tail gate and opened the back door of the camper shell, then climbed inside. He slid open the small windows and closed the screen part. "This will keep out the mosquitoes, but let in some air." He groped through the sacks of food they'd stolen. "Got a few items in here that should be kept cool. What made you take a jar of mayonnaise?"

Ray peered at him through the opening. "Got tired of dry sandwiches."

"Okay, before I implement my idea for keeping this stuff cold, let's fix us a bite out of this partial package of baloney."

The men sat on a big boulder near the stream and ate.

"Now, that was a feast," Ray said, rubbing his stomach.

Jack stood and stretched his arms above his head. "I think I've got an idea that will keep this stuff from spoiling. And also keep the bears from tearing up our sleeping quarters."

"Yeah?"

Ray followed his dad back to the camper and watched him pull the sheet off the small mattress. "We don't need this with our sleeping bags." He tore it in half, tied it into a satchel shaped holder, then dropped in the jars and a couple of wiener packages. He grabbed a small piece of rope lying on the floor, slung it over his shoulder, and headed toward the creek with Ray at his heels. "The water in the stream is down right cold. If I can find a good place to anchor this, it will keep everything nice and cool."

"Great idea."

They soon had the bundle submerged, tied to a big log and the top weighted down with a large rock. Jack stood, and dried his hands on his jeans. "Should do the trick. Now, let's see if that little stove works; otherwise, we'll have to gather some kindling."

Ray eyed his dad. "You act like you're enjoying all this camping. When are we going to talk about getting rid of Tom Casey?"

Jack strolled toward the pickup. "As soon as we have everything set up. We're only a couple of miles, as the crow flies, from his house. We've postponed it this long; a few more days isn't going to matter."

He removed the small stove and set it on the fender of the truck. "This is one neat little unit. It's for backpacking and can even be run on unleaded gas. Sure glad I nabbed a pan out of the woman's cabinet. If this works it will insure us a nice cup of coffee for breakfast." He fiddled with the controls for a moment, struck a match and had the flare of a nice flame. Smiling, he turned it off, let it cool a few minutes, then returned it to the protection of the truck.

"Okay, Dad, you've got the campsite under control. So what's our next move?"

Jack sat down on a boulder opposite his son and gazed into his face. "You know you've probably lost your job by pairing up with me."

Ray nodded. "I'm sure Casey has already alerted my superiors."

"So do you plan on running the rest of your life?"

"This is the most excitement I've had in ten years. If we get out of here alive, I've got plans to leave the country. You're welcome to come along."

Jack sighed. "Why don't you take the truck and escape now. You're still young and have plenty of years ahead. You've done nothing to cause any problems yet, so you might even be able to get your job back. But if you kill or try to eliminate Casey, you'll be put into prison. Then your life's over."

"What about you?"

"I'm already in deep trouble. It's not going to matter what I do now. If I'm caught, I'll be put behind bars and left to rot, regardless."

"Well, I'm not leaving. You're not able to fight this guy alone. It'll take both of us to get him. And nothing will give me more pleasure than to see him squirming on the ground with my bullets in his gut. In fact, it would give me even more joy to hurt him just enough, so he'd suffer for the rest of his life."

In the shrinking light, Jack studied his son's expression. "You really mean it, don't you?"

"I've dreamed about it for years."

"It's strange, I never saw the sign of revenge in you, until now."

"I never wanted you to, but I dropped little hints for several years, because I knew I'd need your help."

"Then we better decide how we're going to do this deed, cause it ain't gonna be easy. And you're the organizer, so I'm going to leave the rest up to you."

Jack pulled his cell phone from his jacket pocket. "This is of no use anymore. The battery's dead and I don't have a way of charging it. Too risky to use Casey's place, or for that matter, any home. I'm sure the people of the community have been warned about us by now. So harassment by phone is out. In fact, we're going to have to be careful, as people will be on the lookout for two shaggy looking mountain men. We'll have to keep to the back country."

Ray ran a hand over his chin. "Yeah, we must be pretty pathetic. You really look bad, like a weird monster with those green eyes of yours. They stand out like they're perched on a stick."

"I've got a couple of weeks' growth on you," Jack said, chuckling.

"A plan has been forming in my mind while we were camping in the hills. Let me lay it out and see what you think."

Jack placed his cell back in his pocket and sat down on the rock next to his son. Ray picked up a stick and began to draw a picture in the dirt.

"Here's what I've been thinking."

❧

Hawkman watched Jennifer pace the floor. "Honey, sit down. You're making me crazy."

She flopped on the couch, her hands clenched into fists. "We need to find those two men and have them arrested."

He leaned forward. "Think about it. They haven't done anything but harass us, and that's not enough to warrant a sheriff, police force or a helicopter searching the hills."

"One of them shot at me."

"Can't prove it."

"What about all the threatening calls we've recorded?"

"Those will help in a court of law, but not in apprehending them."

"What about the rock through the window?"

"Have no idea who did it."

"How about the stolen pickup from the ranch, the jeep and running Rita off the road?"

"The reports have been made and all officers are on the lookout. The Willys has been found in good condition. No reports as of yet, on who took it. Even if they have Jack's fingerprints, no one knows where he is."

She threw up her hands in disgust. "What has to happen? One of us get killed?"

He nodded. "Yep."

"Wonderful!" She jumped up, went over to the sliding glass door and opened the drapes. Then yanked the cord on the ones over the large window exposing the living room.

Hawkman hurried behind her and closed them. "What the hell are you doing?"

Putting her hands to her face, she let out a sob. "I can't stand being a prisoner in my own home."

He took her into his arms. "Honey, this isn't going to last forever. They're going to make a mistake and then we've got them. But let's not risk our lives and be a sitting target."

She pointed toward the window. "Ray knows we sit right there, so we can look out over the lake. All he has to do is aim with a high powered rifle and he could pretty well pick us off even with the drapes closed."

Hawkman gazed at the chairs. "You're right. So until this is over, we'll refrain from using our favorite seats and sit on the couch or hearth instead." Then he pointed at the computer center. "Let's change your room around. Ray would have noticed it, too."

Together they switched the furniture so Jennifer's back wouldn't be toward the east window, but face north toward the kitchen. Hawkman stepped into the living room and eyed the set up. "Hey, you might even like it better this way. Now you'll have a view of the bridge and the lake."

She put a finger to her lips. "You might be right. At least I won't be in the line of fire through the dining room window."

"Exactly. If you don't like it this way, we can move the furniture back later."

Miss Marple moved into the room and immediately jumped up on Jennifer's chair. She sat up on her haunches and began cleaning her paws. Jennifer stared at her suspiciously. "What's she been into?" She leaned over and gave her a whiff. "I can smell something." Dashing into her bathroom, she discovered the small can of baby powder she used to dust the inside of her shoes, had been bounced all over the bathroom floor. She'd obviously left it open on the counter top, and Miss Marple had a lot of fun rolling it all over the floor, making one big mess. "This cat is going to be the death of me before any gunman is," she mumbled picking up the container, closing the lid, and placing it in the cabinet.

Hawkman walked up behind her as she collected the throw rugs. "This cat has a white dust all over her. Whatever it is smells good."

"Yes, I know. She's had a wonderful time with my talcum."

"Think it will hurt her?"

"I doubt it. After I shake and vacuum these rugs, I'll give her a good brushing." She pushed past him with her arms loaded.

"Go out the front," he called.

In her frustration, she grabbed the door handle and opened the door. The alarm siren built to a loud volume before she could drop the load on the steps and dash back inside to turn it off. She grabbed the rugs and shook them with vigor, grumbling under her breath. "Damn cat, damn alarm, damn Ray and Jack."

Jack and Ray lifted their heads as the piercing sound echoed over the hills.

"You hear that? I hope it's not a siren warning there's a forest fire nearby." Jack stood and sniffed the air. You smell smoke?"

Ray inhaled. "Nope. But I sure as hell wouldn't want to be caught in this place with an inferno licking at my heels. I wouldn't know which way to run to get out of here."

"We'll keep a vigilance for the next couple of hours. Hopefully, it's just an emergency on the lake."

CHAPTER THIRTY-FIVE

Jennifer bent over to pick up one of the rugs from the ground, when the crunch of tires on the gravel driveway made her glance up.

Peggy, holstering her gun, leaped out of the Chevy Tahoe. "Is there a problem?"

Waving her hand, Jennifer looked at her with disgust. "Stupid me ran out the front door without switching off the alarm."

Hawkman stood in the doorway, grinning like a Cheshire cat. "Miss Marple is going to kill off my wife before she gets old."

Putting a hand to her mouth, Peggy stifled a laugh. "What'd she do this time?"

"Come on in and I'll tell you."

Jennifer dropped the rugs on the kitchen floor. Miss Marple strolled over, sniffed them, and sneezed.

"Serves you right, you curious little outfit." She then turned to Peggy and related the story. "I've got to get in there with the vacuum before I can put the rugs down. She really made a mess. Powder all over the place."

"I won't keep you. When I heard the alarm, I dashed right over. Must say I'm relieved to find out there's nothing to worry about."

"I feel so bad you have to jump every time something crazy happens."

Peggy reached over and patted her on the shoulder. "It's my job and I love it. So don't you fret."

Jennifer gave a feeble smile and walked her to the door. "Thanks."

Back inside, she pulled the vacuum and attachments from the closet, then proceeded to clean up the white mess. When she'd finished, she studied the soft brush and bit her lip thoughtfully.

"Hawkman, bring Miss Marple in here, please."

He came in with the cat draped over his arm. When Jennifer raised the brush toward the animal, he stepped back and put up his free hand. "Oh, no, you don't. Not with me holding her. The minute you turn that loud machine on, this cat will go over my head with her claws extended. I don't need more stitches."

"She's been around when I've vacuumed and it doesn't seem to bother her."

He pointed to the brush. "Have you ever used it on her?"

Jennifer scrunched up her nose. "Well, no. But it would sure get the powder off."

He put the cat on the bed and took the hose. "Turn it on and let me clean off my shirt." Then he handed the nozzle back. "Okay, try it on the kitten."

She advanced slowly toward the feline. Miss Marple swatted playfully at the brush as Jennifer ran it gently over her fur."

Hawkman watched for a moment. "That's the weirdest animal I've ever seen." Shaking his head, he left the room, and headed back to his chair, then gave it a second thought and moved to the hearth.

Soon, Miss Marple romped into the living room with her tail held high, as if she were queen for the day. She sidled up to him, purring as she rubbed against his boot.

"Are you trying to tell me you're all nice and clean now?"

She stared up at him with big blue eyes and licked her mouth, as if to say, 'that's right'.

Jennifer entered and headed for her chair. Hawkman snapped his fingers. "Don't sit in front of the window."

She rolled her eyes. "I forgot." And flopped down on the couch.

He pointed to Miss Marple. "Your pet wants attention."

"Well, give her some. She's had enough from me."

Hawkman leaned over and gave the cat a rub across the back. She immediately pounced into his lap and bumped her head against his chin several times. He leaned back and pulled her away. "What the heck?"

Jennifer laughed. "She's telling you she loves you."

"Those were about the hardest love pat I've ever received." He frowned. "Does she do head knocking on you?"

"Occasionally." She scooted forward on the cushion. "I read an interesting article on the Ragdoll."

"Oh, yeah? "

"She can never be let outside on her own. The breed is not aggressive, so Miss Marple wouldn't defend herself against an attacker."

Hawkman expression turned apprehensive as he continued to stroke the cat. "Hey, little gal, someone stole a very important gene from you. We'll have to make sure you're always protected. You will definitely stay inside. Too many critters live around here that could hurt you."

Jennifer and Hawkman tried to relax and enjoy a cocktail. He picked up the paper, but couldn't stop watching Miss Marple scamper across the room and bounce on the toys Jennifer tossed across the floor.

He guffawed when the cat misjudged, rolled over the stuffed bunny, then bounced on it like a tiger. "I have to say, her antics are a far better show than anything you can watch on television"

"She does help keep me from my worries. My mind is at least at ease knowing Jack isn't in town stalking Marie's little girls or after Rita again."

"No, he's after us in full force, and even with the distraction of Miss Marple, we can't forget it."

Jennifer threw one of the cat's toys in the air and caught it. "I know."

They prepared for bed and once they were snuggled close

together, Miss Marple climbed upon the foot of the mattress and wedged herself between them.

Hawkman raised his head and glared at her. "Now, just a moment, little lady. I can be mighty tolerant, but this is going just a bit far." He lifted her off the covers and gently placed her on the floor. "Go get in your own bed."

Jack and Ray prepared the items they needed for their mission and stored them in the backpack. Ray slung it over his shoulder and they began their walk over the hill, both thankful for the cloud cover. Their sight grew accustomed to the darkness, so fallen branches and gullies caused little problem. They finally reached the road and the first fishing access.

"We won't find a boat here," Jack said. "This is where the rafters unload and no one ties up in this area. We're going to have to get closer to the lake where there are docks along the river bank."

They stayed on the edge of the road and headed west inside the protection of the trees. When a lone car came down the road, they dropped to their haunches and hid behind boulders or tree trunks.

Soon, Jack pointed toward the water and whispered. "Let's get closer to the river so we can see what's anchored near the shore."

They stumbled down the steep embankment, sending the night critters running for their lives. They soon came upon a rickety dock, but no water craft. They continued their journey and the next pier supported a large pontoon party boat.

Ray eyed it. "I don't think we want to mess with something this big. I'd prefer a fishing vessel or even a canoe."

"We've almost reached the bridge near Casey's place," Jack said. "We can either go past and approach his house from the other direction, or we can cross over onto the other side. There are more berths, but the houses are closer together and our risk of getting caught is greater."

"It won't make any difference in which direction we come. We just have to find something reliable to get us out of there in a hurry, so we can get back to the campsite without being spotted. We can leave the boat anywhere or even adrift."

"Let's move up the south bank of the river. The houses are farther away from the docks and the occupants are less likely to hear us kicking on a motor."

Struggling to keep from slipping into the water, they moved slowly along the sheer bank. The first pier stood empty, but the next one they could see held promise. A ski vessel, which appeared to have plenty of power, rocked at the end of the dock.

Ray calculated the distance before they approached. "The cabin is a long way from the water," he whispered. "We might be able to float this baby out to the middle of the lake before we rev it up. If we're lucky, no one will hear us and they won't even know the boat is gone until morning."

"Good idea. All water craft by law are supposed to have oars aboard, so we should be able to row it without any problem. Let's just hope it's full of gas and a working machine."

The two men crept upon the gangplank, each put on gloves, then trod softly out to the end. Jack eased into the boat, scooted across the seat and took his mini flashlight from his jacket pocket. After running the beam under the dashboard, he turned it off and sat up. "No problem, I can hot wire this one in the dark."

Ray untied the boat from the clamps as Jack held it steady so he could climb aboard. Once they were both situated in the seat, Ray took an oar and pushed them away. Together the two men rowed the craft toward the center of the lake.

Knowing their voices could carry a long distance over the water, they kept quiet as they worked. Once they reached the halfway mark, they slid the oars into the holders and let the boat drift. The clouds had floated away and a half moon cast an eerie light across the surface. A fish jumped here and there, making a large splash in the deep silence. Jack's nimble fingers worked on the wires, while Ray slid the backpack off his shoulders and propped it between his legs.

"How's it going?" Ray whispered.

"Just about got it," he said, through the gloves he held clenched in his teeth. At that moment, a low rumble issued from the rear and the craft leaped forward. Jack grabbed the wheel and put it into a low gear so the boat cruised slowly through the water with hardly a ripple. "Looks like we've got a full tank of gas."

Ray grinned. "Sweet. You did a great job."

Jack tugged on the gloves, then turned the boat eastward and headed toward the bridge. "Let's take a swing by Casey's place and see the best area for the target. Then I'll know how close to get."

Making a slow pass, Ray took out his night binoculars and studied the rear side of the house . "Just as I thought, the back deck is wood. Perfect. All you'll have to do is glide as close to his dock as you can, then I'll see if my pitching arm is still as good as it used to be."

CHAPTER THIRTY-SIX

Hawkman opened his eyes and glanced at the clock on the bedside table. "It's only two in the morning. What woke me?" he muttered. He lay there a moment and swore he could hear the low rumble of a motor. Getting up, he crossed the room to the sliding glass door, and pulled back the corner of the drape. In the moonlight, he spotted a boat puttering toward the bridge. Dropping the curtain, he made his way back to bed.

Jennifer sat up when he flopped onto the mattress. "What's wrong?"

"Nothing," he said, crawling beneath the covers. "Looks like someone's out on the lake fishing for catfish."

"I love the sport, but not at two in the morning. He must be some dedicated fisherman." She yawned, lay back down, and rolled to her side, pulling the comforter up to her shoulders.

Jack and Ray made a turn around the pillars of the bridge and glided toward the back of Tom Casey's house. Ray removed one of the small bottles of gasoline and sugar he'd previously mixed. Taking off the cap, he inserted a rag into the narrow opening.

"Are you ready," Jack said, pulling up close to Hawkman's dock.

"Yep." Ray took a cigarette lighter from his pocket, ignited the cloth, stood up and heaved the Molotov cocktail straight for the wooden porch. It hit with a crash and flames leaped across the back of the house. "Perfect. Now, let's get the hell out of here."

Jack turned the boat around and threw the engine into full throttle. The front end leaped out of the water as he sped toward the bridge. They were out of sight within seconds.

Meowing loudly, Miss Marple jumped upon the bed, and bounced from Jennifer to Hawkman. Both awoke with a start. When they spotted the orange glow coming through their bedroom glass door and smelled smoke, they leaped out of bed.

"Fire! get out quick," Hawkman yelled. He yanked open the window above his head so their alarm would sound. Running into the kitchen, he grabbed a tee towel off the counter, wet it, and held it to his face as he dashed to the slider in the dining room. He shoved it open and raced to the falcon's cage. She squawked with fear as flames sprang up eating around the edges of the wooden porch and licked at the bottom of the aviary. Not having the key to the lock, Hawkman wrenched off the flimsy latch with his bare hands and flung open the door. Hopping around to keep his feet from burning, he waved his hand and yelled. "Hurry up, Pretty Girl, take flight!"

The bird flapped her wings, brushed past him, and flew upward out of the smoke. He could hear the alarm singing above the crackling of the fire as he hurried back inside and closed the slider behind him. Racing toward the front door, still holding the towel to his nose, he grabbed a pair of boots he'd left in the hallway, and fled outside. He dropped the damp cloth from his face and coughed several times.

Jennifer had run across the street and set off the firehouse alarm. The wailing sirens, pierced the serenity of the night. She hurried toward Hawkman, and grabbed his arm. "Are you okay?, she asked, her voice quivering.

"Yeah."

"Where'd you go? It scared me when you didn't follow me out."

"I had to release Pretty Girl, or she'd have burned up. We can't waste any more time or we're going to lose everything."

He pulled on the boots, dashed to the side of the house and yanked the hose from under the porch. Turning on the spigot full bore, he sprayed the flames. Jennifer dragged the one from the front lawn around to the opposite side and aimed water onto the orange blaze licking up the west side of the porch. In only minutes, what seemed like hours, the volunteer firemen showed up in their yard. They drove the tanker trunk up into the lot next door and as close to the burning structure as possible Using much larger hoses, the men stepped close to Hawkman and began dousing the burning house. Soon, they searched the underneath side of the porch and the outside walls looking for hot spots, then announced the fire was extinguished.

Jennifer stood in shock as she stared at the charred back of her beloved home. Tears ran down her soot covered cheeks. She dropped the hose, covered her face and sobbed. The volunteer nurse, who'd accompanied the firefighters, put an arm around Jennifer's shoulders, and guided her to the front yard.

One of the volunteers strolled over to Hawkman and held up a plastic bag containing a partially melted bottle. "Mr. Casey, I think someone tried to burn your house down with a Molotov cocktail."

About that time, Ken and Peggy hurried around the corner of the house. Ken held out his hand. "I'll take it to the lab."

Hawkman narrowed his eyes and glared at the grotesquely shaped glass.

"Where's Jennifer?" Peggy asked.

Hawkman stared at her as if coming out of a trance. He left the group and rushed around to the front where he found the nurse holding his wife in her arms. Pulling Jennifer to his chest, he hugged her tightly. "Honey, we'll get everything fixed. It'll be good as new or better."

She looked up at him. "If it hadn't been for Miss Marple, we could have died from smoke inhalation." Suddenly, she pushed away. "Where is she?" Jennifer dashed for the front door, with Hawkman at her heels. They ran through the smoke filled house and into the bedroom, softly calling their pet's name. Searching under the bed, the closets and in the bathroom, Jennifer finally turned toward Hawkman, her eyes welled with tears. "She's not here."

"She's bound to be in the house somewhere. Let's keep looking."

"What if she couldn't get enough air and died."

"Remember, she's low to the ground. If anyone could find fresh air, she could."

They searched every nook and cranny to no avail.

Jennifer, wringing her hands, paced the floor. "Could she somehow have managed to get outside?"

"It's possible." He pointed at the slider. "See how the frame buckled and part of the glass fell away. She could have definitely escaped through it."

"But she could die in the jaws of a predator."

Hawkman put an arm around her shoulders. "Try not to think about it. Hopefully, she'll turn up. If not, we'll get another kitten."

She wiped her eyes. "There'll never be a replacement for Miss Marple."

He gave her a squeeze, then went outside to thank the firemen.

CHAPTER THIRTY-SEVEN

After the fire crew left, Hawkman and Jennifer opened up the house to see if they could get rid of the intense smell of burned wood. Streaks of sunlight penetrated the sky, and Hawkman could feel the light aggravating his vision. He went back to the bedroom, slipped on a pair of jeans, and found his eye-patch on the floor where he'd knocked it off the bedside table in his haste to flee. All his clothes reeked of smoke.

Coming back into the living room, he ventured out on the deck, and stepped lightly, testing the remaining boards to see if they'd hold his weight. The fireman had pulled down the plastic overhead awning and stacked the twisted debris in a pile. The black wrought iron railing curled in agony. The falcon's home had disappeared.

Hawkman let out an audible sigh and gazed heavenward. "Where are you, Pretty Girl? Did you decide, after such a scare, to leave forever?" He strolled down the unburned steps, walked to the center of the side yard and whistled.

Jennifer stood at the dining room window hugging herself, and watched him through the hazy glass. "Oh, Hawkman how could I be so selfish. You've lost your wonderful pet too."

He stood several moments searching the heavens, then with slumped shoulders entered the house through the laundry room door.

"If Pretty Girl comes home before we get the back deck repaired and a new aviary built, I'm going to have to figure out a new place for her.

Jennifer took a deep breath. "We can't put her in the house if Miss Marple shows up."

"I thought maybe the guest room, if we make sure to keep the door secured at all times. Your feisty little kitten doesn't usually go in there. She likes to hang out wherever we are."

"I'm not so sure we're going to be able to stay in this house for a few nights, it smells ghastly."

Hawkman scratched his sideburn. "Yeah, it stinks pretty bad. But we need to try and stand it, because if we're not here when Miss Marple or Pretty Girl come back, they'll figure in their little pea brains we're gone and then they'll leave."

Jennifer nodded. "You're right. If we keep airing out the house, it'll help and I'll get busy cleaning. I'm afraid we're going to have to replace a lot of stuff."

He scowled. "Before I can help with any of the clean up or build a new cage for Pretty Girl, I'm going to find Jack and Ray."

Jennifer searched his face. "You're not going to try and do it on your own, are you?"

"No. Ken told me he'd be by sometime today, after he's talked with his department."

"I think we've got these guys on a pretty stiff charge. Not only arson, but attempted murder."

❦

Jack drove the boat up to the number one fishing access and the two men hopped out and dragged it up partially onto the dirt. "That'll hold until someone discovers it, which might not be until late this afternoon when the groups of rafters come down the Klamath River."

Ray slung the backpack over his shoulder, then stopped a moment and glanced toward the lake. "I can hear more than one siren going off." He turned abruptly and climbed up the embankment.

Jack followed. "Just remember, the siren's calling in the volunteers, so watch for vehicles on the road. Get across as fast as you can."

Jack jogged past Ray as he crested the knoll.

"Slow down, Dad, I can't keep up with you.

He cut his pace down to a fast walk, and the men didn't stop until they were hidden from view. They arrived at their campsite within an hour, crawled into the camper and fell into a sound sleep.

Late the next morning, Jack climbed out of the truck and searched the horizon. Seeing no helicopters or search planes, he carried the small camp stove to the boulder near the creek, balanced it on the flat surface and proceeded to heat water so he could make coffee.

Ray crawled out of the sack and joined Jack at the water's edge. "Well, I wonder how much damage we did? Do you think we got them in the fire?"

Jack shrugged. "Hard to say. That house has a tile roof and aluminum siding, it wouldn't burn easily. About the only thing we can hope for is Casey died of smoke inhalation. Regardless, I think we better flee this area, because the whole law enforcement clan will be hunting for us."

Ray chuckled. "No way are we leaving until I know the mission has been accomplished."

Jack moved to the back of the truck and pulled out some of the food. "About time for a bite to eat. How about a packet of instant oats in water?"

"Sounds good to me."

Rummaging in his backpack, Jack pulled out his cooking gear and separated two metal army bowls, then found a couple of plastic spoons. He handed one to Ray. "Don't throw the spoon away, we're running low on utensils."

As the men ate, Ray glanced at his dad. "That truck have a radio?"

Jack knitted his brow. "You mean just a regular AM, FM?"

"Yeah."

"I think so, but not sure it works. Why?"

Ray grinned. "I'd like to hear the local news. It might tell us if the famous Tom Casey met his death in a house fire last night."

Jack handed him the keys. "You can try, but don't leave it on too long and run down the battery. And you sure don't want to start up the pickup, and use excess fuel."

Ray carried his bowl and went to the truck. He opened the door and slid into the passenger side. He punched the radio button, then turned the knob to accessories, but heard nothing. After fiddling with the dial for several minutes, he gave up, turned it off and closed the door. Shaking his head, he walked back to the boulder, and pitched the keys to Jack. "Naw, it doesn't work. Should have noticed, the antenna's been knocked off. Guess we're going to have to sneak back down there and take a peek."

Jack let out a sigh. "Don't you think you've done enough? Let's just get out of here while we can. Before we end up in a casket."

Ray set his breakfast on the rock and stared at Jack. "Look, Dad, if you don't want to stick with me on this, go ahead and take off. But I'm staying. I'm going to kill Tom Casey."

Silently, Jack walked down to the creek, rinsed out his bowl, and checked the items he'd placed in the cloth sack to stay cool. "We've got enough food to last a few more days. Guess I'm staying."

Sidling in next to his dad, Ray gave him a slap on the back. "Great, because I need your help."

❧

Ken Bronson pulled his Tahoe into Hawkman's driveway and jumped out.

Hawkman met him at the door. "Come on in. Doesn't look like you slept much either."

"Not with this job." Ken stepped into the living room and glanced around the walls. "How much got destroyed?"

"Quite a bit. The whole back side of the house is going to have to be rebuilt and I'm sure there's some furniture we're going to have to replace, unless we can get the stench out."

Jennifer walked through carrying a load of washing. "Hi, Ken."

"I'm really sorry so much damage occurred. At least, you two are safe."

She stopped at the door of the laundry room. "Pretty Girl, and Miss Marple are missing. We're hoping they're both alive."

"If you haven't found their carcasses, they're probably just hiding. Fire really scares animals."

"We're keeping our fingers crossed they'll show up."

Ken nodded and directed his attention to Hawkman. "I'm here to tell you there were no fingerprints on the bottle the firemen discovered, which is par for the course when a fire is involved, but it definitely contained a Molotov Cocktail. Remnants of gasoline and sugar were found on the inside, plus threads of burnt cloth. We also had a report of a stolen ski boat, but found it at the number one fishing access. No damage and also no fingerprints. Our guys must have worn gloves."

"Doesn't surprise me. And to think I saw that boat going down river in the middle of the night." He poked a thumb into his chest. "And dummy here went back to bed, thinking they were some crazy men cat fishing."

"Hey, you had no way of knowing their plans. But now we're getting more than one police force interested in this case. It's developed into arson and attempted murder. Detective Williams from Medford told us if we need more manpower we can call on his group. I'm going to check on getting a helicopter to help with the search."

"Good. I think we better start moving in on them, before they end up killing someone."

Ken shifted his stance. "I just hope they haven't had time to get away completely."

Hawkman waggled a hand in the air. "They're not going anywhere. They haven't taken care of me yet, and that's their objective."

Moving toward the door, Ken held out his hand. "Sure glad you and Jennifer are okay. I'll get back to you as soon as we've organized the search. I expect we'll be ready to go tomorrow morning."

Hawkman walked him outside. "Be sure and let me know what time. I want to be there."

"Will do," Ken said, waving as he climbed into his vehicle.

Going back into the house, Hawkman heard Jennifer crooning in the other room. He meandered back and found her sitting on the end of the guest room bed holding a wiggly ball of fur. She glanced up with a big smile. "Look who I found."

CHAPTER THIRTY-EIGHT

Hawkman sat beside Jennifer and ran a finger down Miss Marple's paw. "Hey, little girl, you gave us quite a scare. You doing okay?" He glanced at Jennifer. "Where the heck did she hide? I thought we'd searched in here."

"We did," Jennifer said, rubbing the cat's head. "While checking to see how bad the smoke had affected this room, I heard a noise under the bed. I pulled out a box where I'd stored some of Sam's stuff. It didn't have a lid, and I found her curled up under one of the tee shirts with just her nose sticking out."

"I'm surprised she didn't come out sooner, just to investigate."

Jennifer shrugged. "Who knows? She probably felt safe cuddled up in those clothes. But she smells awful. I think she's going to experience her first bath real soon."

Hawkman reared back, and extended both arms, palms forward. "Don't count me in on that duty. Cat's don't like water."

"It won't be for a few days as I'm sure she's hungry, thirsty and still a little scared. I want her to adjust and realize she's safe before I even think about it."

"Good idea. No need to give her another shock."

Jennifer pointed toward the front door. "Did I hear Ken's voice a while ago?"

"Yes." He told her about their conversation. "Tomorrow, if everything goes as planned, I'll be off in the hills with the search party."

"I hope you find those two and they give up without a fight."

"I'll worry about it tomorrow." He put a hand on her shoulder. "With the electricity out, I've placed the two burner camp stove on the kitchen counter. At least we can make a cup of coffee or warm up food. Also, we have a couple of those battery operated lanterns. I found one, but can't find the mate."

"It's on the shelf in my closet."

"I'll get it and we'll have those handy for tonight. Of course, the alarm isn't working, so we'll need to be vigilant. It wouldn't surprise me for Jack and Ray to make a trip to their lookout and find out we're still alive and kicking."

Jennifer stood with Miss Marple cradled in her arms. "Tonight we'll take turns sleeping. I want you to get plenty of rest before you take off with a search team."

"Tomorrow there should be several workman around, as I talked with a contractor and Pacific Power. They'll be here in the morning and probably stay most of the day. I can't see any problems developing with so many people milling around the house. You just make sure you stay in the midst of them, especially while outside. Don't let yourself be a target."

"Don't worry, I learned my lesson."

He pointed at the cat. "You're going to have to shut her in the bathroom if you're busy doing something. There are too many open spots where she could get out." He chuckled. "You might even give her your can of baby powder to play with, she'd smell a heck of a lot better than she does now."

Jennifer grinned. "Stop it. I'm not so sure such a fine dust is good for her to breathe."

Hawkman left the room and retrieved the other lantern. He checked the batteries, then placed it on the kitchen counter beside the camp stove, along with a couple of flashlights. Assured all the items were working properly, he went outside.

Jennifer refreshed Miss Marple's bed, food and water. She examined the cat's toys and decided once the electricity was on, she'd run them through the air cycle of the dryer to see if that wouldn't help get rid of the smoky odor.

She took the worst smelling ones to the laundry room and dropped them in the basket when she heard Hawkman's whistle. Hurrying to the dining room window, she hoped he'd spotted Pretty Girl. But to her disappointment, he stood in the center of the side yard, his fists on his hips, turning around in a circle, looking skyward. It dawned on her how dangerously exposed he appeared, and quickly opened the window. "Hawkman, you're a wonderful target."

He hustled toward the back steps and came in the laundry room door. "You're right. Dumb stunt on my part."

She put an arm around his waist. "No sign of Pretty Girl?"

"None. The trauma of the fire probably frightened her so much, she might never come back."

"Don't give up hope. It hasn't even been twenty-four hours yet. At least you know she didn't die in her cage."

Jack and Ray, rifles slung across their backs, tramped over the hill. They skirted the roads, and stayed within the tree line as they made their way toward the lookout point they'd used before.

"We're apt to come across a scouting party looking for us," Jack said, as he scooted behind the large boulder.

Ray rested his rifle against the rock and adjusted his binoculars. "They haven't had time to get organized. I suspect tomorrow at the earliest." He chuckled. "More than likely they've got roadblocks set up all over the northern part of the state."

Jack shot him a dirty look. "You think it's funny?"

He took the glasses from his eyes and gazed at his father. "Yeah, especially when we're hiking around here on foot."

"Tom Casey knows we're here."

"How do you know what he's thinking? He might be in the hospital or dead."

Jack adjusted his jacket and sat down on a stump. "I doubt it. He's a smart son-of-a-gun. One of the topnotch guys when he worked for the Agency. I read a lot about the man and figure I'll probably die pursuing him."

"No man is indestructible. If he's still alive, he'll let his guard down; and when he does, I'm going to be there to take him out."

Ray put the glasses back to his eyes and focused on the destruction at the back of Casey's house. "Damn."

"What's the problem?"

"Casey's still alive. I just missed a great opportunity. He was standing out in the yard next to his house in plain view."

"That surprises me. What was he doing?"

"Looking at the sky."

"Maybe he's searching for a helicopter."

Ray rubbed his beard. "It appears he got out of the place without so much as a scorched hair. And I'm sure he saved his wife. So we're back at square one."

Jack pointed. "Doubt they have any electricity from the looks of the damage. Which means their alarm won't work."

Ray studied the house. "Good observation. Tonight might be a good chance to get him."

"How can we be sure they're staying there? We have no idea how much damage was done to the inside. I'm sure it smells strongly of smoke. A neighbor may have offered them a place to stay until theirs is cleaned up and fixed."

"We'll just keep watching."

❧

Hawkman glanced out the kitchen window when he heard a noise and it surprised him to see the Pacific Power truck pull into their driveway. He walked outside. "Didn't expect you guys until tomorrow."

"We got through earlier on a job than we expected, so decided to come out and see if we could get your power back on. Understand you had a fire?"

"Right. It's mighty nice of you to drive all the way out here. It would really be helpful to have electricity. At least in part of the house, particularly the kitchen."

The workman laughed. "I think we can probably fix it up. We'll wire it so your construction company will be able to feed right into the power source once they get everything completed."

"Great." He motioned for the men to follow him. "Come on in."

Peggy turned in behind the Pacific Power crew, then swerved around the truck and parked in the lot next to the house. She jumped out and hurried toward the entry.

Poking her head inside the opened door, she called, "Jennifer."

Hearing her name, Jennifer wove her way past the men standing throughout the house. She reached the door with Miss Marple dangling over her arm. "Hi, Peggy. What's up?"

"Don't come outside, we'll just talk in the doorway." Then she grinned and ran a hand over the cat's head. "Oh, thank goodness, you found her. Is she okay?"

"Yes. Other than smelling like smoke, she seems fine."

"Did she hide inside or outside?"

"Under the guest room bed in a box."

"The little rascal." Peggy leaned against the rock siding. "I want you, Hawkman and Miss Marple to stay at my place until they get yours repaired. It's just not safe with no electricity. Even if the workmen can restore your power partially, the back will still be open and without protection."

"That'd be such an imposition."

"I'm afraid I'm going to have to insist or else you'll have to go into town and stay at a motel. Ken and I spoke with the department. They feel the house is too open and dangerous with Jack and Ray on the loose. Especially with no functioning alarm."

Jennifer frowned. "I'll have to talk with Hawkman."

"Another reason I'm insisting. He'll be heading out with the men in the morning. I don't want you alone."

"The contractor will be here early tomorrow."

"All well and good. I'll bring you over when they get here and stay with you until the men return from the search."

Hawkman stepped up behind the women. "What are you two discussing?"

Jennifer quickly told him what Peggy had offered.

"I think it's a good idea. We'll be over when it turns dark."

"Drive, it's safer."

After Peggy left, Jennifer took Miss Marple back to the bathroom. "I'm sorry little girl, you're going to have to stay in here while the men are working. I can't watch you with so many people in and out of the house." She placed her in the straw bed with a toy, then closed the door.

The electricians worked on the house until almost dark. The foreman approached them in the kitchen. "We've been able to get the power restored on the north side of the house so you'll at least have some lights and can cook. Your refrigerator is working, and so is the freezer in the garage. This should keep you in pretty good shape until the rest is repaired."

Hawkman put out his hand. "Really appreciate you guys coming out today and getting this done. Makes life a lot easier."

"Glad to be of help. When the contractors get ready to do the electrical, they won't have any problems."

"Great. Thanks."

After the crew left, Hawkman peeked out the kitchen window as he punched the garage door opener. "It's working, too. I'll go check the freezer and make sure the food is all okay. At least you can get your vehicle out now. It's a bugger opening that door manually."

"At least, I didn't have to go anywhere," Jennifer said. "I assume the food in the freezer is fine. It will last up to about three days, if the door hasn't been opened." She looked in the refrigerator. "We should eat these wieners, they're fine now, but might not be in a day or two. How about a hot dog and soup for dinner?"

"Sounds good."

After eating, they prepared to go over to the Bronson's. Each packed a small duffle with their personal gear, then Jennifer put some assorted toys in Miss Marple's bed along with a small plastic bag of cat food. "This is like getting a kid ready to go on a sleep over."

Hawkman laughed. "This should be an interesting evening. Wonder how Du is going to take to our little invader coming into her territory?"

Jennifer furrowed her brow. "Oh, my. I'd completely forgotten about their huge black lab. She could crunch Miss Marple with one clamp of her jaws."

CHAPTER THIRTY-NINE

Ray dropped his binoculars on his chest. "Doesn't look like getting Casey tonight is a good idea."

Jack had sprawled in the shade of a tree and watched his son eyeing the house. "Oh, yeah, how come?"

"Pacific Power trucks just left, and they have lights at least in the front of the house. I doubt they were able to do anything about the burned area, so the back side is probably without any kind of electricity. So the alarm won't do them any good."

Jack spat out the twig he had in his mouth and stood. "See anyone around the place that looks like a guard or police officer?"

"Nope. Oh, hold on a minute. Casey and his wife just drove out of the driveway and are headed straight down the street. You're probably right, they're staying with a neighbor." He shrugged. "Guess we could go down and blow up the rest of the house."

Jack meandered over to the rock. "I don't think that's a good idea. People are on the lookout for a couple of vandals. If anyone spotted us messing around, they'd shoot first and ask questions later. Anyway we don't have the ingredients to make an explosive. Besides, what good would it do without Casey inside?"

Ray swung his backpack onto his shoulders. "We might as well head back to our campsite, and prepare for a showdown. I have a feeling the old posse will be coming down on us. By the way, you have enough ammo?"

"Couple of boxes. Didn't pack much as it's too heavy to carry."

"Any stored in the pickup?"

"Nope."

Looking back at the house, Ray rubbed his hands together and licked his lips.

Jack raised a brow. "What've you got in mind?"

"We'll wait until it's good and dark. You stay here and guard our stuff while I go down and ransack Casey's place for shells. You know he's probably got plenty."

"I don't like the idea. You'll have to get on the bridge and your limp will give you away."

"The minute I get across the river, I'll get off the road and go in next to the blackberry bushes. No one will ever see me."

Jack ran a hand across his forehead. "We could use more ammo, that's for sure. Maybe we should both go."

"If someone spotted us together, it'd be a dead giveaway who we are. They may not pay too much attention to just one guy walking along. I'll walk close to the railing on the bridge and if a car comes by, I'll just stop and look out over the water as if I'm out for my nightly stroll. Also, I've been in the house, so I know the layout."

"It might work," Jack said, settling back down under the tree.

∽

Peggy greeted Hawkman, Jennifer and Miss Marple at the door, showed the trio to their room, then invited them to come back into the living room with the kitten, so she and Ken could introduce Du to their house guests.

Nervously, Jennifer handed Miss Marple to Peggy. "Do you think your dog will hurt her?"

"Not at all. Once Ken has given Du instructions, she'll protect the cat."

Hawkman and Jennifer stood back as Ken took Miss Marple. He held her in his lap as he spoke to Du.

"That cat is so weird. She doesn't even hiss," Hawkman said, rubbing the back of his neck. "I've never seen anything like it."

"She's never encountered a dog before," Jennifer said. "She doesn't even realize the animal is an enemy."

The big lab sat on her haunches at Ken's knee, then suddenly placed a big slobbery kiss on Miss Marple's face. The cat immediately ran both paws over her wet fur and everyone laughed. Ken instructed Du to lay down, then placed Miss Marple on the floor in front of her. The cat stared at the big black lab, and Du tilted her head back and forth observing the kitten, as if expecting her to do something. Soon Miss Marple extended her head toward the big animal and they touched noses. When Du kissed her again, the feline jumped back. The dog dropped her head onto her paws, gave a little whine and watched the kitten.

Ken stood, gave his dog some final commands, then motioned for Hawkman to join him in the kitchen where they could discuss plans for the next morning.

Jennifer, still edgy over the two animals, slid into a chair nearest Miss Marple. She prepared to grab her precious pet in case the dog made an advance. But it turned out Miss Marple made the overtures and the dog handled the situation, either by not paying attention to her, or giving her a nudge with her big black nose. Before bedtime, the two animals were lying side by side on the floor.

When everyone retired to their rooms, Jennifer put Miss Marple's bed on the floor next to her side and tucked the cat in with her favorite stuffed bunny. Just as she got comfortable, hugging Hawkman's back, she felt the furry little ball wedging herself between them.

"Miss Marple, get back in your bed," Jennifer said sternly.

She could feel Hawkman's body shake as he chuckled. "Sometimes that cat is a real comic, but other times she's a real pain."

Jennifer rose up on her elbow. "So what are your plans for tomorrow?"

Hawkman rolled over and faced her. "We're meeting in front of the fire station at five-thirty in the morning. Ken's even got some K-9 units coming in to help in the search, along with a helicopter."

"Do you have any notion where you'll begin looking?"

"No. But we've got a couple of plans, and we'll act on them first. If they fail, then the team will regroup and brainstorm." He ran a hand down her arm. "Promise me you'll be careful."

"I will. Peggy said she'd take me over to the house to meet the contractors and stay with me until you guys return. But I'm sure she'd like to be with Ken. Maybe she'd be happy if I got Amelia from the store to come down."

"I don't care how you work it, as long as you're not alone. We could be gone all day and even then we might not find them. Hard to say where they've hidden in these hills. It's a big territory and two men won't be easy to find. And they could backtrack and end up at our house, the farthest place from where we'd be looking."

"We better get some sleep. You have a long day ahead of you."

They'd no more than closed their eyes when a furry little critter pounced upon the foot of the bed, crawled between them and curled into a ball.

CHAPTER FORTY

Jack and Ray waited for darkness and as soon as the sun dropped over the hills, a cool breeze blew across the area.

"Glad I brought this jacket, the wind's mighty nippy," Jack said, shrugging on the coat as he stood.

"It won't be long before I head down to the house. Keep watching in case I run into any trouble."

Jack leaned on the large boulder and waved a hand toward the lake. "People in this community close their shutters as soon as it gets dark. Just hustle across that bridge as fast as you can. That's where you'll run into a problem, if any at all." He pointed toward the west. "Cars coming down the road from town will more than likely turn, so keep your eyes open."

Ray moved around Jack. "Will do. Think I'll start my journey now."

"Be careful. This is rugged country, especially navigating it at night."

Choosing his footing carefully, Ray made his way down the steep incline. He slipped a couple of times and grabbed a tree trunk to keep from falling down the hillside. Finally, he approached the area directly across from the bridge. He checked both directions. Seeing no headlights, he quickly hobbled across the road to the span over the river. Staying close to the railing, he turned his gaze westward. When he spotted a car approaching, he grasped the balustrade, and heaved himself forward at a faster pace.

By the time the vehicle reached the turnoff, Ray had made it almost to the end. He swung over the last bit of railing and hurled to the ground. He lost his footing, tumbled down the embankment, but quickly scrambled to his feet and flattened himself against the concrete abutment. The pickup passed without slowing. Ray exhaled in relief.

He leaned against the cool surface for several seconds and observed the distance between himself and the house. It appeared about a half block away, and he'd have the blackberry bushes to use as cover the whole distance. Ray pushed away from the wall, and climbed up the slight incline. He sidled close to the brambles, and could hear the rustling of the nocturnal animals as they scurried around inside the depth of the tightly woven twigs. He always wondered how the critters avoided getting poked in the eyes by the thorns.

When he approached the back of the house, he spotted a piece of loose plywood on one corner. If he could tug it off, he'd be able to easily crawl inside. He fixed his gaze on the board, then stepped forward, not realizing he'd cornered a skunk. The animal raised his tail and let go with a powerful spray, soaking Ray's pant's leg. He jumped back and had to bite his tongue to keep from screaming at the horrible stench. "Damn you!" he hissed, hurrying back toward the bushes. The critter ambled away in the opposite direction, his tail held high.

Ray's eyes watered, but he couldn't do much but suffer the consequences. He'd hurry and collect what ammunition he could carry, and suffer with the stench until they got back to the campsite where he could change into some different pants. Then he snickered. Or better yet, *I'll borrow a pair of Casey's and leave these as my calling card.*

He yanked on the piece of plywood and it suddenly gave way, falling to the ground with a clatter. Ducking behind a part of the barrier, he waited several minutes to make sure no one heard the loud noise. When no porch lights popped on or people rushed outside to investigate, he crawled inside the dark house.

Searching his pockets for the small penlight, he could feel the wetness of the skunk's spray on his trousers and the putrid smell made his nose sting. He finally found the small light and flipped it on. Keeping the beam below the windows, he maneuvered his way back to the master bedroom. He checked in both closets and discovered a pair of camouflage pants that would suit his needs. Quickly emptying his pockets onto the bed, he stripped off the stinking pants and let them drop to the floor. "That should add flavor to the nice smoky smell," he smirked.

Once he had on the trousers, he discovered he'd have to roll up the legs, as Casey had much longer limbs than he. Shining the light over the closet shelves, he found several boxes of ammunition and crammed them into his pockets. He kicked a few pairs of shoes out of the way, knocked over a lamp, and left open all the searched drawers. He ventured into Casey's office. While gathering more boxes of bullets, he scattered papers and knocked desk supplies onto the floor. When he'd collected all he could carry, he headed out the back, but before continuing his journey, made sure the skunk had disappeared.

He hurried across the bridge without incident and started the climb back up the hill to the lookout point where he'd left his dad. Panting, he finally reaching the big boulder, and leaned heavily against it.

Jack sniffed the air and wrinkled his nose. "Oh, man, you must have disturbed a skunk. I can sure smell him."

Ray laughed. "It's not up here. The damn thing sprayed me outside Casey's place. If you think this is bad, you should smell the pants I left in his bedroom."

"I hope the odor fades by the time we get back to the campsite, I don't cherish the thought of sleeping in an enclosed area with you."

"You'll get used to it." He unloaded some of the ammunition from his pockets and handed them to his dad. "Take some of these boxes and as soon as I catch my breath, we'll hit the trail."

Jack led the way, and the two men disappeared over the knoll.

❧

The next morning, Hawkman scooted Miss Marple away from his leg, then quietly rolled out of bed. After dressing, he opened the door, and the smell of coffee drifted into the bedroom.

Jennifer raised her head off the pillow. "Be careful, hon."

He crossed to her side and planted a kiss on her lips. "I will. Promise you'll be very observant."

"Don't worry, I'll be here when you return."

He hastened out of the room and into the kitchen.

"Good morning," Peggy said, pouring him a cup of coffee. "Breakfast is on the run." She shoved a box of donuts toward him. "Take your pick. Ken has already left, but will meet you in front of the fire station in about thirty minutes."

"Good, I'll have time to run over and check the house." He grabbed a pastry, took a gulp of coffee, then scooted out the door.

Jennifer soon padded into the room. "Peggy, I know you want to be included in this search. I'm going to give Amelia a call at the store. If she can stay with me, you'll be able to join the men in this hunt."

Peggy raised a brow. "I don't think that's a good idea. I'd really rather stay with you, as we have no idea where these men have hidden. They could backtrack behind the search team and end up taking you as a hostage." She patted Jennifer on the shoulder. "Thanks for the consideration, but my job is to protect you."

Jennifer slumped into a chair. "I hate this whole mess. It's turned into a horrible nightmare. And I'm sure you'll find hanging out with me is not going to be nearly as exciting as being in the field."

Peggy grinned. "Who knows, it might be more thrilling."

Hawkman barreled into the house, his mouth set in a grim expression and his uncovered eye flaring with anger. "You won't be able to stay at our place, Jennifer."

She jumped up and looked at him in shock. "Why?"

"Someone broke in last night. They must have come in contact with a skunk, took a pair of my pants, ransacked the house and stole a ton of ammunition." He pointed a finger in the air. "But he left the putrid scented trousers in the middle of our bedroom floor. The whole house reeks."

Jennifer covered her face and plopped back down in the chair. "What more can they do?"

Hawkman paced back and forth. "I don't know, but you'll have to go over long enough to talk to the contractors. They're going to love working in our smelly house."

"Were you able to get the pants out of there?" Jennifer asked.

"Yes, I threw them into the side yard. The sun and air should help. Then we'll bundle them up and throw them away."

"Don't fret," Peggy said, giving Hawkman a pat on the back. "We'll manage. You just find those guys and bring them in." She smiled. "If they're the ones who broke into your house, you might have an easier time following the trail than you thought."

Jennifer couldn't help but laugh. "She's right, just follow the stink."

Hawkman jerked his head around. "You know, you might have a point. I'll fetch those pants, put them into a plastic bag and let the dogs get a good whiff. It will definitely give them a strong aroma to follow."

CHAPTER FORTY-ONE

As they waited in front of the fire station for the rest of the team, Hawkman told Ken about what had happened at his house and held up a plastic bag.

"I don't know if you have any hounds in this group of K-9s, but if you do, I have the scent."

Ken scratched his head and grimaced. "No blood hounds in this group, however, the problem with the skunk smell, is we have lots of those critters around the area. Especially up in the hills. It might throw off the dogs, and instead of finding the men we're looking for we might end up chasing varmints."

Hawkman glanced at the parcel. "Guess this isn't such a good idea after all."

"If Ray or Jack got sprayed somewhere along the way and then broke into your house, I think we'll get a whiff without having to depend on the dogs. You don't wash off that scent easily."

"You've got a point." Hawkman walked over to the side of the building and dropped the stinky package on the ground. "We might need the pants for evidence, but I don't think we want to carry them around."

The Fire Chief pulled up and opened the fire station so Ken could get the portable lanterns for the arrival of the helicopter. Hawkman helped place them around the perimeter of the pad. After turning them on, they moved back to the road to wait for the assisting crews.

Soon, several uniformed men in marked cars, two K-9 teams and a SWAT team arrived, along with the Incident Commander, Jim Bates. Ken called them forward and introduced Tom Casey as an ex-agent, now a private investigator, then explained the connection between him and the two men.

Ken unfolded a map on the hood of his Chevy Tahoe and pointed to the area where he thought the two villains might possibly be hiding. "I figure they'll camp close to a creek as they'll need water. We'll set up the command post at the old hotel and start a sweep south."

Jim then took over and pointed at the patrol officers. I want you guys to set up roadblocks on the other side of the bridge and at the Oregon border." Then he gave a quick description of the men they were after. "Ray has a definite limp, and both have grown shaggy beards to the point of looking like they've lived in the hills for years. Don't let anyone pass through the barriers fitting these descriptions. Any questions?"

One raised a hand. "Are we going to have air support?"

"Yes, the helicopter will be here shortly. Bronson will ride with the pilot as the spotter." Jim glanced around to make sure everyone understood. When no one else spoke up, he motioned toward the vehicles. "Okay, let's go." He gestured for Hawkman to join him.

"I hear the chopper," someone called.

Another pointed toward the sky. "There she flies."

Ken headed toward the back of the fire station. "Talk to you guys later," he yelled over his shoulder.

The team scrambled into their cars and followed the commander. After all passed over the bridge and turned east on Ager Beswick Road, one of the uniformed officers parked his marked car across the entry into the guarded area.

It was still dark when they reached the old hotel. Hawkman watched the K-9 teams as they prepared the dogs and took the lead. The men knew to stay behind these canines as the animals couldn't distinguish between the good guys and the bad. They just attacked on command from their masters. Carrying their weapons in a poised ready position, the men spread out in a wide line and walked south. The land held rocks and was full of small gullies, making each step hard to manage. Most of the time, they had the protection of the forest, but as the sun peeked over the hills you could see the spots of sparse foliage. They would hurry across the exposed areas to hide amongst the trees.

Ray tried desperately to wash off the skunk scent in the stream, but without soap, he made little headway. Exhausted, he finally gave up, stumbled back to the pickup and climbed into his bedroll.

Jack tossed and turned, putting his head deep into his sleeping bag, hoping to get some relief from the horrible stench that permeated the camper shell. Finally, he gave up and decided he'd try the cab. If he could get away from the pungent smell, he might be able to snatch a few winks. He quietly climbed out the back, opened the driver's side door and slipped under the steering wheel. The night had turned still and stuffy, so he rolled down the window, then crunched up his jacket behind his head. He'd no more dozed off, when he jerked up and listened. He hastened out of the pickup and woke up Ray.

"Just heard a copter. We've got to make sure we can't be seen from the air."

Jack pulled the truck farther into the grove of trees, then the two men chopped limbs off a nearby oak and placed them around the front and tail end of the vehicle. Finally, he stood back in the predawn hazy light and scrutinized the effect. "I think we did it. At least it will keep the reflection from the sun down to a minimum."

Ray's gaze searched the landscape. "We need a place to hide. Somewhere away from the truck. Damn, I wish we knew the area better."

Jack pointed toward a hill in the distance. "Let's gather our guns and ammo, then hike up to that ridge. Maybe we can find a small cave where we're protected at the back. Also, high enough so we can see them coming."

"Good idea," Ray said, grabbing his guns. He loaded the backpack with boxes of bullets and slung it over his shoulders. "Let's go."

Jack shoved the remaining cartons into his pockets, stuck his pistol into the waistband of his pants and hefted his rifle. "I'm ready."

Ray trekked a few yards ahead, but Jack knew he'd have no trouble catching up, so he grabbed a couple of the canteens. Food they could do without, but water would be essential. He quickly filled them at the creek, then took off in a trot after his son.

The hill stood a lot farther away than it appeared and it seemed to take them forever before they finally reached the base. The two scaled the side and soon came upon a perfect hideout where a huge piece of rock had separated from the side leaving a gap big enough for them to slip behind, see over the top ridge and yet be well hidden by the ledge jutting out above their heads.

"This is perfect," Ray said, placing his rifle on the rock. He dropped the backpack to the ground, put the binoculars to his eyes and searched the horizon. "Don't see any sign of the posse." Leaning against the rock, he wiped the sweat from his brow with the back of his arm.

Jack held out a canteen. "Good thing I stopped and filled these."

Ray smiled and took a big gulp. "I tend to forget the essential items in the heat of the battle. Thanks." He capped the bottle and placed it in the shade of the big boulder.

The two divided up the ammo and situated themselves so they both had a view of the whole area, including where they'd hidden the truck.

"Man, that was one hell of a walk," Ray said. "My legs are still trembling."

"Yeah, our eyes play tricks on us. Things tend to look closer than they really are."

"At least we can see what's coming. I didn't like the idea of hanging around the tree covered area. They could've surrounded us and we would never have known it. This way, they might never find us, even if they locate the pickup." Ray raised a hand. "So don't shoot unless absolutely necessary."

Jack remained silent as he scanned the sky. The sun rays were peeking over the hills and daylight would be in full swing within thirty minutes. He felt his stomach tighten and pointed toward the small speck that shot up over the distant hills. "They're on the way."

CHAPTER FORTY-TWO

Hawkman hopped out of the car at the hotel ruins, and followed the Commander to the rear of the vehicle. He opened the trunk and fished around in a couple of boxes, then handed Hawkman a bullet proof vest and radio.

"You better wear one of these if you plan on traveling with the men."

"Thanks." Hawkman shrugged into the heavy attire and adjusted it over his broad chest and shoulders.

"Fit okay?"

"Yeah, it's fine."

"Know how to use the squawk box?"

Hawkman studied the controls for a moment and nodded. "Yep. I can work it."

"Good." The Commander closed the trunk lid. "The vest will be warm, but it's better than being dead." He then ambled over to the group of men gathered in the center of the lot. They were struggling into their gear and checking their guns. "About ready?"

"Yes, sir," several said, as they fell in behind the K-9 teams, who were already marching forward.

"You know where we're headed and the two we want. We'd like to take them alive, but if you have no choice, don't hesitate to fire. Both are armed and considered dangerous."

Hawkman counted twelve men, including the two K-9 handlers, going into the field. Carrying the AR-15 Assault Rifle Ken had given him before leaving the fire station, he joined the last group of four heading out. They made their way silently toward the cover of the trees. About the time they fell into the shadows, he heard the rotors of the helicopter and glanced up as it soared overhead to the front of the line.

The sun made its way over the hills, and as the rays hit the trees they gave off steam, making them appear on fire. A haze covered the area for several minutes before it burned off.

Hawkman felt good about being with this group. They were following Shovel Creek as it worked its way through the hills. Knowing Jack and Ray would need water, he felt strongly that they'd set up camp near a stream. At least the police might find some evidence the two men had left behind. Of course, there were other small brooks, but this one seemed the most logical, as it flowed close to his place. And he was their target.

As he trudged along, his thoughts went to Jennifer. He prayed Jack and Ray had not backtracked. At least Peggy would be with her. He couldn't help but grimace, thinking of his wife going into the house and getting a whiff of the skunk.

They hiked for thirty minutes over the rugged terrain before taking a break. The helicopter kept a steady pace flying back and forth ahead of them. The radios were used to let the Commander and each group know the others' location. Ken had called several times, reporting no sign of a vehicle or men. They'd stay up for about an hour before having to refuel. Hawkman had seen the truck parked in a small flat pasture before they reached the command post.

He walked out to the edge of the tree line and studied the landscape. He'd been in this area before, but wasn't as familiar with it as other parts. There were logging roads all over the place and you could get a vehicle into many of them, if you didn't mind the rough ride. He figured hiking in a fast walk to his place by foot, as the crow flies, would take anywhere from thirty minutes to an hour.

Getting his bearings, he doubted Jack and Ray would camp too far from the main road. He figured another thirty minutes of searching would about do for this stretch. Then they'd have to go to plan number two. Pulling a toothpick from his pocket, he put it between his teeth and gnawed as he stared at the hills ahead.

Taking the radio from his belt, he cued in Ken aboard the Hughes 500. "I think a fly over of the next row of hills should do it for this round. If they aren't hiding in the valley, we probably should go to the next step."

"We're heading there now. Over," Ken responded.

Hawkman watched the helicopter make a turn and head toward the low lying mounds. The group reached the top of a small knoll when the radio crackled.

"Suspicious looking obstruction up ahead. A group of trees near the creek. Be on the alert."

The men of Hawkman's group held their weapons in a poised position as they circled the odd looking barricade. Slowly advancing, and not receiving any gun fire, they soon uncovered the stolen pickup. Hawkman stuck his head inside the camper shell, but quickly backed away. It pretty well told him, from the telltale skunk scent, the culprit who'd stolen ammunition out of his home had definitely left his calling card.

The absence of Jack and Ray worried Hawkman. Had they spotted the helicopter and taken off toward his place? Two men would have had time to sneak through before the troops had covered the region. His stomach tightened at the thought. They'd know he'd be with the search party, leaving Jennifer vulnerable.

Again, Ken's voice came over the radio. "Any sign of Jack and Ray?"

Hawkman quickly flipped on his transmit button. "None. Call Peggy and alert her to be on the lookout."

"Will do. We're heading west to see if there's any sign of them on foot. Then we'll go refuel."

Peggy hopped under the steering wheel as Jennifer slid into the passenger side of the Chevy Tahoe.

"Are you sure Miss Marple will be safe with Du? You know when the master isn't around sometimes dogs disobey."

Peggy tittered. "Not this one. Don't you worry. Your pet is probably safer with Du than she'd be with you."

Jennifer twisted around and gazed with apprehension toward Peggy's place.

When they pulled up in front of her home, the carpenter's van was parked in the driveway. Jennifer quickly got out and hurried toward the vehicle. "Hi Scott, I hope you haven't been waiting long."

He smiled. "Nope, just pulled in. The rest of the crew should be here shortly."

Jennifer led the way to the entry, followed by Scott and Peggy. When she opened the door, she gasped. "Oh, my, I didn't think the odor would be this strong."

Peggy held her nose. "This is bad."

"Uh, oh, smells like a skunk," Scott said, making a face.

Jennifer decided not to elaborate and let him think whatever he wanted. "Yes, Hawkman warned me, but I'd hoped the smell might have dissipated by this morning."

He placed his clipboard on the kitchen cabinet, then strolled over to the glass doors and slid it open. "By the time we open up the house, it should air out pretty good."

Peggy glanced down at the pager on her belt, picked up the phone and called dispatch. Her expression turned solemn as she listened. Not wanting to disturb Jennifer as she hovered over the plans Scott had spread out on the counter, she meandered over to the dining room window and peered out the corner of the drapes toward the bridge.

Another couple of cars pulled in front of the house and Peggy visually checked out each man as he filed into the house. Soon the sound of banging hammers echoed throughout. Then suddenly everything went silent.

CHAPTER FORTY-THREE

Peggy's attention piqued immediately. She grabbed Jennifer's arm. "Quick, duck behind the counter."

Scott looked at her wide eyed. "What's going on?"

She pulled her gun. "Take cover," she instructed, as she eased into the living room, her back against the wall, and her Springfield .40 poised. Peeking out the window, she noticed the workmen standing back and looking toward the area of the burned out porch. When she glanced in the direction of the partially warped wrought iron railing, a smile formed on her lips, and she holstered her gun. "Looks like Pretty Girl has returned."

Jennifer leaped up and dashed toward the window. Her hands covered her mouth, "Thank God." She turned and grabbed the long leather glove off the counter, then headed out the front door.

Peggy raised a hand and yelled. "No, wait!"

Paying no heed to the warning, Jennifer raced to the side yard while slipping the protection over her hand and arm. The falcon glanced toward her, then spread her wings and lifted into the sky.

"Pretty Girl, it's me." Jennifer watched her make lazy circles close to the house. "Come on down," she pleaded, her arm extended.

"Get back in the house," Peggy urged. "You're in danger."

"Don't talk to me right now, I've got to coach her back."

Peggy backed into the shadow of the house, concern written all over her face. She canvassed the outer boundaries of the property, particularly where the blackberry bushes were the thickest. Any stirring of leaves, even from a breeze made her break into a sweat. She held her pistol, ready to fire at the slightest movement.

The workman stood like statues in awe as they watched. It took several minutes before Pretty Girl made a wide circle around the house, glided down, and gently landed on Jennifer's arm. She crooned to the bird and quickly walked into the house.

Hawkman had already placed the portable perch in the guest room. Getting the hawk to step onto the top rung might be a problem, but when she moved her arm to the right position, the falcon climbed aboard. Jennifer breathed a sigh of relief as she tethered her to the perch. "You're such a good girl," she said in a soothing voice. "Hawkman is going to be so thrilled to see you."

Peggy stood in the doorway. "Girl, you scared me out there."

Jennifer frowned. "Why?"

"I didn't have a chance to tell you, but I'd just received word from Ken, the search uncovered the vehicle Jack and Ray were driving. But so far no sign of them. He thinks they may have headed in this direction and wanted me to make sure you stayed safe."

Jennifer put her hand on Peggy's arm. "I'm sorry. I didn't realize why you were so worried." She glanced toward Pretty Girl. "But you know, I'd have taken the chance, as this bird means a lot to Hawkman; and he thought he'd lost her after the fire."

"I don't think he would've wanted you to take the chance. You're more important to him than the falcon." She let out an audible sigh. "No sense in fretting now, it's done. At least you're okay and so is Pretty Girl."

Jennifer smiled. "I better get her some water and food."

After getting the falcon situated, Jennifer talked with Scott and assured him all was well. She persuaded him to work on the aviary as soon as they could reasonably do so, as the bird liked the outdoors better than being cooped up inside. "Keep the door shut to the guest room. Strange people might upset her right now. She's been frightened enough by the fire."

"I'll pass the word to my men. Shouldn't be a problem, I see no reason why we'd even need to go in there."

Once Jennifer had everything under control, she turned to Peggy. "Let's go back to your place. I need to check on Miss Marple."

"I'll feel much more comfortable with you at my house, rather than here. I know Jack and Ray would have a hard time doing you any harm with all these men around, but they're crack shots. And the minute you're in the open, you could be dead in a second."

"I understand," Jennifer said, as they walked out the front door.

Peggy kept to her right, checking the area to the east as they climbed into her vehicle. "I want you to crunch down in the seat when I head up Quail Lane."

"Okay."

As soon as Peggy pulled out of the driveway, Jennifer hunched down until she got the okay to raise her head. They soon pulled in front of the Bronson's and both women hurried into the house. Du and Miss Marple were in the middle of the living room floor. The cat had her back up, ready to pounce on her new buddy. Poor Du covered her nose with her paws, and gazed up at Peggy with mournful eyes.

Jennifer laughed. "Miss Marple, I think you've worn your friend to a frazzle."

Jack leaned back into the shadowed area of the overhang, and let the binoculars fall to his chest. "They've found the truck. Now they'll start looking for us."

Ray placed his rifle on the top of the boulder. "Wonder what they plan on doing? Keep scouting with the ground troops or let the helicopter take over?"

"Get your gun off the rock." Jack pointed. "Keep it back in the shade so the sun doesn't hit it. Whoever's in the helicopter would spot the glare real fast."

"You're right." Ray put his glasses to his face. "Doesn't look like they're moving out; they're all just hovering around the pickup. And the helicopter turned and went westward."

"They may think we've headed for Casey's house or they need to refuel. I have no doubt it'll be back. Keep an eye out for a few minutes. I'm going to see what's behind us."

"What good will that do? We can't outrun them. Our best bet is to stay quiet and hidden."

"Just going to check and see what advantage they might have if they spot us and plan a surprise attack by coming up the backside."

Jack climbed out of their den and started around the side of the hill. He had trouble keeping his footing due to the small rocks and pebbles. He slipped several times skinning the palms of his hands in an attempt to catch himself. Ray would never be able to handle this uneven ground if they had to dash out of there. So best they stay right where they were. He put his hands on his hips and stared out across the landscape. "Guess this is as good a place to die as any," he mumbled.

He stumbled back into their lair. "If they try to come up back there, we'll hear them. And there's no way we can escape if we get cornered. So I hope you're all right with your Maker."

"As good as I'll ever be," Ray said.

Jack rummaged around in his backpack and pulled out a couple of energy bars. "Here, I saved these for later, but I have a feeling we're going to need them."

Ray's mouth widened into a big grin. "Great, my stomach was rumbling. This should calm it down." He took a bite, then picked up the canteen and took a big gulp. "It feels much warmer up here."

Jack settled behind the boulder and put his glasses to his eyes. "Yep. We're away from the water." He straightened.

"Something's going on. They're moving around. I see Tom Casey with the group. The big cowboy hat gives him away."

Ray stood up beside his dad. "He's mine."

CHAPTER FORTY-FOUR

Hawkman searched the hills with his binoculars, but saw no activity. The leader of his group, a big brawny man called Barney, gave a hand wave for the K-9 handler and his dog to go forward. The men followed.

The group spread out and marched along the creek. Their trained gazes traveled along the path for any sign of clues. When the stream veered to their left, Barney signaled for them to keep going straight ahead.

As they moved along, Hawkman noticed the dog straining on the leash and wondered if he'd caught a scent. Even though these animals were not bloodhounds, they could smell a human trail.

The whirling rotors of the helicopter could be heard in the distance. Soon, they came over the knoll and hovered for a few seconds in front of the advancing men, then proceeded on toward the rising mounds. Hawkman put his binoculars to his eyes and studied the craggy appearance of the large mass in front of them. He pointed toward a rocky area. "Lots of hiding places up there. We'd be easy targets, so stay undercover as much as you can."

Barney walked over to Hawkman. "You from here? You sound familiar with this area?"

"Yes . I used to hike it with my son. I don't remember every crevice, but I know there are caves and places you could hide. Very rocky and steep."

"Why don't you come up front. This is all strange territory to me. Even though I was born and raised in Montague, I never spent much time in this neck of the woods."

"Sure, be happy to assist." As the two men walked to the front, Hawkman nudged Barney's arm. "Don't let the men get away from the tree line." Then he pointed. "When you get to that open space, let the helicopter pilot and spotter do their job. Also, I've been watching that dog straining on the leash. I have a feeling he's sensing a trail. If so, it's pretty fresh."

"The handler will probably let him loose shortly."

Hawkman frowned. "Not so sure that's a good idea."

"Why?"

"Jack and Ray are bound to know we're close due to the copter, but they might not have seen us yet. The minute that dog charges into the clearing, they'll know we're right behind him."

Barney hurried toward the K-9 handler and spoke with him for several seconds, then joined Hawkman. "He's aware of the problem and will keep the dog on the leash until the Commander gives the word."

"That's a better plan."

The men soon reached the edge of the trees and stopped. Barney held his radio close to his lips and transmitted their position to the Commander. As they waited for instructions, Hawkman's gaze followed the plane as it made several passes in front of the knoll and glided over the top out of sight, only to appear again from a different direction.

Barney turned to Hawkman. "He's waiting to see what the spotter says."

The sun climbed higher in the sky, and Hawkman felt the heat of the bulletproof vest as the rays played across his back. After stepping into the deeper shade, he glanced out over the barren ground, but couldn't spot the other team. They were good, and had kept well hidden. If Jack and Ray were high in those crevices, they had a good vantage point. They were definitely in for the kill and would have the opportunity to pick off the dog and several men before they could locate them. This worried Hawkman.

He put his binoculars to his face and studied the hill starting at the top. He worked his view slowly down the front side.

Suddenly, he straightened. Focusing on an area about halfway, he adjusted the lens. The sun rays reflected off of something shiny. Possibly the barrel of a rifle. Or it could be just a piece of glass or shiny rock, but definitely worth reporting. He took the radio from his belt and called in to the Command post, hoping Ken could hear the report in the copter.

Jim immediately instructed all the men to halt in their positions until they made a fly over of the area to check it out.

Hawkman watched the plane bank and come back toward the location he'd suggested they examine. Soon, Ken came over the air waves.

"There's definitely a bright reflection, but don't think it's a gun barrel. However, the jutting rock formation prevents us from getting close. It appears there's a large space under the hangover. The ground crew will have to investigate. It'll be dangerous. The men will be in the open if they go straight in, as the tree line stops at the foot of the hills."

"You men stay in position until I give the word," Jim's booming voice announced. "Let me check out a safer way. Ken, how familiar are you with this area?"

"Not much. Tom Casey might be able to help."

"Are you there, Casey?"

"Yes."

"What's your feeling?"

"This is rugged country, and it'll be tough. But I think it would be safer if the men stayed in the protection of the forest until they get to the south side. If Jack and Ray are hiding in the suspected area, they won't see the men making their way up the back."

"Good idea. Let's go for it. Ken, distract our felons."

"Be happy to."

The helicopter made a steep turn and then hovered, kicking up dust and small pebbles over the spot where they'd detected the reflection.

❧

Jack and Ray hunkered down behind the boulder as dirt and rock were hurled into their hideout.

"What the hell is going on," Ray swore.

He grabbed his gun, but Jack put a hand on his arm. "Don't do anything stupid. We don't know if they know we're here or just playing a game. The minute you make yourself visible or shoot, they'll kill us."

Ray put his rifle down beside him and coughed. "This flying debris is killing me, I can hardly breath."

"They won't stay here long. Just keep down and hold on. They can't get close enough to see us or the blades would hit the rock. So we're safe."

Ray pulled his shirt up around his nose. "I hope you're right."

Soon, the helicopter pulled away, and swerved around the side of the hill.

When Ray started to stand, Jack pulled him back down. "Are you crazy? Stay down. They'll spot any movement as long as they're this close."

"I need a breath of fresh air."

"If you get shot in the head, it won't make any difference. Don't worry, it will clear in a few minutes. Let's just hope they don't come back."

"What do you think is going on?"

"I'm not sure. Something made them look for us up here." Jack glanced around the small hideout. He reached across and grabbed the metal canteen Ray had placed beside his feet. "There's our culprit. When the sun got at high noon, and the shade moved, this little tin can sent out a signal as bright as a spotlight. Someone spotted the reflection and they're checking it out." Jack picked up his rifle, placed it across his lap, then removed a box of shells from his pocket. "I think we better get ready for an ambush. They'll be coming in from all sides."

CHAPTER FORTY-FIVE

Once the men made it to the south side, they spread out along the base of the hill and the K-9 handler took off up the side with the dog still leashed. Hawkman could tell the canine had lost whatever scent he'd followed earlier, as he acted a bit distracted.

Ken had told them over the radio they couldn't spot any activity in the area where they'd seen the reflection, but it didn't mean Jack and Ray weren't there. The pilot couldn't get the copter close enough to see deep into the cavern due to the overhanging rock. They'd hoped the kicking up of dirt would drive the men out, or they might spot some movement. But they observed nothing.

Hawkman knew Jack and Ray were tough. Both having been trained by the Agency, they could withstand a lot before caving into a little discomfort. He scanned toward the other group and noted a couple of the men hiding behind what few trees were scattered along the hillside. Also he spotted the other dog and handler leading the pack, as they made their way upward. He scrutinized the hill and calculated where the crevice appeared on the other side. Instead of going over the top, he'd prefer to come in from the side. He shifted over to the right, joining the men moving in that direction. To his relief, he noticed the K-9 had moved into position ahead of them. He didn't want to get ahead of the dog and take the chance of being attacked. So far the dog was held on a tight leash, but more than likely, the handler would soon turn him loose and give the command.

It amazed him how stealthily the men moved. He couldn't hear a sound, other than the chopping blades of the copter.

If Jack and Ray were holed up in that crevice, would they try a shoot out or give up? They obviously figured they'd been spotted. Hawkman concluded what with Jack's strange thinking and Ray's intent to kill him, they'd use their guns.

He stopped a moment and shifted the rifle to his other hand, took a toothpick out of his pocket and poked it between his teeth. Eyeing the landscape. he calculated they'd be in position in another ten minutes. Adjusting his hat, he moved forward again.

&

When the helicopter veered away and the sound of the rotors were lost in the distance, Jack wiped his forehead with the back of his arm. Clutching the rifle, he stood up and peered over the boulder. He took his binoculars and searched the trees at the base, then swung around and studied each side of the hideout. "Where are they?"

Ray hoisted himself up next to his dad and put his glasses to his face. "Beats the hell out of me. You know there's a bunch out there. They didn't bring in the aircraft for nothing. They have the advantage, they know the territory."

Jack glanced up as a smattering of pebbles rolled off the overhang and fell to the ground below. "They're coming over the top," he whispered.

Both men backed up against the rock. Suddenly, Jack jerked his head to the right. "Hear that?"

"Yeah," Ray said, a grin forming on his lips. "A dog. They've even got the K-9s out after us. We must be pretty damned important."

Jack shot him a look. "You ready?"

"As I'll ever be." Ray brought up his rifle to firing position. "Bring 'em on. And let Casey be right out in front."

Jack grimaced as he hoisted his rifle and placed the pistol on the boulder for easy access. "I have a feeling the dogs will be first."

"Let 'em come. They'll have trouble attacking since they won't be able to get a good footing on this steep terrain."

Jack remained silent as he viewed each side of their cubbyhole, then gazed straight ahead. Even if the animals couldn't make it, the men could. He felt in his gut they were cornered. He studied his son's expression and noticed how his eyes glazed. His mouth was set in an odd smile as the tic throbbed at the base of his jaw. "What are you thinking?"

"I'm finally going to get the man that caused me such pain."

"He didn't send you to get hurt and you know it. He was on the other side of the building when you stepped on the land mine."

Ray's eyes flared. "Casey should have briefed us about those mines, so we'd have been aware."

"I read the report. But at the time I was so angry, I wanted to blame someone so bad for the accident, I didn't believe what I read."

"What'd you read?"

"The Agency didn't know there were any mines a hundred miles within the area they were investigating. It had never been in a war zone. They wondered if someone had leaked their plans, and planted a bomb. Casey wouldn't have known anything about it."

"They were covering their asses," Ray spat.

"Whether they were or not, I don't think you should kill an innocent man."

Ray grabbed his father's arm. "I thought you were all for this. Now, you're going to chicken out on me?"

"You planted seeds of horror into my brain. At the time you did this, you knew I was not in a good frame of mind. And I bought it, hook, line and sinker, because it made me think of something besides your mother's death. Now I've had time to mull it over, and came to the realization I was wrong. We've made a stupid move and gotten ourselves cornered. As soon as they come into sight, I'm going to give myself up."

Ray, his eyelids blinking wildly, yanked his father around by the neck of his shirt and banged him up against the rock.

"You bastard. You're not going to chicken out on me now." He jammed his pistol into Jack's belly and pulled the trigger.

Jack slid down the rock, staring in disbelief at his son. Blood flowed from his mouth, but he managed to aim his rifle. When the shot rang out, Ray clutched his chest and crumbled to the ground.

CHAPTER FORTY-SIX

When the first shot rang through the air, the whole police team dropped to the ground. Hawkman crawled behind a boulder and waited. Soon the second shot echoed through the hills. Silence reigned for several minutes before the Commander came over the air waves.

"What the hell's going on?" his voice boomed.

Hawkman didn't feel it his place to respond to the head man. Instead, he focused on the area he thought to be the origin of the shots. They couldn't have possibly come from the other team. He glanced at the dog handler, who gripped the catch to release the animal, and signaled him to hold the canine. "I'm going in," he mouthed.

Crawling on his belly, he edged toward the break he'd spotted on the side of the hill. Pieces of rock erupted out of the ground like huge castles, but this section had broken away, leaving a small slit separating it from the mother mountain. When he reached the rim, he moved next to a boulder, and peeked around the edge.

His gaze riveted on the view of two bloody bodies. "Oh my God," he said aloud. He slowly rose and motioned for the men in his team to come forward. He pointed toward the opening. "Lots of blood and both men down. Can't tell if they're dead or injured. Haven't seen any movement."

An officer moved up and stood beside Hawkman, aiming his gun at Ray and Jack. "Stay back. You're their target. It could be a ploy to get you within their sights."

"Only one way to find out," Hawkman said, as he quickly made his way toward the opening.

⌘

Peggy paced, studied her watch, and checked the radio several times.

"Any news?" Jennifer asked.

"Nothing," she said in an agitated voice. "I thought by now, they'd have found them, or were regrouping for another plan. But no word about the search has come over the air." She flopped down in the overstuffed chair.

"Is that good or bad?"

Peggy brushed a hand across her forehead. "I'm not sure. I just hope no news is good news."

The big black lab, Du, moseyed over and sprawled at her mistress' feet. Peggy reached down and stroked the dog's back.

Miss Marple jumped off Jennifer's lap and slowly made her way toward the big canine. Du eyed her as she approached, as if to say, 'Oh, no, what's this little monster up to this time'.

The cat cocked her ears and gave her new friend a head rub down the side of her black coat, then rolled over and batted at the dog's collar. Du turned and gave her a big sloppy kiss, causing the feline to jump away and rub both paws over her face.

Jennifer put her hand to her mouth to stifle a laugh. "Miss Marple, you got what you deserved." She let out a sigh. "I hate to ask you, Peggy, but it's about time for the workmen to leave the house. Would you mind driving me over to check on their progress and see what I can expect for the next few days? Also, I'd like to see how Pretty Girl is doing."

Peggy rose from the chair. "Sure. It'll give us something to do, besides waiting around for some sort of news."

Jennifer left Miss Marple in the care of Du, feeling more confident than earlier. As they drove toward the house, Jennifer was on the north side of the car, so she didn't have to huddle down. Peggy remained vigilant until they turned into the Casey's driveway.

"Go through the house instead of walking around the side to see how far they've gotten on the structure. It's safer."

Jennifer nodded as she hopped out of the vehicle. Peggy followed close at her heels. When they entered the front door, Jennifer sniffed the air. "Thank goodness the odor has faded."

"Yes, it's much better," Peggy said. "Probably because the workmen are in and out, causing the smell to dissipate."

Jennifer opened the guest room door. "Hello, Pretty Girl. You look good as new. Hawkman is sure going to be glad to see you."

The bird spread her wings and flapped them a couple of times, then settled back on the perch.

Looking over Jennifer's shoulder, Peggy laughed. "She looks very content. I think she's glad to be home."

"I agree," Jennifer said, closing the door. She walked out to the deck area, and let out a gasp of delight. "Wow, you guys have gotten a lot done."

Scott pushed back the brim of his baseball cap with his finger. "Hi, Mrs. Casey. The aviary is almost completed. You think Tom will like it?"

She gazed at the beautifully constructed, oversized cage. "I can tell you right now, he's going to love it and so will Pretty Girl. That's so much nicer than the last one."

"I'd say we'll have the project completed in the next couple of days. In fact, you can probably come back to your home tomorrow evening." He waved a hand toward the back wall. "We'll have this side enclosed and the electricity hooked up. The rest will be outside work."

"Wonderful."

"Have they caught those guys yet?"

"We don't know. Peggy hasn't heard anything."

"I hope they nail the bastards. You don't need this kind of harassment."

Jennifer sighed. "You're right. I don't think I can take much more." She stepped back toward the sliding glass door. "I'll leave you guys to your work, unless you have any questions."

Scott checked his watch. "No. Things are moving along rather smoothly. We'll be leaving in less than hour. See you tomorrow morning."

She waved, closed the glass door and turned toward Peggy. "Everything's moving along real well." A wave of concern crossed her face. "What's the matter? You look like you've seen a ghost."

"I just saw the coroner's wagon go by while you were talking with Scott."

Jennifer paled, sped to the window and looked out. Her expression somber, she headed for the front door. "Let's get back to your place. Maybe something's come over the radio."

They hurried out to the Chevy Tahoe and jumped inside. Peggy gunned the engine, turned around and practically skidded onto the asphalt road. Jennifer didn't even bother to hide as they flew past the turnoff to the bridge. Skidding to a halt in front of the Bronsons' house, the two women dashed inside.

Peggy ran to the radio, put on the headset, pushed buttons, fiddled with the knobs and asked questions. "Dang it, nothing."

Jennifer stood over her shoulder. "Why wouldn't they report in?"

"Too busy or they don't want us to know."

Jennifer grabbed the back of Peggy's chair. "Are you saying something could have happened to Ken or Hawkman?"

She grimaced. "Yes."

They went into the living room where Peggy balanced on the edge of the overstuffed chair, and Jennifer took the straight back. They both sat rigidly, hands clenched. Miss Marple jumped into Jennifer's lap, as Du hunkered down at her mistress' feet.

Time seemed to drag, when suddenly Du perked her ears, thumped her tail on the floor and stared at the entry. Both women clutched the arms of their chairs as Ken swung open the front door. And Hawkman walked in behind him.

Jennifer and Peggy grabbed their men, giving them hugs and kisses.

Ken guffawed. My goodness, what's this all about?"

"We've been worried sick about you guys," Peggy said. "While we were at Jennifer's house, we saw the coroner's wagon head up Ager Beswick. and we've heard nothing on the radio."

Ken walked toward the wet bar. "We'll tell you all about it, but first, I think we need a drink. After mixing the cocktails they sat down in the living room. The women were entranced as Ken and Hawkman related the events.

"When I spotted all the blood, I figured neither one was alive. So I decided to take a closer look. I called out to both men, and neither answered. When I reached the scene, I checked their pulses and found nothing."

Jennifer gasped. "They shot each other?"

"Sure appeared that way."

"But why?"

Hawkman shook his head. "We'll never know."

"How'd you get them out of there?" Peggy asked.

Ken leaned forward, rolling the glass between his hands. "We thought about having the helicopter hoist them out, but decided it would be just as easy for the men to do the job. So we dropped a couple of stretchers and the team carried the two bodies into the base camp."

"I got a little concerned when I couldn't get any communication about what'd happened," Peggy said.

"Sorry," Ken said. "We just had too much going on. We let the Commander know; and if he didn't call it in to dispatch, then it didn't get reported. We pretty much had everything under control, and all we needed was the coroner. He took care of the rest."

Hawkman stretched. "Man, I'm beat. Been a long time since I've been mountain climbing."

Ken laughed. "Me too, I think it's time to hit the sack."

Jennifer patted Hawkman on the thigh. "We could go home tonight, since both men are gone."

"Hey, don't worry about putting us out. You guys are more than welcome to stay here until your place is fixed," Peggy said. "And Du will definitely miss her new little playmate."

"Yeah, I'm sure," Jennifer said, laughing. "She's going to be glad to get the little pest out of here."

"We really appreciate your hospitality, but I think we'll head home." Hawkman said, standing and extending his hand to Ken.

CHAPTER FORTY-SEVEN

Jennifer gathered Miss Marple's gear, while *Hawkman loaded* their duffel bags into his SUV. When they arrived home, Jennifer suggested he go out and look at the work the men had completed. She hurriedly placed Miss Marple in the bathroom and closed the door, then went out the sliding glass door in the dining room to join her husband.

Hawkman stood admiring the aviary. Then with a solemn look, he glanced up at the sky. "I wonder if Pretty Girl will ever come home?"

Stifling a smile, she said, "Oh, I think she will. After all, look at her beautiful new home."

"They did do a great job. Even attached awnings that can be dropped down during the colder months." He released the latch to one and let it slide down over the exposed side of the cage. "Those will be so much better than my having to tarp the sides."

They moved back inside and Jennifer noticed the answering machine light blinking. "Appears we have some calls."

"At least we know they're not from Jack." He crossed the room and his finger almost hit the button when he heard a squawk. He whirled around. "That sounded like Pretty Girl."

"Oh, I almost forgot. We have a house guest." Chuckling, she followed as he dashed to the back of the house. Tears welled in her eyes when he opened the extra bedroom door and a big grin erupted on his face.

He quickly turned and took Jennifer into his arms. "When did my falcon come home?" He then moved toward the bird. Pretty Girl raised her wings and squawked loudly.

"I'll tell you all about it later, but right now you better pay attention to your pet. She's definitely glad to see you."

Jennifer went into her bedroom to check on Miss Marple. "I'm sorry little girl, but you can't come out yet. As soon as Pretty Girl goes into her new home, you'll have free run of the house again." She gave her an affectionate hug, put her back on the floor and wiggled one of her toys along the floor, then grinned as the cat batted it with her paws. "I'll play with you later. Right now I've got some things to do." She pitched the stuffed bunny into the corner and the cat jumped on it. "You take care of him for awhile and I'll be back."

She went into the living room and crossed over to the phone. Punching the red button, she smiled at Rita Rawlings' soft voice.

"Jennifer, I'm worried about you. There's talk in town your house burned down and that horrible man has been after your husband. Jack, Jud or whatever the bastard called himself, has not been seen in town for several days. Please give me a jingle, so I'll know everything's okay."

Hawkman walked up beside Jennifer as she listened. "She's quite a woman. Doesn't mention a thing about how he scared her so badly."

"Yes, a very sweet person. I'm so happy she didn't get hurt real bad in the accident Jack caused."

Hawkman pointed to the machine. "There's another call."

She pushed the button. "Mr. Casey, this is Marie Paulson. There's a lot of rumors going around town concerning the man you warned me about. He supposedly set fire to your house. I also heard your cat and falcon were destroyed. I will definitely replace Jennifer's kitten if she wants another. I feel so badly for you two. Please give me a call if you have a moment and let me know what's happened. I've been on high alert ever since you visited me. I'll certainly be glad when that horrible man is caught."

He shot a look at Jennifer. "I think we better make some calls and nip this gossip in the bud. It reminds me of the game we used to play as kids called Telephone. Everyone sits in a circle and the first person whispers to the next and so on. By the time it reaches the last in the line, it doesn't sound anything like the original statement."

After they called the two women and cleared up the misconceptions, they had a bite to eat and went to bed exhausted.

The next morning, Hawkman went out to the deck and put the finishing touches on the aviary, while the other men worked on the rest of the deck. Within two days, the repairs were completed and Hawkman put Pretty Girl into her new home. She immediately settled in and he knew she loved it.

When he walked back into the house, Jennifer put finger to her lips and pointed toward the window. He laughed as he hooked his thumbs into his jeans pockets and strolled toward Miss Marple where she sat on the sill. Her tail twitched as she stared out at the big bird in her new cage.

"Don't even think about it, little girl; you wouldn't have a chance." He turned toward Jennifer and smiled. "Now where were we in our life before we were so rudely interrupted!"

THE END

Made in the USA